Avenger of Blood

RYAN CALLAWAY

ISBN:0615590454
ISBN-13:9780615590455

The Avenger of Blood himself shall slay the murderer, when he meets him, he shall slay him.

Numbers 35:19

To Cheryl Palmer, the biggest fan and supporter of the Avenger of Blood.

Bioweapon

1

"She's not dead, is she?"

"Not yet," The male nurse replied, glancing up at his coworker.

"What happened?" She asked, her eyes glued to the prone body resting atop the stretcher. She squinted and examined the middle aged woman's face. Though she was unconscious, her eyebrows were scrunched and her lips parted to show clenched teeth. Her face and curly brown-gray hair were drenched in a clear liquid. It had already soaked the sheet under and around her head. "Fred?"

"She came in complaining that she couldn't breathe well," Fred shook his head. "Three minutes ago she started perspiring profusely—passed out when she came out of triage. She was burning up a fever in there. 104."

"Excuse me," A black woman sitting among the patients in the waiting area spoke up. "Can you guys get things moving back there before the rest of us pass out?"

Some of the others voiced similar sentiments. A few looked too worn or in too much pain to pitch in, even if it was obvious that they wanted to. They leaned on the shoulders of whoever had accompanied them, sweating and sporting miserable expressions on their faces. Those who were alone were hunched over their knees, heads down.

"We're doing all that we can, folks." The female nurse held her hands up. "As quickly as we can, but we have to be efficient, and we have to be careful." She nodded to Fred, and he immediately pushed the unconscious woman toward the double doors leading to the E.R. "Check the rest of her vitals and consult Dr. Chase. The whole city's going to be in here by tomorrow morning at this rate."

"We need to talk, Brenda," A fair skinned Asian woman stepped forward. She stopped an arm's length away and slightly lowered her head. "And maybe that situation can be avoided."

Brenda gave a nervous smile and returned the bow while extending her right hand. "Good evening Detective Miyoshi. Nice to see you as always."

Miyoshi had managed to blend in with the civilians until she spoke. Brenda didn't seem to have noticed her standing in the corner. She wore a jacket and jeans, both matching black denim. The jacket, perhaps a size or two larger than she needed, concealed her petite frame. She stood at 5'2", about four inches shorter than Brenda. Her wide, light brown, almond shaped eyes were sometimes piercing, and often made up for her lack of stature. She firmly shook the nurse's hand and said, "My pleasure."

"It's been rough tonight," Brenda said, glancing over Miyoshi's shoulder at the room full of sickly patients. Some glared back at her. "How can I help you?"

"I'm here on police business officially, but I also wanted to check on my roommate Cassandra Farrington. I brought her here on my way back to work after a lunch break. She was coughing up a storm. And she was very warm—complaining about the heat and sweating in a 65 degree apartment. I'm assuming she's still here?"

"Yes, I'll take you to her right now." Brenda turned and walked into the E.R. with the detective close behind. The hallway was crowded. Patients sat in chairs or laid on gurneys against the walls on both sides. Whatever loved one had accompanied them stood or sat in chairs nearby. Some glared at Brenda and whoever else happened to go by. *Friendly faces for the staff tonight, I guess,* Kana noted.

"Didn't know you had a roommate," Brenda said. "She joins the not so exclusive club today. There are 49 patients exhibiting similar symptoms. All arrived within the last eleven hours and it's been hectic as you can probably see. Dozens of complaints and threats and two incidents of physical violence. Worst of all, the night is still young."

"Lourdes is the best," Miyoshi replied. "That's why I brought Cassandra here. Just stay strong."

"Thanks Kana, I appreciate that." Brenda stopped next to a closed door and pointed to the square window in its center. "One of our doctors reported in for work this afternoon and went down **bad.**"

Miyoshi peeked inside. A man lied on his side in the bed facing the door. His eyes were closed and the lower part of his face was covered by a mask. It was connected by wire to a large machine on the table beside his bed. A white band attached to the top of the mask had been wrapped around his head, right above the ears.

"James resuscitated an eight year old girl through CPR yesterday. Her family and the staff called him a hero." Brenda shook her head, her eyes growing tender. "Now his own life is maintained by a mechanical ventilator. He showed the typical symptoms and suffered respiratory failure two hours ago. We made an unofficial diagnosis, which I'm assuming is what may have brought you here."

"Affirmative." Kana followed her across the hall to another closed door. "The other three hospitals in the city are filled with patients who checked in during the last ten to eleven hours. Besides whatever happened here – there have been 12 incidents of violence thus far."

Brenda started to push the door open and paused, leaving it open a crack. She looked back to the detective, her expression dark. "So what conclusion have you come to? If it's not classified."

"We haven't reached one that we like. The one answer that really fits scares me. We're thinking that Minikin Capital may have fallen victim to a biochemical warfare agent within the last 24 hours."

"Man. This can't just be some nasty bug?"

"We both know the answer is no. And I was hoping you could provide some specific suggestions as to what it may be."

"I think it's Ricin, although—"

"That my girl Kana's voice I hear?" A weak woman's voice called through the doorway.

Brenda opened the door and moved inside, holding it open for the detective. Kana thanked her and stepped into the medium sized room. Besides the usual hospital appliances and machines, a television monitor attached to the upper wall overlooked a bed in the floor's center. Lying back on the bed was Cassandra, Miyoshi's roommate of two years. Her purple and black hair was disheveled and spread out under her head. As expected, there were sweat stains on the bed sheet but she appeared dry. Her blue eyes were narrowed tiredly. She watched Kana come to her side and smiled, showing all her teeth.

"Hiya Cassie." Kana giggled, taking her hand in both of hers. "I know you said not to worry about you but I had to see you."

"Can't keep yourself away, huh?" Cassie teased. "Even though you're going to get married, move out, and forget all about little old me."

"That'll never happen." Kana squeezed her hand. "How are you feeling Cass?"

"Same as I look." She shrugged. To Kana, she didn't look *bad*. "Whatever that means. I've gone through 12 cartons of orange juice and they have me on all sorts of fluids. Still ain't working. I'm thirsty as a vampire in a desert."

"Cass... sickness isn't an excuse for remarks like that. What does a vampire have to do with a desert? Or do I want to know?"

"Probably not."

"As for the thirst, the I.V. is there doing its job. You just relax and try not to talk too much. I'll be here for you tonight."

"You don't have to miss work for me. Joe said he'd be here soon. I doubt he'll stick around for the whole night, but..."

"I want to be here for you."

"Look, someone has to pay my half of the rent next week. We both know it won't be me. Anyway, I'll be fine. You know I wouldn't let some little flu beat me. Though I will gladly take the opportunity to get more sleep."

The room was quiet for a moment. Cassandra's eyes were closed and her lips pursed. Kana opened her mouth to speak when Cassie quietly called her name. "Kana?"

"Yes Cassandra?"

"Don't you call me Cassandra. Kana... please don't leave me alone tonight. I'm scared—and thirsty. I'm afraid that... I'm afraid to be by myself."

"I'll be here tonight. I may have to go back to the department but you won't spend the night alone. I promise."

"Thanks."

"Do you remember how soon Joe said he'd show up? Knowing him, he meant it biblically. 'A day with Joe is as a week or two,' as you say."

Cassandra remained silent, her eyes still closed. Her stomach raised and lowered upon each shallow breath. Kana's head began to fill with dozens of unpleasant thoughts. What if Cassie ended up staying in the hospital for weeks? Or what if she got worse and had to go on the respirator like James? For that matter, there was the possibility of her never coming home. No one had died yet, but with the way things were going... it seemed like a matter of time.

"Cassie?" Kana shook her hand gently.

"She's sleep." Brenda placed her hands on Kana's shoulders. "And better off. The more she talks the more difficult her respiration becomes."

"It's okay that she just passed out like that?"

"Sure—she's been in and out all day," Brenda said. She sighed. "I think it's Ricin. When I examined her I heard crackling at the end of each breath through my stethoscope. Pulmonary edema. 34 of the other 49 had it as well."

Kana's eyes returned to the still face of her unconscious friend. She silently prayed that her immune system and the medical staff would succeed in fighting off the sickness.

"She's been experiencing diaphoresis – which has contributed to her water and electrolyte loss. She was crying from the pain but a Tylenol dropped the level from eight out of ten to three. Fortunately, she's a strong girl. Hanging in there."

"Please do all that you can." Kana leaned over Cassandra's face and pressed her lips against her warm, damp forehead. "I don't know what I'll do if something happens to her."

"We'll do our best and nothing less, Miyoshi. For now the plan is to continue supporting her fluids. She hasn't been getting worse like some—so I'm confident she'll pull through."

"Thank you."

"It's what we do. And I like Cassie. Let's leave her in peace for a moment, okay?"

Kana nodded, and after running her hand through Cassandra's hair, followed Brenda into the hallway. Brenda closed the door behind them and crossed her arms over her chest. She frowned and surveyed the frantic scene outside. It was a far cry from the quiet calm inside Cassandra's room. Kana took the opportunity to wipe the tears under her eyes away. *Have to remember I'm here for business, too.* She cleared her throat.

"So, what is Ricin?" She asked.

"It's a poison that's made from the waste left over during Castor oil production," Brenda explained, thoughtfully rubbing her chin. She spoke slow, her eyes squinted as if she were trying hard to remember. "It works by inhibiting protein synthesis—basically killing off the cells."

"It has to be made, huh? So this wasn't some type of an accident if it is Ricin."

"Oh no. It's relatively easy to make but... at the rate people are coming in showing symptoms, there's no way this is an accident."

"How are the people being infected?"

"Most likely inhalation. You know... most of the people showing symptoms were at the mall today at some point."

A muffled musical tune played and Kana reached in her inside jacket pocket and withdrew a cell phone. "I'll look into that." She flipped the phone open and spoke into it, "Miyoshi."

"Hi Detective, where are you?" A woman inquired.

"Still at the hospital," Kana replied. "What's up, Lieutenant?"

"A housewife called my office a minute ago. Even though I wanted to keep it quiet initially, the epidemic has been all over the news. She said she has information and evidence that may be relevant to the case. I'm heading there myself to chat with her, but I want you to come with me."

"Where?"

"Be at the police department in ten minutes."

"Yes ma'am. Lieutenant?"

"Uh-huh?"

"Look up whatever you can on Ricin if you have time."

"Ricin? Will do."

Kana closed the phone and nodded to Nancy. "Thank you."

"I hope you guys figure this out before it gets any worse." Brenda sighed.

"Me too." Kana turned and strode down the hall.

2

Lizzy and her parents sat in wooden chairs around their dining room table. She had a plate filled with green peas, macaroni and cheese, and one tender piece of steak. Her parents were already halfway through their meals. Her father was a big burly man who looked intimidating but was more like a giant teddy bear to his loved ones. He glanced up at her from his plate every thirty seconds. Then he would look toward his wife and resume eating. She had long blonde hair with gray streaks overtaking it, and wore thick, large framed spectacles. Lizzy had her mother's big eyes, thin nose and lips, set on her father's rounder face. Her hair was dark brown, down to her shoulders, and all over the place.

Though her Dad was obviously wondering why she hadn't touched her food, an occasional icy stare from his wife encouraged him to keep his comments to himself. Lizzy's elbows were propped on the table on either side of her plate. Her chin rested in the palms of both hands and her fingers cupped her cheeks. She peered back and forth between the faces of her parents. Her mother finally paused after swallowing a spoonful of peas and said, in a voice that indicated how little she cared, "Your food is getting cold, honey."

"Yup." Lizzy glanced down at it and let out a sigh.

"The steak is delicious—better have it warm." Her Dad presented the juicy piece of steak impaled on the prongs of his fork.

"Right," Lizzy replied.

Her Dad let down his fork and stared at his daughter, looking exasperated. This time he ignored his wife's piercing eyes and spoke, "Lizzy, your mom is getting worried about you. You should eat now."

"I am absolutely *not* going to eat my last meal." Lizzy shook her head. "You can drive me to the chamber but I'm choosing if I eat or not."

"Last meal? Chamber?"

"Lizzy, that's quite enough now," Mom said. "You can choose not to eat if you want to, but you will not talk like that at this table."

"Charlotte, maybe we ought to—" Her father began.

"No, Bill." His wife raised her index finger and held it inches from his lips. "We've pampered and made excuses for her for far too long. It ends today. She will be a strong, independent woman and *she will* grow up. For goodness' sake, I'm just asking her to walk home after work. Is that so bad?"

"No," Lizzy said, giving a phony smile. "Not at all, Mom. Only when you happen to live in the most dangerous city in the United States. Where you'll be lucky to be murdered before they do anything else to you. So, how high are the murder rates this year? Lost count already?"

"Lizzy." Mom rolled her eyes and talked slow, as if to a four year old. "We live in one of the best neighborhoods in Minikin Capital. Those murders and crimes you hear about, for the most part, happen in M.C. South. I used to walk to and from work seven days a week. If I was fine all that time, walking three miles home at eleven p.m., what are you so worried about?"

"Okay and gas was what? 25 cents a gallon back then?"

"Ha, ha."

"Times have changed since then," Lizzy reasoned. "Look, when my friends and I—"

"Friends?" Her mom made a face.

"Fine, Melissa. When she and I drive through the streets at night, you should see how they stare at us. I'm telling you, if they catch me outside the car I won't make it home alive."

"Most likely they're staring at your ridiculously large glasses. Who wears those anymore?"

Lizzy gasped, and then she and her mother shared a laugh. Few people wore glasses as thick as Lizzy's. Charlotte happened to be one of them.

"Honey, you'll be okay, trust me." Charlotte reached across the table and cupped her daughter's chin. "Don't I love you?"

"Yes." Lizzy frowned.

"Think I want you to get hurt?" Charlotte asked.

"Nooo."

"You're my precious little lady. If I say you'll be fine, I mean it. It's only seven blocks and you should be finished the interview by 9:30 at the very latest. You'll be alright."

"You know your mom is protective of you—even if she is pushing you a bit," Her father added.

"Yeah, yeah," Lizzy agreed reluctantly. Then she was reminded of something she'd seen in the news the past few days. The thought of it brought back the nightmares she'd suffered lately. Her heart pounded as she saw herself being chased down a dark alley by something that she couldn't shake. A persistent creature blending in with the shadows of the night. Its grotesque outline visible only due to the moonlight. She'd smirked at similar scenes in horror movies. It didn't bring a smile to her face this time.

"What's wrong?" Her Dad asked. Both of her parents looked bewildered.

"What about..." She swallowed, and realized how ridiculous it would sound before she said it. "What about that thing people have been seeing? You know—the demon."

"I know you're joking," Her mom said.

"You've seen the reports in the news, haven't you?"

"I've seen 'em," Dad said, once again eating his steak. "You should be more afraid of the gangs than that thing. It's just the weirdness of the people around here. Okay?"

"Okay, Dad."

"Eat honey," Charlotte admonished her. "We leave in fifteen minutes."

"Yay." Lizzy clapped and picked up her fork.

3

Kana watched the houses and small buildings rush by from inside Lieutenant Brooke's gray Lincoln Continental. They were traveling in one of the few quieter neighborhoods in Minikin Capital. It afforded peaceful sights that Kana preferred to the bright lights and sky scrapers of busier areas. The orange glow emitted by the sun was slowly fading into the purple abyss. Both colors were a beautiful, haunting display, showing over the shadowed roofs and treetops. An occasional scattered orange cloud passed by overhead.

The detective glanced at Brooke in the passenger's seat. A faint white light illuminated the lieutenant's face as she stared intently into the lap top screen. The portable computer rested on her lengthy thighs. She looked like a tall geek, hunched over it, but Kana kept her thoughts to herself. Brooke was likeable and well respected by her employees, although some were taken aback by her beauty. She had blonde hair that hung five inches past her shoulders, plush light pink lips, green eyes, and a shapely build. One unlucky officer remarked that she belonged in modeling instead of law enforcement. The black eye he sported for the next three weeks said otherwise.

"This is…" Brooke muttered. "This could be bad. Real bad."

"Found something interesting, finally?"

"I had to weed through all the technical gobblety goop." Brooke shook her head. "I'll need your nurse friend to translate most of this for me."

"I'm not sure if she speaks gobblety goop. Might speak Spanish, though."

Brooke snickered, then took a deep breath. "Well, it turns out that you can be infected by Ricin through three methods. Inhalation, ingestion, or skin and eye contact. Some sites include injection as well. That's about as deadly as ingestion, which is the worst… and it's not likely that 119 people were injected. Unless someone working in a medical office is doing it. Which…"

"Isn't likely."

"Right. Interesting tidbit here though. In 1978 a writer named Georgi Markov died of Ricin poisoning. A man stabbed him in the leg with an umbrella. Claimed that he had just dropped it, got into a cab, and disappeared. He died within three days. An autopsy turned up a tiny pellet that was injected under his skin by the umbrella. It contained Ricin."

"Was the guy who killed him the Penguin by any chance?"

Brooke laughed. "Might as well have been."

"Have we confirmed that all of the victims were at the mall today?"

"I've got officers and detectives making the rounds on that one. So far, 42 of the 119 have said they visited the mall between ten and twelve this morning. And six others were confirmed by friends and relatives to have been there. That was at least one location of infection.

By ingestion or inhalation is the question. And what was—turn right here."

Kana followed her directions and turned down a well lit but relatively empty street. The orange in the sky had lost out to the enclosing dark purple. It was the pale blue glow from the street lights, and the house or porch lights, that provided illumination to the road. A citizen here and there sat on their porch or looked out from house windows.

"Ricin can be used as a powder, a mist, or a pellet," Brooke continued. "It can be dissolved in water or weak acid. So, seems like there's a ton of ways this could have been used at the mall. Um... it's not contagious thank God. Casual contact isn't harmful."

"That's a relief." Kana scanned the houses on her side of the road. 3217. 3219. The address of their destination was 3253.

"It works by getting inside cells in a victim's body, and keeping them from making proteins. With the proteins gone, the cells die and that's what often causes death. Skin or eye exposure isn't usually fatal. The other two, or three, can cause death between 36 and 72 hours after symptoms appear. Usually due to kidney failure, respiratory failure, circulatory collapse—whatever that is—and fluid loss. There is no cure. Only symptoms are treatable."

An image of Cassie lying prone on the hospital bed forced itself into Kana's mind. She hadn't expected anything on the level of what she was hearing. No one had died yet but time would be the real test. That meant Kana might have to sit by helplessly and watch her best friend die a slow death. Confined to a hospital bed and drifting in and out of consciousness. A mere pathetic shell of the lively young woman Kana loved.

The numbers 3253 passed before her eyes and she stomped on the gas pedal. The car lurched to a halt as the tires screeched. Brooke grabbed the laptop to prevent it from crashing into the dashboard and turned to her detective. "Something I said?"

"Sorry." Kana blinked back tears, carefully parked the car, and exited. She waited for Brooke to join her on the sidewalk and then the two proceeded toward the house. It was a nice, one story brick flat decorated with beautiful flowers. They were in pots visible in two windows on either side of the front door, and a variety were grown in flowerbeds underneath the windowsills. Of course, the grass was neatly trimmed without a weed in sight. *I guess when you're not hearing gunshots too often you would be brave enough to do this outside.*

As they neared the door, it opened inward and a slender, forty something Hispanic woman stepped out to greet them. "Hello." She glanced back and forth at the two younger women with wide brown eyes. "Are you Lieutenant Brooke Morgan?"

"Yes." Brooke gestured to Kana and said, "This is my partner, Detective Kana Miyoshi. May we come in?"

Montoya Freeman invited her guests inside and led them to a comfortable living room. A large round plastic table occupied the center of the floor. Montoya sat in a throne-like cushioned chair on one side of it and pointed them to the loveseat across the table. "Sorry, but we never had children and visitors are rare. Can I get either of you a drink?" She grabbed the armrests and prepared to push herself up.

"No, I'm fine." Brooke had already sat down.

"I'm okay." Kana settled beside the Lieutenant, still observing the room. She was surprised upon noticing that there was no television. In its place, it seemed, two bookcases were set against the walls to either side. They were six and a half feet tall and three wide. Both were filled with roughly a hundred books. She skimmed a few of the titles while Brooke began the conversation.

"Mrs. Freeman, you said you had some information for us related to the epidemic," Brooke said, discreetly nudging Kana with her elbow.

The detective grabbed a miniature notepad from a jacket pocket and flipped it open. She scribbled in some of the titles in the bookcases. *Mein Kampf. Three Weeks in October: The Manhunt for the Serial Killer Sniper. Ted Bundy: Conversations with a Killer. Child of Satan, Child of God.*

"Yes, I think my husband Thomas may be involved," Montoya admitted, her eyes watering. "I usually don't pry into his work because he asked me not to. But the way he's been acting the past few weeks—I knew something was wrong. I didn't think he'd go this far, though. I just figured he was having an affair or..."

"Where is your husband right now?"

"At work. He's an employee at the Sentinel Building on the eighth floor. He does software design, creation and repair. A lot of technical stuff. This was supposed to be one of his off days but his boss called a couple of days ago and asked him to go in. She wanted him to interview some new girl. To my surprise he was all for it."

"In what way has he been acting strange?"

"Going out late at night. Sometimes I'd find him in the backyard doing exercises or meditating. Other times he'd be in the green house working on strange plants and vegetation. He forbid me to even go in after a while, and he was never like that before. We were always open and honest about everything. He leaves and doesn't come back for the night... and two weeks ago he was arrested for hiding in the mall overnight."

"I heard about that," Kana said. "No charges were pressed because he didn't attempt to steal anything. Any idea why he did... oh." It hit her that instant and she looked to Brooke, whose eyes were stretched in realization.

"Well, I don't know exactly." Montoya rubbed the side of her head.

"We do," Brooke mumbled. "What about those plants you mentioned?"

"He's been growing castor plants back there," She said. "I've seen them. The beans are there too. I think he's making that poison."

"How do you know about all that?"

"I found his key and looked in his green house when he went out. I had a bad feeling when I saw one of the plants so I checked up on his internet activities. I had to go back a few weeks but I found articles on Ricin. A lot of them. So I printed out pictures and took them to the green house to compare. Exactly alike."

"You still have that key?"

"No, he took it with him earlier."

"I'm going to call—"

"Lieutenant Brooke?" A man's voice spoke through heavy static.

The three women jumped, startled, and then Brooke retrieved her radio from her belt and answered, "Brooke here. Doyle, I need two units to come out to 3253 Ephraim, and three to go to the Sentinel Building."

"All available units report to the Sentinel Building." A third voice cut in.

"Uh oh," Kana said.

"Uh oh indeed." Brooke stood.

4

Dread of future events often had the ability to cause time to pass quickly. In high school, students were barely able to enjoy the average two day weekend. Reluctance to return to the prison on Monday made 48 hours seem more like ten. Lizzy had expected her time spent waiting for her interview to whiz by as well. The walk home had consumed her mind on the way to the Sentinel Building. She managed to calm herself during the elevator ride up to the eighth floor.

Now, instead of trepidation, she was bored. Almost bored enough to wish the interview would come and go already. She sat in a cafeteria, watching the twenty people gathered at the wooden fold up tables spread throughout the room's center. People of all sizes, shapes, colors and styles sat, talking animatedly about things that only added to their observer's ennui. *Man, how exciting can a round of golf be? Then again, who am I to talk?* She was ready to embark on a career in programming and computers. She planned to start at the bottom of the ladder as an executive assistant. If the interview was successful, at least.

Yawning, Lizzy stretched her arms above her head and glanced at the clock on the wall across from her. She'd arrived early and the interview had been scheduled to begin eleven minutes ago. This wasn't a promising start. *On the plus side, if I die of boredom I won't have to walk home.*

The doors under the clock burst open and a short, plump, brunette woman stormed in. She immediately marched toward Lizzy, shaking her head and muttering under her breath. The employees stole glances at her and exchanged knowing smirks. *What did I do?* Lizzy stood as the red faced woman reached her.

"He hasn't been back here yet?" Mrs. McDougle asked, putting her hands on her hips.

"No, ma'am," Lizzy replied. *Thank God it's not me she's peeved at.*

"The nerve of him," Mrs. McDougle said. "Hold on, child. I'm so sorry you had to wait all this time. Thomas used to be a good, reliable worker until recently. Trust me, our company is not like this."

"I know, that's why I'm eager to work with Software Tech." Lizzy smiled. *You butt kisser.* "I'm sure he's just busy. I don't mind waiting."

"Thank you, but this is inexcusable. He had three days notice that you'd be here at 8:30 p.m. And daily reminders. He'll be giving his two weeks notice soon if—"

"How about today?" The double doors ten feet to Lizzy's left opened and a tall man waltzed in. He carried a large black duffle bag with its strap hung on his right shoulder. His left hand seemed to be occupied but it was hidden from Lizzy's point of view. She was suspicious instantly. Something about his voice, his demeanor, and the look in his eyes frightened her. He was tall and possessed an average build. Slender yet powerful arms were visible through his white and black striped dress shirt.

"What's been the matter with you?" Mrs. McDougle took three steps in his direction. Lizzy wanted to hold her back, but didn't. "You used to be hardworking—dedicated, a team player. Lately you've acted like this job means absolutely nothing to you."

"I've had an epiphany, Mrs. McDougle." He ran a hand through his dirty blonde hair, keeping his shoulder elevated to balance the bag. His hair, probably once a crew cut, was longer in some places and had odd clumps scattered throughout. Stubble was also growing on his chin and where his sideburns would be. His narrow facial features and expensive looking shirt suggested that he was normally careful about his appearance. Perhaps that had changed with his work habits.

"I realized that hardworking, dedicated, honorable men are trampled by a fast paced and unappreciative world. Lost in the shuffle of desensitized humanity. No one cares anymore. Not like they used to."

The employees seated at the tables were silent. They intently watched the disturbing scenes unfolding before their eyes. Lizzy felt a heaviness growing in the pit of her stomach.

"What on earth are you talking about?" Mrs. McDougle asked. Apparently she was the only person in the room who didn't feel the tension in the air. Who didn't sense the dread building. "Have you lost your mind?"

"Oh no, let me demonstrate," He said. "You see Doreen, if I came in here and worked hard every single day, was diligent to keep up with my tasks and appointments, was never late and refused to clock in early, if I was always available to work overtime—if I was the perfect employee—no one would care. I was, and none of you cared. You liked it, sure, but you still treated me like crap. In the end, fifty years from now, no one will care, right? Now, if I do this..."

He turned to face her and raised the previously hidden hand. Lizzy gasped. *That's not what I think it is. Can't be.*

"No one in this room will *ever* forget."

BOOM! Doreen McDougle and Lizzy screamed. The older woman clamped her hands over her stomach and crumpled to the floor. Lizzy looked down to see specks of blood covering her trembling hands and her clothes. The liquid had formed a puddle under Doreen. She lied on her side, writhing in pain while clutching her abdomen.

"No," Lizzy stammered as an explosion inside her body brought her to her knees. Her head suddenly felt light, but her limbs weighed a thousand pounds. The throbbing in her chest was hard enough to hurt, and much faster than it should have been.

"Alright, the rest of you sit down," Thomas ordered. He waved the gun in the direction of the tables and those that had risen sat immediately. The others cried out and ducked to avoid the line of fire. "Just relax, and don't make any stupid moves."

He unzipped his bag with his free hand and reached inside, keeping the gun in place. No one moved a muscle. Grinning, he withdrew a book sized piece of machinery and slipped it through the opening in the double doors' handles. He tapped a few buttons, producing a loud beep from the device.

"What are you doing?" Someone at the tables asked.

"Setting a dramatic example." Thomas stepped over to Lizzy and grabbed her forearm. He gave a tug. "You're coming with me."

"No, please don't." Lizzy resisted, fighting to keep herself low to the ground.

"Up now." Thomas pointed the gun at her forehead. "I won't tolerate disobedience. You give me a hard time and you die. You don't get up right now—they're going to pick your brains off the floor."

Lizzy peeled her eyes away from that horrible, black hole of death. She wouldn't be able to move if it stayed before her eyes for long. Even knowing it was inches from her head terrified her. Though Thomas expected it to, the gun didn't motivate her to move faster. Instead it added additional weight to her already heavy limbs. She ceased resisting, however, and the gunman easily pulled her to her feet.

"You won't—won't hurt me if I come?" She asked.

"No, no," Thomas said. He pushed her around the tables, once again aiming the gun at the seated employees. They held their hands up in surrender. "Today Lizzy, I was supposed to be introducing you to the world of computer programming. Instead, I will introduce you to the broader world. To the truth. Just don't do anything stupid."

They reached the other side of the room and he released her arm to dig inside his bag. He pulled out a device similar to the one he'd placed on the other door. Up close, Lizzy knew what it was. It was a black rectangular object with wires, buttons, and a switch decorating its surface. *None of us is making it out of here alive.* Thomas punched in a code on the buttons and numbers appeared on a screen near the top of the gadget. 00:25. Then 00:24.

"Alright folks, here's what's happening," Thomas spoke. "If you attempt to open either of these doors, you'll detonate the bombs. They're set to explode simultaneously so don't try to be slick. Detonator is with me, and so is the disabler. In the meantime, help poor old Doreen McDougle over there. Stop the bleeding, call the cops. Tell them I want my wife, Montoya Freeman, here. Do a good job and you all live."

Thomas opened one of the double doors, pushed Lizzy through the opening, and stepped in after her. She moved back and watched him hold the bomb against the thin crack between the doors. He placed the gun at his feet, snatched a roll of duct tape from his bag, and began taping the bomb to the doors. Lizzy tensed. She had an opportunity to stop him now. His back was turned, the gun was on the floor, and there was nothing to stop her. She could throw herself into him, knock him past the weapon and pick it up. *As weak as you feel, you may just kill yourself trying something like that.* Conversely, he might be planning to kill her anyway. Now could be the last chance she'd have to save herself.

"Done, just in time." Thomas scooped up the gun and turned to face her. A beep sounded behind him and he smiled. Lizzy's opportunity had come and gone. Her heart sank. *Too late now you coward. You're a failure and you blew it. Don't even deserve to live.* Lizzy's eyes filled with tears as Thomas pointed down the hall and said, "Shall we go on, dear?"

Without waiting for a response, he pushed her toward the elevators close by.

5

"I want my wife, Montoya Freeman, brought to me immediately," Thomas' voice demanded through Brooke's car radio. Kana once again sat behind the wheel, this time with Montoya in the passenger's seat. The Lieutenant stood outside the driver's door with her arms crossed over her chest. All three listened to Thomas' message for the third time. They ignored the dozens of officers surrounding the Freeman home. Some went in and out of the house, others stayed in the backyard, and a few waited by the eight cruisers parked in the street.

"No one will be hurt as long as the police don't try to pull anything," He continued. "Isn't that right, Lizzy? Lizzy?"

"Y-yes," A quiet voice replied.

"I don't want your money, just your cooperation. Get television cameras here, news anchors, especially Julia Newman, and put me on LIVE. I have a message I want to give to the sheep of this city, and the rest of the world. You'll have 25 minutes to set up all of those conditions. And just so you know, I'm in the control room. I'm sure old Rick will tell you that I can see *everything* from here. And I don't want to see ANYONE enter this building without my direct permission. No SWAT or snipers on the roofs, either. If you even begin to break one rule, everyone in the cafeteria dies. When all is in place and I see my wife here—I'll call with further instructions."

Brooke rested her hands on the top of the car door and leaned down to the open window. "Alright, it'll take you 15 minutes to get down there. There are several news reporters on the way already. Montoya, you're still okay going through with this, right? I won't let you be put in harm's way, and neither will Kana."

"My husband won't hurt me." Montoya shook her head. "I can assure you of that."

"Okay ladies, get a move on it." Brooke slapped the top of the car and backed away. "Kana, keep charge over there and keep the peace until I show up. I'll authorize you to go in undercover if you can. Think of something."

"Yes ma'am," Kana replied. She rolled the window up and began driving forward, glancing at the officers and other personnel nearby. They had discovered an impressive collection of guns and knives in a room under Thomas' greenhouse. There were also more signs of castor oil production. Although he had yet to confirm it, the authorities had their suspect. No one had died yet and hopefully it would stay that way. The shooting of a Doreen McDougle, however, meant that they had to act with urgency.

The detective made a quick left turn while taking her cell phone out of her jacket pocket. She took her eyes off of the road and stared into the small object's screen. Her thumb slipped over the six and she paused. *Should I call him? More specifically, do we need him?* The police might be capable of handling matters without any deaths occurring. Yet, something told her that his involvement would be the safest bet. She didn't trust Thomas' promise not to hurt anyone. Since when was the word of a criminal reliable? Before Kana realized what she was doing, she punched in the number.

Three rings later, he answered. "Hey Kana."

She took a deep breath. "Hey. Where are you?"

"Here with Cassie."

"Feeling better than ever!" Cassie called out.

"I bet she is." Kana grinned. "Joe have you heard about what's happening down at the Sentinel Building?"

"No."

She gave him a brief overview, concluding with, "No one is dead yet, but that could change at any moment. Our hands are tied because he has the situation pretty well scouted. And frankly, although his wife says he's never been violent before, that merely makes this that much more unpredictable. Somehow, I doubt he plans to let those people live."

"And you want me to..."

"Yeah."

"How can I get past the cameras?"

"Hm..." Kana narrowed her eyes. He wasn't invisible even if he was better off than the police. "Well..."

"To keep track of every important place in that building, there has to be a lot of monitors. He can't watch all of them at the same time if he's working alone."

"You're brilliant." Kana smiled. "Keep your phone on you. Stay out of sight, and I'll call you when I get there."

"Will do."

As she tucked her phone away, Montoya asked, "Detective, what are they going to do to my Thomas?"

She sighed. "Right now, Montoya, that's completely up to your husband. He hasn't killed anyone but he has threatened lives. No one will shoot him on sight unless he does kill or is attempting to."

"You have to understand, Thomas has just been driven to this by something. We've had a lot of setbacks in our lives and every time it seems like things are improving—there was another problem waiting. He is a good man. So please do all that you can to save him."

"Good men do good things, Montoya," Kana spoke before she could stop herself. "What *he* does in the next hour will determine what he's all about."

6

If causing a stir was what Thomas Freeman planned to do, he had succeeded. The Sentinel Building's parking lot was crowded with police officers, other law enforcement agents, reporters, journalists, and employee vehicles. Concerned loved ones had also shown up and been restrained by the authorities. They were joined by onlookers watching from outside the area the police had cordoned off. The majority of the employees had evacuated the building and were in the process of being questioned.

Detective Miyoshi peered around at the scene. Thomas had undoubtedly gotten what he wanted. The news teams were having a field day capturing it all on camera. A SWAT truck was parked closest to the building's entrance doors. Unmasked members of the team stood around it with their guns at the ready. They repeatedly had to warn the reporters to keep their distance. 14 police cruisers were positioned to block off the small area surrounding the SWAT team.

Kana stood in a small circle consisting of the SWAT leader James O'Donnel, a negotiator named Albert Diamant, bomb expert and task force leader Bob Hop, Sentintel Building security guard Rick Jones, and

Montoya Freeman—who stood beside Kana. The popular news anchorwoman Julia Newman and a camerawoman waited behind the detective. They occasionally drew icy stares from their fellow media members, who were not permitted to be within 15 yards of the group.

"So, he really does have visual access to the entire building?" James asked. He was a tall, eager looking man with a dented chin and blonde hair.

"Oh yes." Rick nodded. "He can observe all of the entrances and the rooftop from that one room. The cameras also give him a view of the roofs of the surrounding structures. We can't make a move without him knowing it."

"How is sewer access?" James, though well intentioned, was grasping at the wind.

"There is one and there aren't any cameras so you could probably get in without him knowing. Good luck finding a way past the basement cameras if you choose that route, though."

"Damn," James muttered.

"Let's settle down and talk about the possibility of resolving this peacefully, shall we?" Albert suggested, rubbing his brown and white beard. "He hasn't asked for an unreasonable amount of cash and a trip to Cuba so... thus far he's been rational. Is there any reason to distrust him?"

"I can give you about 23," Kana said. "He has that many hostages up there at the least. And the ones with cell phones say he critically wounded a woman. I won't take the little *sense* he's shown us and take it to mean he's reasonable."

"I suppose you don't believe in giving someone the benefit of—"

"No. And especially not when it comes to criminals."

"You have a way to resolve this situation without putting lives at stake?" Albert crossed his arms.

"Yeah, I do," Kana replied, ignoring the noises coming through the Blue Tooth in her left ear. The device was hidden by her hair. "For now, we can't risk any big or obvious moves. Not until he starts killing people. So we send in his wife Montoya, like he asked, along with Julia Newman and a camera."

"Yes!" Julia made a fist and cocked her arm downward. Her camerawoman extended her open hand and Julia slapped her a high five. "We're in Monica."

"However, to keep track of things, and to ensure no one is hurt…" Kana turned and sized up the camerawoman. "We're about the same height and hair color. I'll go in disguised as her."

The camerawoman stared at Miyoshi, open-mouthed.

"Sounds smart to me," James said.

"Me too." The quiet bomb expert, Bob, chimed in. "But don't we need some sort of a contingency plan? You know, in case he is just planning to kill everyone? Or already has?"

"Since we are on a time limit I'll leave that up to you guys," Kane said, glancing down at her watch. She turned to Julia and approached her and the camerawoman, who wore a blue vest with yellow letters over the left breast reading: *MC News Today*. "I'm going to need that."

"This isn't fair," Monica fretted. "Why can't you just be a second camera?"

"Obstruction of justice. Need I say more?"

"Fine." Monica handed the camera to Julia and slipped the vest off over her head.

"Don't worry," Kana said, removing her jacket and handing it to her. She had a shoulder strap on which held an occupied pistol holster and a pouch for her badge. "All credit will go to you."

"Rick," Kana called. She waited until he stepped away from the group and approached. Once he was near enough she lowered her voice and said, "Tell me, can he really see every camera at once? He has to have a blind spot."

"Well, of course the bathrooms are clear," He told her. "And unless he's a spider he can't see all the monitors at the same time. There are 57 screens spread on a wall about seven feet wide. If you take the West Staircase, past the elevators, he'll have to turn his head to see the monitors showing the roofs and upper floors. But it's unlikely he'll focus on the stairwell cameras long enough for SWAT to move in. Otherwise I would have brought that up."

"Understood. Thanks."

"Ask him what's on the floor right above the Control Room," A raspy voice asked through the speaker in her Blue Tooth.

"What's on the floor above the Control Room?" She asked, trying to sound casual.

"A dance class." Rick shrugged. "They sure do make a lot of noise for a bunch of girls with little feet. Maybe you shouldn't have allowed the evacuation. The noise on the floor might have driven Thomas crazy."

"Too late for that I guess," Kana said. She turned to Mrs. Newman and took the camera from her. "Ready to go?"

"I was born for this." Julia smiled.

"Let's go, Montoya." Kana took her hand and gave it a firm squeeze. "Just act natural, don't give me away no matter what, and maybe we can resolve this peacefully."

"You'll…" Montoya's voice cracked. She stared up at the higher floors of the Sentinel Building, eyes wide and wet. "I don't think he will, but if he attacks me… you'll protect me, right?"

Kana couldn't imagine how terrible Montoya Freeman felt uttering the possibility. The denial had faded. She had to know that the man waiting on the eighth floor wasn't who she thought he was. Not anymore. Kana spoke softly, "I won't let him hurt you, Montoya."

"Thank you," Montoya whispered, briefly squeezing the detective's hand in appreciation.

"Let me know when you're on the second flight," The voice spoke in her ear again.

Kana lowered her head to keep the voice muffled to the ears of others around her.

"Just apologize for something and that'll be my cue."

"M-hm," Kana hummed. *I pray to God that this works.*

7

God, please get me out of this, Lizzy pleaded in silence. She sat with her back against the far wall of the control room. Her hands were clasped on top of her knees, and her head hung only a few inches above them. Her eyes went back and forth between the floor and the door fifteen feet across the room. She avoided looking in her captor's direction to keep from setting him off. He was probably only a wrong look away from snapping.

Thomas sat in one of two black, cushioned chairs, his eyes roaming the dozens of screens displayed before him. They took up more than three fourths of the wall. Behind him were alarms, buttons, and various pieces of machinery. The chair five feet to his left, close to the door, was occupied by his black duffle bag. On top of it say the detonator. *Funny how such an insignificant looking object can be so deadly.*

"Good," Thomas said, petting the barrel of the rifle in his lap as if it was a cat. "See? They're doing everything I asked them to do. Julia Newman is here, too. You get interviewed by her and it'll be all over the U.S. Since you've been so good, I might let you go on, too."

Man this guy is nuts, Lizzy closed her eyes.

"Let me tell you what led us here, okay?" Thomas glanced at her, not waiting for a response. "You see, this isn't a simple case of an underappreciated worker trying to get his cheap fifteen minutes of fame. No. Try an entire lifetime of not being appreciated, and being completely ignored by the mainstream. It can—"

Kana, Julia, and Montoya were ascending the second flight of plastic stairs. They walked in silence, besides the occasional comment uttered here and there. That left them listening to the clicking sounds made by the detective's boots and Julia's suede blue high heels. Each step echoed through the 100-foot tall staircase. It sounded as if an army was advancing instead of three relatively thin women.

Julia was several steps ahead of the other two, adjusting her hair as if she was going on a date. Montoya was next to Kana, who purposely made sure they stayed close. She looked up and noticed a camera perched in the upper left corner of the landing between the second and third floors. Returning her eyes to the wall ahead, she stepped up onto the second to last stair, placing her foot a few inches over into Mrs. Freeman's path. She prayed that the deliberateness of the movement had gone unnoticed.

"Oh." Montoya's ankle crossed Kana's and she tripped immediately, falling forward onto her hands and knees. Kana fell with her and landed on one knee, throwing her arm behind Mrs. Freeman and balancing the camera with the other hand.

"I'm so sorry," Kana said.

"You two okay?" Julia stepped toward them.

"I'm okay." Montoya nodded. "Sorry Kana."

"It was my fault," Kana replied, helping her up to her feet.

"Clumsy fools," Thomas muttered. He shook his head, watching the staircases shown on the far left monitors. Lizzy noticed an odd shadow on one of the screens closest to her. It was gone in an instant however. Probably her imagination.

"So... I was providing you with some insight into the truth," He went on. "I was a typical bad kid, raised in the slums of Ivory City. Joined one of the nastier gangs when my parents kicked me out for bringing drugs home. Ran with them for most of my teenage years. Learned all about the bad side of life. Desperation, drug addiction, rape... seen people killed right before my eyes. Robbed more stores and hurt more people than I can count. At 20 I was arrested for assault and battery and rape. I spent five years in prison. Had a lot of time to think and consider where my life was headed. I realized that I wanted to make an impact in this world—and a good one."

Thomas looked to Lizzy, who continued to stare at the floor.

"So I began studying, got my GED, and enrolled in a county college. When I got out I studied law, politics, criminal justice, and government. I also got involved in my community. And eventually some of my friends urged me to run for mayor. Not only them, but even some of the poor people I visited on the streets. Twice a week I'd go with a church organization to feed them. Quite a number of them got back on their feet thanks to me, and they pulled for me. As did many former criminals who believed in true redemption.

"Some people in the elite, unfortunately, were dead set against me. They had nothing on me so they dug up my past, did commercials with the people I had hurt and turned the town against me—despite all the good I'd done. So I went back to the streets, continued to help people, built well maintained shelters, and created programs. Crime rates dropped. I was asked to run again and guess what? They spurned me."

Thomas sighed, and shook his head. "So then I came to Minikin Capital. I brought all of my experiences, ideas, statistics, and zeal ready to change this evil city. If I had worked wonders for Ivory, I could undoubtedly do it in Minikin Capital. When I arrived, only one news station even mentioned me—and their supposedly unbiased *report* was a complete mockery. 'A young upstart has come to Minikin Capital with a lot of whacky ideas, and enough enthusiasm to make it sound credible—almost.' That's all Julia Newman had to say about me then.

"Of course that was the last bit of coverage I ever got. They ignored me afterwards, as did the officials. They're all corrupt, you know? In the police department, in the board, in the mayor's office. Either they're owned by the Mafia or the Yakuza. Doesn't matter which. Everything I tried to do was effectively snuffed out by the liberal media and wolves in sheep's clothing. Why do you think that is? Lizzy?"

She lowered her eyes to avoid his gaze and recapture her voice. "I... I don't know." She understood his gripe with society. But it was difficult to be sympathetic toward a man who had threatened her at gunpoint.

"If I knew you'd be this stupid, I'd have left you downstairs," Thomas muttered. He stood, put the gun on the floor in front of his chair, and stretched his arms over his head. "Do you want to die?"

"No!" Lizzy pleaded, fresh tears welling up in her eyes.

"Why not? Don't you realize that in this evil world you either fail or become a monster? There is no true success and no one cares about good guys like I used to be. They rejected me—mocked me. So what's the point of it all?"

Lizzy searched her mind for something other than *I don't know.* "Well... maybe we shouldn't be... working just to be successful. Maybe it's just important to do our best. For the people who do care."

"Why?"

"I don't..."

"Well, I do. And I'm going to make it crystal clear for you. If you want to make an impact in this life, and be recognized, you have to be a monster. Think about it, there were countless heroes in World War 2, right? But do you know any of their names? No. They and their names are forgotten. Hitler, however, was immortalized and his book is a top seller. Same with Stalin, Bundy, and soon... yours truly.

"Bundy raped and murdered at least 30 women. He found religion in prison and warned that pornography started his descent into perversion. Didn't know about that one did you? See my point? They glorified his atrocities, *not* his redemption!"

"What are you going to do?" Lizzy asked. She had a terrible feeling about where this was headed.

"Talk to Julia Newman, share the truth of life with the United States... and murder the sheep in the cafeteria downstairs. That, along with the hundreds of people who will probably die from Ricin poisoning, will cement the name Thomas Freeman in history."

"You can't." Lizzy's head dropped. *This is all my fault.* Had she acted earlier, she could have prevented it from getting this far. If she'd died, she at least wouldn't have the deaths of the others on her conscience.

"Can't I?" A devilish smile spread across his face.

Beeeep. An electronic, muffled beep came from somewhere nearby. Lizzy recognized it, lifted her head, and exchanged a glance with her captor. He appeared as baffled as she felt. It had sounded identical to...

BOOM! An explosion sounded overhead as the ceiling became engulfed in flames. Lizzy screamed and covered her head with her arms and hands. She saw Thomas drop onto the ground face first and protect his head as well. The fire above ceased instantly. In its place debris, plaster, and concrete rained down. Hundreds of pieces poured through the murky cloud of smoke hovering where the ceiling had been seconds ago.

What now? Lizzy closed her eyes to protect them from the dust cloud rising up.

Thomas remained motionless on the floor, waiting for the shower of destruction to end. He was continuously pelted by hot materials landing on or bouncing off of his back. Something solid fell on his right hand and rolled off. He grunted. At least it wasn't his head. *But still, what the hell was that?* Scowling, he pushed himself up to his hands and knees. The floor was almost completely covered in a layer of rubble. He could barely see the tile except on the room's edges. The girl appeared okay. Scared as usual but physically unharmed.

That noise had sounded like one of his own specialized explosives. The beep informed whoever set the bomb that it had been successfully armed. The girl had heard it too, which meant it wasn't his imagination. Who had been bold and reckless enough to perform such an attack?

Thomas felt anger building inside him as he climbed to his feet. He stood on trembling legs and peered into the mist above. It was beginning to clear but he still couldn't see beyond it. His heart fluttered within his chest. Anger wasn't able to drive the fear from him. Fear of what? The person or persons who had endangered his and his hostages' lives. Definitely not police protocol. *But who else could it be?*

A massive black form cut through the smoke and filled Thomas' vision. He cried out and tried to move out of its way. In an instant he was struck in the chest by two stiff objects. Pain jolted through his torso as the impact pushed him back. He stumbled and fell on his butt, a few feet from the door. The wind had been knocked out of him and he coughed, trying to recover. *What in the?*

Caressing his sore chest, he looked up to see what had happened. He gasped. A creature stood in the center of the room, staring down at him. With the lights broken, he wasn't able to make out much besides the monstrous outline. It appeared to have wings. Three fin-like shapes were erected behind broad shoulders. A leathery fabric hung from the shoulders down to the being's ankles. The cape or shroud concealed its bodily shape, though a large silver emblem was visible where its chest would be.

Thomas' eyes rose to its horned head. The face was a metallic skull with empty, gazing, eye sockets and a mouth filled with sharp fangs. The monitors cast a faint blue, eerie light on its form.

"What in the name of..." Thomas gawked. *Get up stupid. Run.*

A cough cut into the uncomfortable silence. The monster turned sideways and its head whirled around to see Lizzy. She sat against the wall, her face buried in her arms and her sides shaking. The dust was getting to her. *Thank God I brought you.* Thomas rolled onto his knees, sprang to his feet, and charged toward the chair where the bag rested. The detonator was still there. That meant he could accomplish his glory before the devil took him. *Not yet.*

He reached out for the device but the creature stepped forward and seized his wrist. Thomas instinctively reached in his vest pocket and ripped a knife lose from its holster. With blinding speed he turned to the demon and swiped at its face. It leaned away to avoid the blade and brought its knee up between them. The sole of its foot extended and struck Thomas in the chest. He was thrown back into the door and crashed through it, tumbling into the darkened hallway.

The sound of something heavy slamming into the door startled Lizzy. She jumped and immediately lowered her arms from her head. Staying inside her little protective shell wasn't an option any longer. Even if she wasn't able to save herself, sitting in the corner with her eyes closed was foolish. She opened them and observed the damage that been wrought. *Wow.*

As expected, there was a giant hole in the ceiling. Through it she could see the ceiling of the room on the next level. The material that had once been there was strewn over the tiles before her. Some pieces had broken seven of the monitors on the wall to her right. Two bits of concrete were still embedded in the screens. Lizzy breathed a sigh of relief upon realizing what could have happened to her. She had only felt dust and small bits of debris. She'd survived the explosion and apparently Thomas had as well. He was nowhere to be seen.

The door on the other side of the room was also gone. No way it had been blown off its hinges. An explosion that powerful would have injured or killed Lizzy. Something else had occurred, then. Perhaps he had panicked, thinking the police had infiltrated the building, and fled the scene? That was possible, but unlikely. Why not just open the door and run instead of barging right through it?

Does it matter what happened? She shook her head, and pushed herself up with her feet, using her palms on the wall for support. Shards of glass were scattered throughout the floor. They'd come from the fluorescent lights that had been on the ceiling. Again, she'd been fortunate not to get cut. Taking a deep breath to build her courage, she took two shaky steps toward the doorway. A dim light source was visible beyond it, but too far away to provide a clear picture. Hopefully her memory would work in case the power was out.

She stopped to listen and heard nothing. No screams, no footsteps. If Thomas had run off he most likely wouldn't dare to stay close by. He'd want to get as far away as possible. At the same time, he was a madman and predicting his behavior wasn't an easy task. *Still, I'd rather take my chances out there.* Otherwise she might end up on the receiving end of his anger. *Come on, girl.* She forced herself to inch across the room, nearing the hallway.

A twisted, frightening silhouette appeared in the doorway. She saw the horns on its head and the fin-like tops of its wings behind the shoulders. *No way.* Lizzy's heart melted like wax and her breath caught in her throat. She sucked it in and screamed, started to step away.

The demon seemed to glide across the floor, devouring the distance in less than a second. He grabbed her shoulders with firm, yet gentle hands and spoke, "Relax, Lizzy. I'm here to help you." Though quiet and raspy, his voice was human. And his fingers were as well. She didn't feel talons on the tips of them as she expected. Still, she was gripped with fear and continued to scream.

"Quiet," The demon ordered, raising his voice.

Lizzy stopped herself in mid-scream and stared up into the black, soulless eye sockets a mere inches from her eyes. She hadn't believed that her evening could get any worse until now. Though it was probably human, it had to be the demon she'd heard of in the news. The one her parents insisted was nothing to worry about. *Easy for them to say!*

"What do you want from me?" Lizzy asked, finding the strength to speak. "You're that demon everyone's been seeing."

"I'm not a demon," it replied, releasing her arms. "The only person who should be afraid of me is Thomas Freeman. You're safe."

"Hey, you promise?"

"Yes. Have you been exposed to the Ricin?"

"Ricin?" Lizzy's mind wasn't working properly yet. She was shocked that she was capable of communicating with him. He didn't seem to be there to harm her after all. Regardless, his fearsome features prompted her to exercise caution. *The Ricin.* "Oh yeah, the guy mentioned it earlier. He said he poisoned a lot of people with it. I don't know what it is. He hasn't touched me, though."

"Hasn't given you anything to eat or drink?" He pressed. "It can be ingested or inhaled."

"No, he hasn't given me anything. I am a little hungry, though." *Like he cares, bonehead. Don't make him think of food—you don't know if those teeth are real or not.*

"Relax and keep your head down." He turned around. "I'm going to take care of him. I want you to stay in here until I get back. Don't go anywhere unless the police come. Got it?"

"Yes, sir," Lizzy stammered.

He rushed out the door, a long cape trailing him, and joined the darkness beyond it. *Wow.* Lizzy wondered what she had gotten herself into. She was stuck in the room again, this time with a sliver of hope.

The Avenger of Blood walked quietly down the hallway. The hall lights were off but some of the rooms on either side were lit. Either his prey had turned them off on his way to the control room, or the explosion had caused a partial blackout. He didn't mind. He preferred the darkness. It was usually his ally. Right now, because he had gotten a head start, Thomas had the edge. He could be hiding in one of the open doorways or in the alcoves.

The Avenger allowed himself a quick glance into each open space as he passed. He wasn't able to see much but the doorways were clear. At the moment, he didn't have time for a thorough search. Thomas was obviously a dangerous man. The speed and precision he'd demonstrated when he took a swipe at the Avenger's face was consistent with someone well trained. Whether that training was professional or not, treating him lightly would be a mistake.

He approached two perfectly adjacent doors, cracked open, on opposite sides of the hallway. To avoid putting himself in a vulnerable position, he paused three feet behind them. On his left was A8. It was partly lit, but the door wasn't open enough for him to see inside. There was nothing else peculiar about it. It fit in with the rest of the rooms around it. The door to the right was marked B15: Storage Room, and light from the hallway showed a large area beyond it. Though A9 and A10 were just ahead, B15 seemed to be the last room on its side, which would make it twice the length of the normal rooms.

Narrowing his eyes, the Avenger refocused his attention on the hall ahead and began forward. There were twenty feet before the end of this section and the staircase was probably nearby. *Can't afford to let him get too far.* He'd advanced a mere four steps when something metallic clattered inside the storage room. He hurried back to it, shoved the door open, and stepped inside. Thomas had picked a good hiding spot.

The room was filled with hospital beds. They were set in six rows of eight, their heads facing the wall to the Avenger's right. Some equipment lied around the sides of the room. None of it, not even the piles, were big enough for a grown man to hide behind. That left one place. The Avenger stepped closer to the first bed in the nearest row, placed his right hand on the edge, and stooped down. He lowered his head and peeked underneath. The hallway light allowed him to see under the nearest beds as well. No Thomas. But at the head of the first bed in the second row, he spotted a knife. *A trick I usually play on my enemies.*

He didn't hear or see anything initially. He felt it. Knew it. The Avenger dropped flat onto his stomach, his body aligned with the bed, and rolled under it. He briefly saw the form of Thomas standing beside him, and heard a quiet ripping sound as a sharp blade slashed through the fabric over his shoulder. *That was stupid,* he berated himself. Thomas stepped closer to the bed and an empty hand gripped under the mattress. The Avenger grabbed the steel supports under the mattress and brought his knees up to his chest. He took a quick, deep breath, and upon exhaling kicked the bed up and toward the door.

It overturned on top of Thomas and the force knocked him to the ground. Immediately he batted it aside and got onto his hands and knees. He ignored the Avenger and frantically crawled past him to the second row. The Avenger climbed to his feet just as Thomas scooped up the knife he'd thrown earlier. He jumped up and thrust it at his opponent from overhead, aiming for the neck.

The Avenger ducked and the blade went by harmlessly. Thomas rebounded without pause and turned his wrist over to take another swing. The Avenger raised both of his arms, and blocked the attempted cut by striking the outside of his left wrist against Thomas'. He brought down the right arm sideways with his fingers extended, and the edge of his hand hit Thomas' thumb. His grip loosened involuntarily and the knife was swatted to the floor. The Avenger quickly closed his hand into a fist, and swung his arm back toward Thomas. He struck him near the temple and Thomas turned and staggered across the threshold.

He's good. The Avenger rushed after him. He wanted to end the fight before any more surprises were pulled. Unfortunately, Thomas spotted his other knife in the middle of the hallway and picked it up. He spun around to face the Avenger and brandished the weapon between them. *Too late.* The Avenger halted and stood a little more than an arm's length away. He kept his arms loose at his sides and his knees slightly bent. Ready to retreat or spring into action.

Thomas grinned a humorless scowl that revealed his bloody teeth and gums. Fire danced in his eyes, wild with anger and insanity. He kept them focused on the Avenger's face while stepping sideways toward the end of the hall.

"You know, for a moment there I wasn't sure if you were human," Thomas said. "I'm normally a guy who laughs at religious people and their fear and condemnation. But, I'll admit, I thought you were a devil here to steal my glory. To transport me to hell."

Thomas chuckled, and lowered his eyes to the "creature's" torso. He wore a black apron of sorts held on by a thick martial arts-like belt tied around his waist. Under the belt, the apron ended in a loin cloth that hung down to his knees. The edges of it were lined with silver. His pants, shirt, and boots were also black. On both arms, from the elbows down to the wrists were dark gauntlets with compartments presumably concealing weapons. Thomas only glanced at them. He seemed fascinated by the large, bold, light gray cross decorating the center of the apron.

"Now, I'm curious as to who you are and what you want," Thomas went on. He continued making his way toward the end of the hall. Behind him it branched off to the left and right. A sign on the wall fifteen feet away read, STAIRS. An arrow directly under it pointed to the right.

Can't let him create too much distance between us. The Avenger held his alert posture and crept forward, maintaining his distance.

"Not going to tell me, I suppose?" Thomas shrugged. "Suit yourself. Even if you are mute, you're obviously intelligent. You know I'm good with this knife. So you'll be in a bit of a tough spot trying to stop me from getting downstairs. Get too close and I slit your throat. Lay off, and nothing will stop me from detonating one of those bombs just down the stairs. You know I can set them off manually, I suppose? That was one of mine you used to take out the ceiling. Neat trick. Caught me off guard. I guess you found my van."

Thomas stepped back into the open hall and started moving to his left. *Oh, no.* The Avenger knew he couldn't afford to lose sight of him, not even for a second. He was far too fast, and too *good* to give him that much slack. *Can't risk the lives of the people in that room down there. And God only knows where Kana is.* The Avenger put his back to the wall on his left and cross-stepped toward Thomas. He moved quick and managed to catch up in seconds, leaving five feet between them.

The terrorist inched backwards, daring his pursuer with his eyes. There were three rooms along the left side of the hall—across from the middle one was the opening to a narrower hallway. Five feet past the third door, the Avenger spied the double doors that led to the stairwell. A total of forty feet or so.

"You know what, Cross?" Thomas grinned and reached into his vest pocket.

He withdrew another knife, an inch or two smaller than the other. The edge and tip of the blade, however, were no less sharp. Thomas lowered himself into a defensive posture while continuing to retreat using cross steps. He held the smaller weapon in his left hand in front of him, close to his hips. The larger knife he positioned across his chest, both blades in a reverse grip.

"I have absolutely nothing to lose in this situation," Thomas boasted. "Nothing. You might have noticed the six pack of Cola sitting on top of a brief case in my van. One of the cans was missing. I put a little case of Ricin inside and brought it in the building with me. For what? Not for cute little Lizzy back there, no. I put it into some of the cups in the cafeteria, and in the food they were preparing to serve. Now... it's possible that the threat of being blown to bits spoiled their appetites. But... it's very likely that after forty five minutes, they got kind of hungry, isn't it?"

The Avenger's hands tightened into fists. He quickened his pace.

"That makes you angry, huh? Well, I can promise you this... whatever happens between you and I—I win. You die, you're just some weirdo. If I die, I'm a legend. So at this point you can't stop me."

"Then why are you fighting?" The Avenger growled.

"Oh, he does talk." Thomas laughed. "I'd rather be known for two. And I want the more immediate approach. It's much more interesting if I killed hundreds with Ricin, and a few more with explosives. I mean, there's a good chance at least twenty five percent of the people I infected at the mall will survive. Yet, if I set the bombs downstairs there won't be any survivors."

Thomas suddenly lunged toward the Avenger, raising the closest knife in a half circle. The Avenger moved his body to the inside of the attack, lifting his right hand. The blade whizzed by his face, missing by inches, and he immediately brought his hand over the top of Thomas' extended arm, grabbing hold of his forearm.

Thomas already had the other knife ready and he slashed across his body at his opponent. The Avenger had expected it and he used the outside edge of his left hand to strike the center of Thomas' right forearm. He hit his target area, a pressure point, and Thomas' hand opened automatically. *Got to move, fast.* The Avenger leaned forward to hit him in the face, but Freeman already had a knee up. He put his foot against his aggressor's stomach and thrust the sole into him. The Avenger stumbled back three steps and dropped to one knee to prevent tripping.

"See you in hell." Thomas waved with the knife and turned to run for the double doors.

The Avenger pushed up and charged after him. Thomas was indeed as fast on his feet as he was using the knives. Despite the blows he'd taken, he seemed to move with relative ease. *Don't concern yourself with that.* Focusing on the target's speed instead of his could make all the difference. He ran as fast as his legs would propel him, using his arms for extra speed. *20 pounds of this costume is slowing me down.*

He forced the negative thoughts from his mind and reached across his body with his right hand. He pressed a button on the side of the left gauntlet and flipped open a lid. The movement slowed him down a little but if his aim was perfect it wouldn't mater. He slipped a four-pointed, black throwing star out, holding one of the edges between his thumb and index finger, and brought it back by his head.

Thomas was two steps from the double doors and he extended his free hand in preparation to grab the nearest handle. The Avenger launched the star, staggered a little, and kept onward. Thomas's fingertips were touching the handle when the star hit it, ricocheted off, and cut his palm. Groaning, he retracted his hand, and crashed into the door. He took a step back and gripped the handle with his bloody hand. As he pushed he turned back to see where the Avenger was. The "monster" had lowered his shoulders and was charging straight at him. Thomas raised the knife threateningly and screamed, "Get away from me you—"

The Avenger plowed right into him, still running. His right shoulder rammed Thomas' stomach, sending the air right out of his lungs. Both men crashed through the door. *Can't let him stab me in the back.* He pushed with his legs, taking Thomas off his feet, and then the ground disappeared under his.

The two were briefly airborne, the Avenger's body up horizontal as if he were going into a dive. Thomas was slumped over the shoulder buried in his abdomen. He still held the knife, though it was useless now. He landed midway down the flight of stairs on his butt and the Avenger toppled over him. Momentum carried them down the rest of the stairs, and the two hit only twice before spilling onto the landing.

They untangled there and Thomas rolled over close to the wall before lying prone on his back. The Avenger hit the ground beside the bottom step and rolled onto his side, facing Thomas. Both remained motionless like two fallen warriors after a long, intense battle. The lone indication of life in them was their stomachs slowly filling with air, and then deflating.

8

The group of four law enforcement agents, along with reporter Julia Newman, ascended the staircase. They were led by Detective Kana Miyoshi, who had abandoned her camera. She moved up one step at a time and held her gun in both hands before her face, the muzzle aimed at the ceiling. Three stairs behind her were two uniformed police officers, Patricia and Andy, and SWAT leader James O Donnell trailed them. He carried an AK-47, currently pressed against his chest to avoid an accident. Two steps to his rear was an irritated looking Julia Newman, trying to peer around the bodies of those ahead of her.

Kana paused and held one of her hands up, signaling for the others to halt. They did, except for Julia who walked right into James' back. He muttered something under his breath but Kana ignored him. She lowered her weapon and aimed it in front of her at chest level. On the landing between the eighth and ninth floors, she could see someone's legs from the calves down. They wore expensive looking shoes and black socks. The rest of the person's body was hidden by the railing, but he or she appeared to be lying down.

Slipping her index fingers inside the trigger guard, she gingerly continued her ascent. She walked closer to the wall on the right as she neared the top. The body came into view more and more until she realized that it was Thomas Freeman. He lied on his back with his right arm sprawled out to the side, and the left pinned between his torso and the wall. His eyes were closed and blood had streamed out of his mouth, down his chin, and soaked the collar of the work shirt he wore. *Oh boy.*

Kana looked to his stomach and saw it rising up and down. He was alive. She lowered her gun and nodded to the others. Patricia sprang up the last few steps and stood next to the detective. The men moved past them to the body. Andy dropped to one knee beside Thomas and checked for a pulse while the SWAT leader scanned the area. He spotted a hunting knife sitting on the third stair that led to the ninth floor.

"Strong pulse on him," Andy announced, shaking his head.

"What happened?" James asked. He glanced back and forth between Thomas and the knife.

Julia paused on the last step and scratched the back of her head.

"Looks like he took a tumble down the stairs to me." Patricia raised an eyebrow and turned to Kana. "Miyoshi?"

"That's what it looks like." Kana shrugged. *Even though that's definitely not what happened.* "Andy, get on the radio and call for medics. And let Brooke know that it's over. We shouldn't touch him yet, because he might be seriously injured. But James, if you will, keep that gun on him—just in case."

"What do you want me to do?" Patricia asked.

"Come with me." Kana moved past the men and climbed the stairs with Patricia a few steps behind.

"Wait a minute," James stammered. "All this and he just fell down the stairs? By himself?"

"He must have been in a hurry," Kana called over her shoulder.

I'm not sure which of the two I'd rather see right now, Lizzy sighed. Since the man in the costume departed ten minutes ago, she had reclaimed her seat on the floor. Her knees were once again drawn into her chest with her arms wrapped around them to hold them in place. Her watch informed her that it had been ten minutes since she watched him disappear out the door. She couldn't trust her own senses, which made it seem like hours.

The entire time, she wondered what she was supposed to be waiting for. Were the police going to show up and leave her doubting her sanity? Had that entire scene been her imagination going into overdrive? Unlikely. Her evidence of its truth was the rubble scattered on the floor before her feet. Then what? Why did the "creature" tell her to wait? For her own protection or did he have ulterior motives? That led her to ask herself whether she wanted him to win the fight or Thomas. The man who'd held her hostage hadn't planned on killing her at least. *As for the other guy...*

Lizzy looked up from her knees to see the masked man standing inside the doorway, leaning against the wall. She climbed to her feet. *How the hell did he get in here so quietly?* She stood warily, hoping she could run past him if he did attempt anything. Besides his frightening appearance he didn't look like a threat. He seemed to be leaning for support, not casual reasons. He stared back at her through the eye-sockets in the mask, breathing steadily.

"Are you hurt?" She asked, taking a cautious step toward him.

"I'll live," He replied in his hoarse voice. "I'm surprised you stuck around."

"Well, something that looks like you tells me to do something, I'm likely to do it," Lizzy admitted. "Unless it's Satan."

Due to the pale blue glow from the monitors, Lizzy noticed a detail in his costume design that she hadn't earlier. In the center of his chest a bold, gray, cross was woven in. The top of it ended near his throat, and the bottom came down to the sash around his waist. The two arms of equal length extended to nearly the width of his chest. Maybe he wasn't a demon after all.

"Thank you." Lizzy took another two steps closer. "You promised that I would be safe and I took your word for it. Thanks."

He nodded. Then, after a deep breath, he pushed himself off of the wall and walked slowly toward her. His eyes were on the large hole in the ceiling. Lizzy clenched her hands into fists and squeezed them for courage. *He's not going to hurt you, just relax.*

"So... who are you?" She asked.

"It's written of me," He replied, lowering his eyes to hers. "That he is God's minister to you for good. But if you do evil, be afraid, for he does not bear the sword in vain.   He is God's minister, an avenger to execute wrath on him who practices evil."

"Avenger," Lizzy repeated. "Fitting... I guess."

They met in the center of the floor and stood three feet apart.

"Oh, is Thomas alive, or..."

"He's going to jail this time," The Avenger said. "No one's dead yet so he gets another chance. For now."

"What about the things that he said?" Lizzy winced. During her time alone, she'd thought about the truth behind Freeman's discourses. They bothered her as much as waiting alone in the dark for the unknown. "You know... about bad people being recognized? He's got a few screws loose and all, but he did make a good point. It does seem to be backwards in our world. People do get recognized for doing evil."

"It depends on why you do what you do. Detective Kana Miyoshi should be here in a minute or two. She can answer that question as good as I can. I've got to go."

"This was supposed to be my big interview today." Lizzy smiled. "You know, first day. My parents had to talk to me for hours to get me to agree to come. I'm terrified of walking home alone. Little did I know, getting through the day itself was going to be hard enough."

He turned his back to her, bent his knees, and jumped straight up. While he was in midair he extended his hands and grasped the edge of the hole in ceiling. Then he pulled himself up, and climbed onto the floor. *Wow.* Despite a few grunts of effort, and the pain he was obviously in, he performed the move with relative ease. Once settled, he turned and looked down at Lizzy.

"Don't be afraid. No one will hurt you."

She opened her mouth to ask—

"I promise," He said. Then he was gone.

"Hey, Lizzy?" An Asian woman stepped into the doorway. Behind her stood a female uniformed officer with sandy red hair.

"Huh?" Lizzy realized that her mouth was hanging open and she closed it. "Detective Migoshi?"

"Close enough." Kana smiled. "Come on, I know you've had quite a day."

The scene at the Our Lady of Lourdes Hospital was far more peaceful, four days removed from the Ricin scare. Even the atmosphere had changed. The people waiting to be taken into the ER were still impatient, and at times rude, but that was typical. They weren't gripped with the same panic that Kana had witnessed days prior. She remembered the sick feeling in her stomach when she stood among them, praying that Cassie was okay.

Though it seemed late, she knew now that her prayers had been answered. She reached the familiar door and pushed it open. Cassie had been reclining on her bed with her hands comfortably interlocked behind her head. She heard the door and peeked out of the corners of her eyes. Her brown irises brightened as she sat up and grinned. "Hey Kana!"

"Hi, how you feeling?" Kana walked over to her and sat on the edge of the bed, facing her friend.

Cassie threw her arms around Kana's waist and squeezed. Kana winced but returned the embrace. She cupped the back of Cassie's head with one hand and held her around the shoulders with the other arm. The younger woman was bigger and stronger than she knew. Through the pain, Kana smiled, content to know that Cassie's strength had returned.

"I love you," Cassie said.

"Love you too, Cass," Kana replied in a weak voice.

"Oops, sorry." Cassie relinquished her bear hug but left her arms around Kana. "Didn't mean to hurt ya. I forgot how little and cute you are."

"Yah, yah." Kana patted her head. "Why are you so emotional today, missy?"

"I'm just happy that all of this is over," Cassie explained. "For a little while there I didn't think I was going to make it. Especially when the third night came. Brenda tried to hide it from me, but I knew that people died after three days from Ricin. Saw it on the news. I thought... I didn't tell you and Joe, but I thought I wasn't going to wake up. That's why I wanted to stay up so late."

"Cass." Kana leaned back and smiled. Fresh tears ran down Cassie's cheeks and Kana felt them on her own face. She pulled Cassie back into her arms, gently running one hand through her hair. "We don't have to worry about that, anymore. You're going to be fine."

"I was probably dreaming, but I remember waking up in the middle of the night and seeing you two sleep next to the bed. You had your security blanket—er, jacket—draped on top of you and Joe was holding you. It was so freaking cute."

"Oh shut up, will you?" Kana released her and they shared a laugh. "But, no. It wasn't a dream. He really was here the whole night, which was very nice. First time we've actually been able to talk in a week and a half. We've both had so much work to do lately. He wanted to be here now but—"

"I understand," Cassie said. "To his defense, it's not like the murder rate in this city ever slows down. I bet he has a lot of makeup work to do from the night he was here. I heard in the news, by the way, that the guy who did it took a tumble down a staircase. They called it in accident but I knew better."

"He'll undoubtedly get a life sentence since he has no mob connections," Kana said. "The guy's logic may have been a bit twisted, but he's quite sane. I feel bad for his wife and all, but a lot of people died. 32 by the latest count."

"Joe's not going to..."

"No, not this time. Apparently HE has other plans for him, although I guess we'll be waiting to see what they are."

"I wish he would get fried, personally," Cassie muttered. "But him aside, I wish I would've actually been able to enjoy my time in bed more. Had a T.V. with cable channels, a nice soft bed, and I was in too much pain to appreciate it. Think they'll let me stay an extra day or two?"

"No chance." Nurse Brenda walked into the room, a curt smile on her face. "Good evening, Detective. Cassie."

"Thanks Brenda, I owe you big time," Cassie admitted. "Kana told me all the trouble you had to go through dealing with my crap. Even though I was terrified most of the time, having you around made me feel a lot better. I knew I was in good hands. Thanks, dude."

"Haven't been called that since high school." Brenda crossed her arms over her chest. "I was just doing my job. Although I'll admit you were a unique and trying patient at times, I enjoyed getting to know you. Since Kana's been a friend of mine for years I'll probably stop by the house to check in on you. You'll need it for a little while. You may feel good now, and you're well enough to go home, but you still need to take it easy for a bit. Okay?"

"Of course." Cassie's eyes dropped to the bed and she blinked a few times, thoughtfully. "I was kind of wondering about something, though. From what I've heard about the Ricin on the news it doesn't sound like it has any good purpose. I mean, can't the government blow all of the Castor plants up? They manage to put everything else on the endangered species list."

"Don't start," Kana warned.

"I would prefer them to not exist, sure." Brenda shrugged. "In fact, a few days ago I wished they didn't. But after I did research I realized that like most things on our planet, it's kind of a double edged sword. There are multiple positive uses for Ricin that are being explored as we speak. Immunotoxins for one."

"What are they?" Cassie asked. Kana's face showed that she was wondering the same thing.

"It's created by linking a tumor seeking antibody to a certain portion of the Ricin toxin. When it finds a cancer cell, the immunotoxin kills it without causing any harm to the healthy cells. Reason being, the antibody specifically targets cancerous cells. So far, experiments have produced promising results in both mice and human subjects. It'll take time to realize the full potential of immunotixins, and an even longer time to gain F.D.A. approval. But it seems to be well on its way. Conversely, cancer research has turned up a possible Ricin vaccine. Pretty neat when you think about it. Two problems may be able to cancel each other out."

"God works in mysterious ways," Kana said.

"Evolution." Cassie rolled her eyes.

"Joe and I won't pray for you next time something happens, then we'll see about that." Kana grinned.

Cassie laughed.

"Well, I've got to go get some discharge papers for you to sign." Brenda moved toward the door. "I'll be back in five or six minutes."

Once she disappeared, Kana took Cassie's nearest hand in both of hers. "I guess you're healthy enough for me to tell you now. They threw out the outfit you wore to come here a few days ago."

"That..." Cassie began. She closed her eyes, took a deep breath, and let it out slowly. "That doesn't bother me too much. Wasn't that expensive."

"But because you were initially exposed to Ricin while wearing the outfit you had on at the mall—I took the liberty of getting rid of that one for you. I wore gloves of course. Didn't want to risk you catching something again, you know?"

Cassie gawked at her in disbelief.

"I know, it cost you almost a whole paycheck. Don't worry about it, though. What matters is that you made it." Kana patted her on the head again. "I have to use the bathroom. Be right back."

Kana stood and walked to the door. She opened it, and turned to say over her shoulder, "I didn't like it that much, anyway."

Cassie bit her bottom lip and nodded. "I'll get you, woman."

Lizzy walked with her hands tucked in her skirt pockets, and her head held low. She felt like a lone jackal traveling through territory marked by a lion pride. Every person who came within half a mile of her was a threat. Every pack of young men, whether they sat on steps or stood on street corners, were hungry lions waiting for an opportunity to pounce. It didn't help her fears that the majority of them stopped whatever they were doing to stare at her. She couldn't see their eyes, nor make out details on their faces, but they were still intimidating.

Don't you guys have anything better to do than hang out on steps at night? She hoped they weren't able to somehow hear her thoughts. *Come on, Lizzy.* She was nervous enough. Ascribing supernatural characteristics to the loiters wouldn't help her any. Then again, neither would walking with her head down looking like a victim. What was it her mom said again?

"When you walk, don't look like a victim and no one will treat you like one. If they see that you're afraid of them, that's when they'll bother you. Just look strong, and pay them no mind. But make sure they know you're alert."

Yep, yep. Sounded nice—sort of. Lizzy had taken the advice to heart when she heard it yesterday. It sounded simple and true. She supposed that predators resembled dogs or other fearsome animals in that way. Fear attracted them, drove them crazy, and tempted them to attack. If only the creatures and humans with that trait weren't so intimidating. Then, her mother's nice theory might have held up.

Now, as she walked along the sidewalk on the left side of Cephas Street, it wasn't the least bit comforting. She was scared out of her wits. Terrified that the next group of *gangsters* that she passed would start trouble. No one had said anything to her, although one deep voiced man had spoken about her. "That little girl better watch herself out here." He knew she heard him, and he'd probably meant for her to. *Thanks to you too, jerk.*

The street was relatively well lit, which alleviated her fears some. It was the lack of non traditional pedestrians that bothered her most. There weren't any policemen in cruisers parked in the shadows, keeping an eye out for unsuspecting speeders. No proper looking men or women walking home from work, either. Just cute little Lizzy, wearing a dark blue denim blouse and matching skirt. The skirt came down to her ankles. She preferred to dress modestly, and she was grateful for that. The onlookers would probably have attempted something already if she were dressed provocatively.

"Yo baby, you need someone to walk you home?" Someone called from across the street.

Lizzy's heart began throbbing, and she looked to where the voice had come from. Five or six young men, roughly 17-21, were huddled together in front of an alleyway between a convenience store and a nail salon. Four of them wore oversized white tee shirts and the others had on tank tops. It was a little cold out for that but they didn't seem to mind. They all watched her, two of them smoking cigarettes, and the rest passing around a 40-ounce bottle of alcohol.

Only three more giant blocks to go and you're home. Lizzy set her eyes on the streetlight on the next block and quickened her pace. She had made it this far, no need to panic now even if they were talking to her.

"Just how I like them," another one remarked. "Short and thick. Mm-mm-mm!"

The group laughed, all except the one who had spoken first. He stood holding the cigarette and glaring at Lizzy.

How dare they talk about me like that, right in front of me! Lizzy swallowed to quench the anger rising up in her chest. *What right do they have to talk about me like that? Didn't they have mothers to teach them manners or something?* She wanted to shout at them, and especially the one who continued to glare. Instead, she turned her head and returned his look. Something about his eyes sent a shiver down her spine. They were ablaze, although she hadn't done or said anything yet. She could see the rage in him from twenty-five feet away. Her heart pounded harder and she turned away immediately.

"Hey, why didn't you answer me?" He called. The fury in his voice now matched his eyes. "I asked you a question you little four eyed freak. You going to play me out like that in front of my boys?"

She quickened her pace more, but removed her right hand from her pocket and reached across herself to hold her purse.

"HEY!" He yelled. His voice was a little closer now, but she didn't want to look again.

"Hulio, calm your butt down, man," one of his friends said. "You get played out all the time. Ain't nothing different."

Two or three others snickered, but Hulio went on talking as if he hadn't heard him. He sounded like he was following her from across the street. "I just asked if you wanted a walk home."

"No... no thank you!" Lizzy forced herself to say. Her voice didn't sound anywhere near as firm as she wanted it to. The words were jumbled together and they came out unsure and shaky. *Should have just kept quiet.*

"No, no thank you," Hulio mocked her, getting laughter from his friends. "Your little ugly self, I wasn't trying to hit on you. I just thought maybe you'd let me hit if I walked you home. You look easy. Ugly girls like you can't get dates otherwise, can you?"

His words cut into her heart like a knife. Even though they were coming from someone whose opinions she couldn't care less about, it still hurt. *Why do they have to be so cruel?* She blinked back tears of heartache and fear.

"I'm going to hit anyway," Hulio said. She could see him approaching out of the corner of her eyes. He was moving fast. "Either you'll let me or I'll just take it."

His friends piped in. "Take it, Hulio!"

"She'll thank you later."

More laughter followed. They were enjoying her torture. Lizzy reached into an open compartment on the front of her purse and pulled out a small cylindrical canister. She had purchased pepper spray from a martial arts instructor three months ago. Now she wished she had taken the class he offered as well.

"I know you're a virgin, too." Hulio was crossing the street, less than fifteen feet away. "It'll hurt a little bit, but..."

"Stay away from me!" Lizzy cried, turning to face him with the pepper spray bottle's dispenser aimed at his head. "I mean it!"

"What are you going to—"

"Hulio, chill!" One of his friends called. He sounded shaken.

"Man, I'm not..." He stopped, seven feet from her, and held up his hands. His lips were moving but no words came out. The fire in his eyes had faded and been replaced with what looked like fear. *These animals feel fear?*

Lizzy watched him as he slowly backed away, keeping his hands up. His friends were staring at her with the same expression on their faces. *Wow.* She waited until he rejoined them in front of the alley before she turned and continued down the street, glancing over her shoulder every five seconds to make sure they didn't approach again.

They didn't. *Thank goodness.* She breathed a sigh of relief, but kept the pepper spray ready in her hand. Just in case.

Fortunately, that "case" never came and she made it to her home three minutes later. She tucked the pepper spray into its compartment in her purse and walked up the lengthy trail to her front door. Upon reaching the steps, she turned around and sat on the bottom step. She could see the majority of the block from her position. There weren't any threats in close proximity to her. Nothing to worry about. Her dad's big gray van was parked in the driveway to her right but other than that, she didn't see anything. All was well... all was quiet.

She raised her head to let the air blow through her hair while calling to mind her brief conversation with Detective Kana Miyoshi. Kana had told her to reflect on them later, but now was the first opportunity she'd had. *Hard to think about philosophical, spiritual things while being terrified on the streets.*

"If you do good things to be seen by men, and to be praised by them, then you can and will fail," Kana had told her during the *long* walk to the first floor. "A lot of people—that's why they become police officers, firemen, and pastors. They want people to see them, and they enjoy the fame, and the positive things said about them. But when that notoriety fades, or if it never comes at all... then they get depressed. Not all people will be appreciated in this life. Doesn't work that way.

"You know, I think that the people whose accomplishments went unnoticed or weren't paraded around... they'll be the ones able to really enjoy what they've done. Especially those who have acted because of conscience toward God."

"But what if you're not religious?" Lizzy had asked.

"Doesn't matter," Kana replied. "I mean, you'll have a lot more problems than lack of recognition if you don't get saved. But, the same holds true in general. If you do what's right for God's sake, or for goodness' sake, then you won't be so disappointed when no one cares.

Because you didn't do it for them in the first place. Does that make sense?"

"Yeah," Lizzy said. "It does."

"And there's something great that I always try to keep in mind. Jesus said not to do your good works before men to be seen by them. If we do, we'll have a reward, but it'll be temporary. But if we do them, and don't make a big deal about them, then He'll reward us in the end. And that one *will* last."

Though Lizzy's family had shied away from religion, she took the answer to heart. It erased the tinge of despair she'd felt listening to Thomas Freeman's complaints. Whether she did it for God or not, if she didn't expect the spotlight she wouldn't miss it. That was a basic summary of Kana's response and it brought a smile to Lizzy's face. *Not like a job in computers gives you that many opportunities to be praised, anyway. After today, though, and Avenger showing up when he did—maybe there is more to this God thing than...*

Lizzy noticed that a shadow had fallen across the walkway right in front of her. She gasped and popped up to her feet, her hand going into the purse pocket for the pepper spray. It was in her grasp when she saw what had cast the shadow. The Avenger stood in the grass, three feet to her right. With the light behind him, he was darker than the shadow emanating from him. The only detail visible on his body or costume was the gray cross on his chest. She knew he was safe to be around, but his appearance still gave her the chills. The fins reaching above his shoulders looked more like wings in the darkness.

"You..." She stammered. "What... what are you doing here?"

"I wanted to make sure you got home safe," He replied

"Well, I almost didn't," she said, taking her hand out of the purse and tucking both into her pockets. "I almost got attacked on the way home."

"I know. They weren't afraid of your pepper spray."

Lizzy's mouth dropped open and she stared up at him, summing up the revelation and her day in, "Wow."

A Fallen Rose

1

The pounding rain had kept the majority of Minikin Capital's population indoors. The latest weather reports predicted that a storm was likely to pass through the city during the evening. There hadn't been any thunder or lightning yet, but everyone heeded the warnings. Except Rose.

Rose Arturo hadn't seen one person since she exited her friend Becky's house fifteen minutes ago. She was walking down a lonely street toward a one story building that occupied a block by itself. There was a white sign with light blue letters decorating it three feet to the front door's left. Probably the name or one of those annoying church signs. Though she'd passed the building several times in the past she didn't recall seeing a sign. Rose peeked up at the roof from under her hood. A white cross was proudly displayed atop a pole in the center of the rooftop.

She sighed and asked herself if she really wanted to go in there. She'd been drawn to it, seemingly by invisible forces, the past few weeks. Today those forces were aided by the ponderous raindrops striking her from every direction. When she left Amanda's home, her friend had given her a hooded sweatshirt. It kept the water out of her face, which was nice, but did little else.

The stores and business places all around were closed. The church was the last option she had for a refuge from the rain. Possibly. There were no vehicles in the parking lot in front of it, but lights were on somewhere inside. Hopefully it wasn't just customary for them to leave lights on even when the building was empty.

Rose was also hoping to talk to someone inside because she needed refuge in more ways than one. She quickened her pace as she reached the vacant parking lot. She needed counsel. Someone to listen to her and tell her what to do. The last two weeks she had been tormented by either her conscience or demons. They had driven her out of a bed in Amanda's house, and into the oncoming storm. Feelings of guilt over a lifestyle that she didn't see a problem with overwhelmed her. She wasn't sure what she was going to say. Right now that wasn't important—she *had* to find an outlet.

She neared the property and felt a tinge of relief upon seeing the letters up close. They read:

Faith Independent Bible Church

Sunday 11 a.m. - Friday 7:30 p.m.

Thank God it's not one of those awful signs. She hated those things with a passion. The church a few blocks away had boasted the words, "Wal-Mart isn't the only Saving Place." That one had turned her stomach. If only God granted whoever came up with those slogans a little of His creativity. Especially if He had created the universe. *And the best they can come up with is, 'Wal-Mart isn't the only Saving Place.' Geez.*

Rose reached her destination, shook those thoughts from her head and knocked on the front door. She noticed a luminous round button on eye level beside it and pressed it twice. Then she reached up and pulled the hood of her shirt back. Didn't want to look like a thug. Whoever, if anyone, was inside, might be inclined to leave her out there if she appeared dangerous. She closed her eyes to enjoy the feel of the cold raindrops in her hair. It had become a little humid and stuffy with the hood on.

The door opened and she looked up to see a black man across from her. *That's a pleasant surprise.* He wore a blue dress shirt, complimented by a black tie and slacks. His face indicated that he wasn't that much older than Rose. She had turned 19 a few months ago and he had to be 26 at the oldest. His hair was closely shaved, nearly bald, and he had a light mustache. He was in good shape, too, judging by his build.

While Rose casually observed him, he stared back at her, blinking often. Finally, he said, "Can I help you?"

"Um, is the pastor here?" Rose asked. She'd seen the pastor before. He was old, white, pudgy, a few inches shorter than the 5'8" man across the threshold, and involuntarily bald.

"No, he won't be in until tomorrow morning," The man replied. He still looked confused. Uneasy.

"Oh, okay." Rose's shoulders sagged. She was *never* going to come to a church again as long as she lived. Why had she been so determined to go tonight if the pastor wasn't even there? *Guess whoever was directing me didn't have good timing.* Rose pulled her hood back over her head and started to back away. "See you."

"Wait," the man called. "I'm the assistant pastor."

Rose stopped, and looked at him hopefully.

"Is there anything I can help you with?" He asked. "I may not be as smart as Russ, but I'm sure I could..."

"Yeah, sure man," Rose nodded.

The assistant pastor stepped aside and held the door open for her. She rushed past him, removing the hood again and immediately unzipped the sweatshirt. It was cool inside the building and the wetness made it uncomfortable. She slipped the extra layer off and approached the coat rack to the left. As she draped it onto a hanger she took in her surroundings. The darkened sanctuary was visible beyond the rack. Across from the door through which she entered was another door, and to the right a lit hallway.

"Follow me." The pastor headed toward the hallway.

A moment later they entered a medium sized room. He went and stood in front of the captain's swivel chair behind the desk. She paused in the doorway to observe what she assumed was his office. Nothing out of the ordinary. Behind his chair was a bookcase filled with Bible commentaries, cassette tapes, and other boring looking items. The walls had Christian posters, a calendar, and reminders and notices pinned to them. Despite the amount of stuff, he'd managed to keep the place neat. Orderly.

The assistant pastor gestured toward a cushioned office chair before the desk and Rose sat in it, eyes still roaming. Once she was settled he sat down as well.

"Okay, so…" He began. "Oh, excuse me. My name's Joe."

"Pastor Joe, or just Joe?"

"Uh, either one. And you are?"

"Rose," she said.

"What can I do for you?"

"Well… I don't know, sir," Rose admitted. She felt large butterflies fluttering around inside her stomach. *Take it easy, girl.* "See, I've just… I've felt like I had to come here tonight. I have a lot to get off my chest. And I need advice, too. Do you have a lot of time?"

"Sure. But we do charge by the hour."

"What?"

"I'm kidding." He grinned.

"Oh, thank God," Rose muttered. "I don't like how some churches are all about money. That's why a lot of my friends don't go anymore. You walk in the door and they shove a collection plate in your face. Then when you don't have anything, they teach a two hour sermon about giving. Know what I mean?"

"I haven't had that experience myself, but I can understand your angst." Joe smiled. "Fact is, to keep a building running, to be able to perform some of the functions of the church you need money. And the people who are provided with spiritual blessings should provide financial blessings if they can."

"Financial blessings. Like... giving your church my money so you can buy a wide screen, high definition TV. That way even the people in the back get to see the sweat on the pastor's forehead when he's preaching. Or you could buy some fancy, gold-laced, ten-dollar get well cards for sick church members. Maybe a new drum set? Or some extra cash to pay bands to come in and play on Friday nights?"

"We don't do any of that here, Rose," Joe said.

"I bet you don't. Those churches usually have a corny behind sign out front."

"Like 'Get out of Facebook, and get into My Book?' I think sometimes those signs are a disservice. Especially when they have bad spelling and grammar. You'd think if they can speak in tongues, they could spell right, you know?"

Rose laughed and clapped her hands, "Yeah, man. That's what I always say."

"But, don't take what some do and apply it to everyone. And certainly, you should never let your problems with a church become a problem with God. That's the mistake a lot of people make. Besides, I feel that as long as you give your money to a worthy cause, you're doing the right thing. If your church is going to buy surround sound or something, then you should probably give to an honest Christian organization. Or just leave the church."

"That sounds fair. But why does God need our money? I mean, can't He just make some if He needs it that bad?"

"Interesting question..." Joe nodded. "Well, the thing is, God's people are considered His ambassadors. And the earth is, in a sense, in our hands. He gave us dominion in the garden of Eden. So really it's up to us to decide what to do with what's ours.

"When it comes to giving money to a church—you do that for various reasons. One is to pay the pastors and teachers who are there to help you seven days a week, to study God's Word and faithfully teach it to you. But as to whether God could just *make money*—of course He could. It's better though to make it available to us and to see what we'll do with it. Something tells me, Mrs. Rose, that money is the least of your worries."

"It is." Rose shifted uncomfortably in her chair. She liked Joe, already. He was kind, seemed to answer honestly, and he was intuitive. Though she was curious about money issues, that wasn't why she had come. She took a deep breath and blew it out slowly. "Okay, listen. I like sex. I don't think sex is as bad as some churches make it out to be. If it's fun, if it's consensual, and no one is getting hurt then it's okay. But I do think there's such a thing as too much, you know? And I've probably crossed that line."

Joe leaned back and his eyes raised to the ceiling. Rose read the "oh boy" in his expression.

"Just listen," she pressed. "It started when I was 12 in my youth group. I would mess around with the boys during trips in the van, or I'd invite them over when my mom was out. Then I started messing around in school, and... we experimented with drugs. Now I know drugs are wrong, even weed, right? Unless it's for medical use."

"If we agree that being in a bad mood or wanting to relax isn't medical use."

"I agree. But I stopped that. I'm not doing drugs anymore. Now, it's just sex. Casual sex, because I don't have a boyfriend yet. I do like this boy named Tony, though."

"Do you think casual sex is okay?"

"Yeah. Why not? I mean, if two people want it, then they should go for it."

"So, why are you here?" Joe asked.

"I don't know."

"I'm assuming it's because your conscience has been bothering you. You may think all that you've been doing is fine, but deep down you know better. You know it's not good, it's not right, and that it's *not* pleasing to God."

"Why?"

"Because God made sex to be enjoyed between husband and wife. And in the bonds of marriage it's a good thing. Bible says so. 'The marriage bed is undefiled.' It's taking it out of that original intention that causes the problem. That's why we have so many marriages falling apart, rampant adultery, and more sexually transmitted diseases than the average person can count."

Rose winced.

"There are natural consequences for sin. You have lewd sex you'll catch something. You murder someone, and the government has the right—the duty, to take your life. If you lie, you'll eventually be caught in that lie. If you steal, you'll probably be found out. So, God has set things in nature to teach us what's right and wrong. It's in all of us. We can choose to listen or not, though."

"But..." A stinging pain shot through Rose's heart. "But why is it all so fun?"

"It's always fun to do wrong until you get caught," Joe replied. "The Bible says that bread gained by deceit is sweet to a man, but afterward his mouth will be filled with gravel. That's how life works, sometimes. Doing drugs is fun, until you realize what it does to your body. An older lady who goes to this church was messing with drugs for years. She quit a long time ago, but she still suffers the effects. God's not punishing her, now that she's saved, but she's reaping what she has sown."

Rose blinked her tears away. His words were cutting into her in a way she hadn't experienced before. Reminding her of her own lifetime of sin, and the consequences she'd discovered recently. She swallowed the lump in her throat, and spoke, "Well, if it's too late to avoid consequences, then what? What's the point of life? Why not just keep doing what you want to do?" Her sadness was turning into anger. "He could have warned me sooner if He wanted to."

"You know, I've heard so many stories and even seen a woman who was dying from lung cancer. On what was going to be her deathbed, with a breathing tube. And she would take the tube out, take a hit of her cigarette, and then put it back on. Or a famous male prostitute who was dying of AIDS, and he was going back out turning tricks. It's futile. And it's *stupid*. Especially because life doesn't end here. When those who have done wrong take their last breath, shortly after, they meet God face to face. It'll be you and Him. And He's the one who knows all of your sins.

Not just the sex... even if you were a virgin right now, you'd still be in trouble."

"How so?" Rose stood. "I'm a very nice person. I'd give an arm and a leg to help my friends if they needed it. So don't you judge me!"

"I'm simply telling you what God's Word says, Rose," Joe said. "Please, have a seat. I'm not here to judge you, I'm trying to keep you from being judged."

"I don't need it."

"Rose, did you come here so I could tell you to live life the way you have been? Or did you come to this church because you wanted the truth? Because you wanted a way out?"

Rose sat down. He'd added to her guilt since she walked in, but if she left she knew she wouldn't be any better off.

"Look, I'm sure you're a nice girl. I haven't been talking to you for more than ten minutes and I like you. Fact is, nice people don't all go to heaven. Let me put it to you this way. Have you ever told a lie before?"

"Yeah. Who hasn't?"

"Jesus. Have you ever stolen something?"

"A few times." Rose scratched the back of her head.

"Have you ever used God's name in vain?"

"Yes... I've been trying to stop."

"Good. But in essence, you've admitted that you're a liar, a thief, and a blasphemer. All sins worthy of punishment when committed in the sight of a holy God. And He will punish those who break His laws. In a place called hell. Infinite punishment for offending an Infinite Being. It's horrible yes, but we deserve it. And without God's mercy and grace we're going to get it. But that doesn't just come with an apology. Or by turning around and having a good life. Your sins remain, no matter what good works you do. In fact, trying to get to heaven that way is like trying to bribe a judge. 'Well, I've given money to charity.' 'Yes, but you've also robbed banks.' Crime is crime, and it must be punished."

"I understand."

"But Rose, God didn't create you nor did He allow you to survive all this time for nothing. Making it to 19 these days in Minikin Capital is rare. But you have. The reason is, God didn't make you to destroy you. He loves you more than anyone else possibly can. And because He loves you, He sent His own perfect Son, Jesus Christ, to die on the cross for your sins. Jesus had been with God... for eternity. They always were.

"And yet Jesus came here, humbled Himself, and was born as a Man. He created men, but He was born as one. And after he lived a perfect life, He was falsely accused, beaten nearly to death, spat on, mocked, and then crucified. All of that He did to pay for your sins. Instead of you suffering in hell forever Jesus did it on the cross. Then three days later, He rose again and was seen by hundreds. What His death and resurrection meant, is that we have a chance at eternal life. God can forgive our sins because of what Jesus did. If we are willing to turn from sin and serving ourselves, to serving our Savior.

"If you do that, you may still suffer the consequences of your sins here, but in heaven you won't. When you die, you'll be forever with the God who loved and died for you. And there won't be pain or suffering there. But the choice is yours. I pray that you make the right one."

Rose lowered her eyes to the floor and leaned forward. What she'd just heard was a lot to take in. She felt a surge of emotions coursing through her. Guilt. Appreciation. Sadness. Love. A God who was going to punish her for the bad things she'd done in life. Yet because of his kindness, He was punished in her place to offer her a chance. *Man.* She didn't feel worse than she had upon coming in. She really didn't know how she felt. Or how to feel.

"It's a lot to take in, I know," Joe said.

"Yeah," Rose accented. "I…" She was a little overwhelmed. "Do I say a prayer or something?"

"You should pray, yes. For God's forgiveness. Thank Him for His mercy, confess your sins, and ask Jesus to save you."

"Do I have to now?"

"You shouldn't put it off. 'Today is the day of salvation.' But I'm not going make you repeat a prayer after me or anything. It's between you and Him. Take your time, think about it—but don't procrastinate."

"Okay, I won't." Rose nodded. She thought for a moment. "So… if I do get *saved* that would mean… no sex before I get married. Not anymore."

"Right."

"Are you married?"

"Yeah." Joe grinned. He turned a silver eight-by-eleven frame on his desk around. The picture inside was of a pale Asian woman with high cheek bones, black hair, and large almond shaped eyes. She was looking off to the side of the camera, her eyes fiery. *She's beautiful.* "That's the first picture of herself she gave me."

"She's hot," Rose noted. "So, you didn't have sex before you were married?"

It was his time to squirm, and she noticed his discomfort. "I did. Not with her, but that was before I became a Christian. I waited five and a half years after that."

"You're the man if you could pull that off."

"Thanks." They both laughed.

"So... you're the assistant pastor. Do you ever teach?"

"Only when the pastor is away, or taking a break," Joe told her. "I do have a Bible Study every Friday night. And I would love for you to come."

"I think I'll do that."

"And... you can call me anytime. Here or at my house, I'll give you my card." He reached into a drawer and brought his hand up ten seconds later with a business card.

Rose took it from him and stood. "Thanks."

"You're welcome." Joe tucked his hands in his pockets and the two walked out into the hallway. She waited for him so they could advance side by side toward the door. Both walked slow.

"So... I believed everything you said. But I don't see too many natural consequences happening here. For the killers. The rates are way too high."

"Don't worry," Joe said. "God's taking care of them. Here and on Judgment Day. Things will get better."

"I hope so."

"Do you need a ride home?"

"Well..." They stepped into the foyer and looked through the windowpane on the door. "I think the rain's done so I should be okay. I'd rather walk and think, anyway. But maybe... maybe after class on Friday you could. I'll buy you a dinner or something."

"The Bible Study is from 8:30 to 9:30. Are places still open then?"

"Taco Bell. Or Olive Garden."

"We'll decide then, I guess. You sure you want to pay? I could."

Rose retrieved her sweatshirt, which had dried considerably, and slipped into it. "Well, you did say earlier that if someone gives someone else a spiritual blessing, then it's fair to give a financial one in return right?" She smiled.

Joe grinned also.

"Thank you so much. I do feel better. I just need to think. And I'll probably call you before I come. Or you can call me. I'll leave my number on your answering machine tomorrow or something. Or with your wife. As long as she won't kill you."

"She won't." He laughed.

"Thanks." Rose stepped closer and hugged him.

Three seconds later, he warmly returned her embrace. Rose wasn't sure what it was, but she was more grateful to him than she had ever been to anyone. There was also something about his demeanor that she liked. Something she was attracted to. Not romantically, but... it was there. By the look in his face, he felt it, too.

They pulled away and Rose thanked him again.

"Anytime," he said, stepping past her to pull the door open. "See you Friday. If you want to stop by before then, that's fine, too."

"I'll keep that in mind—see you then." She nodded and walked through the doorway.

2

Rose stood with her back to the door of the church, eyes on the pale clouds in the dark sky. She searched the heavens for a moment before pulling the hood of her sweatshirt up over her head. After a deep breath, she tucked her hands in her pockets and started across the parking lot. The rain had departed but left large puddles behind. She stepped around them and slowed her pace, presumably to avoid slipping on the pavement, which glistened with fresh moisture.

She passed the same car that had been there when she arrived—one likely belonging to Pastor Joe. In the spot right beside it another vehicle was parked, a black, sleeker model. It was on the opposite side of the younger girl who didn't even glance in its direction. She either hadn't noticed the new arrival or wasn't bothered by it.

From inside the vehicle, Kana glanced after the departing teenager before turning her attention to the church. She snatched up a brown paper bag from the passenger's seat and climbed out of the car. While walking toward the building light reflected off of the badge pinned to her belt beside the buckle. She'd forgotten she still had it on. *One of those days*, she said to herself with an internal sigh.

Minutes later she knocked twice on Joe's office door. Without waiting for a response, she opened it and moved forward to stand in the threshold. Light seeped into the otherwise dark room around her petite frame. It revealed the crowded but organized office that had been allotted to her husband. The chair behind his desk was empty so she squinted and gazed around. She found him seconds later on his knees, bent over one of the guest chairs to the left side of the desk. His eyes were shut and his hands clasped together on the seat in front of him.

Kana paused in the doorway with her free hand still clinging to the knob. He appeared to be deep in prayer, and hadn't moved an inch since she opened the door. If not for her knocking he might not have even known anyone was there. *Don't want to disturb him exactly...*

"I'm finished," he spoke in a deep, menacing voice. One that was too powerful to come naturally to a man his size. A man with his peaceful laid back demeanor. His wife was one of few people, however, who knew about his other side.

"I should've figured you'd be ready to head out by now." Kana stepped inside and closed the door behind herself. She leaned against the wood and rested her head. "I usually drive by after work just in case you are still around."

The other guest chair in the room was against the wall a few feet in front of her husband. A black cape and a black tunic with a cross emblazoned on the front, the main components of the Avenger costume, were draped across the back of the furniture. *That answers that question, I guess.*

"I'm running a little late tonight," Joe said. His voice dropped further into his normal tone with each word. He leaned back from the chair and started up to his feet. "Had a few visits today—one just a few minutes ago. And on top of that I was busy trying to prepare for this Friday's message."

"I'll review it like always." Kana smiled. She flicked a thumb in the direction of the costume pieces. "I'm assuming those weren't out during your last meeting, by the way."

Joe grinned. "They were probably out the whole day."

Kana laughed as the two headed toward each other. She wrapped her arms around his waist and he embraced her, drawing her head into his shoulder. Kana closed her eyes and relaxed her entire body, allowing him to support her weight. She was content to rest in his arms after spending the last eleven hours on her feet. Running around the police department and the entire city of Minikin Capital without a break. She wished he could hold her the remainder of the night but the costume on the chair and what it meant negated that. He had worked most of the day as well but unlike her, he had another job to go out to.

His arms relaxed and Kana gingerly pulled away from him. Then she held up the paper bag on display between them.

"I doubt you'll have time to eat it but I did bring you dinner," she told him, sadly. "Knowing you, you haven't eaten anything since lunch time."

"Busy day." Joe shrugged. He took the bag from her and studied her face with a tenderness in his dark eyes. "How are you?"

"Tired." Kana stepped past him to take a seat on the corner of the desk. He pulled the guest chair in front of her and sat, resting his elbows on her knees. "I didn't even get to take a break today. There's so much to do in this city and even more to catch up with. It seems like every time we even make a dent in the case load there's another five to deal with."

"I know the feeling," he replied.

"You would think with the Mafia and the Yakuza *both* having to replace their heads, and all the personnel problems you caused—you'd think we'd have a little break."

"Doesn't work that way, unfortunately," Joe said. "Big outfits like that are just symptoms of the problem. That problem being the evil in this city. You take them out you still have the low level gangs, the serial killers, and all the other thugs."

Kana nodded before adding, "Not to mention before too long the Mafia will be back up on their feet—and the missing leader's just an opportunity for new guys to come up. Trying to prove their worth to the throne with even more ruthlessness. We might even get new gangs. If we haven't already."

Joe considered that while staring out the window through a narrow slit in the blinds. He narrowed his eyes. "And I'm going out there more tired than usual. Makes me wonder if this was a good idea in the first place."

Kana blinked. "Working here at the church?"

Joe kept silent, although that was enough of an answer.

She sighed. "Well, considering the lives you've been able to impact... possibly even that young girl who was here almost ten o' clock at night... she obviously need*ed something*... if you weren't here, she might've gone without help."

"Maybe," he said. "But meanwhile things aren't getting any better out on the streets."

"Is that why the Avenger of Blood exists, honey?" Kana asked with her eyes widened and eyebrows raised to accentuate the question. She waited until he returned her gaze to continue. "Is what you do at night supposed to *make things better*? Or is it just what God called you to, regardless of the results?"

"I'd think after two years we'd be seeing some improvement though..."

"The way we'll see any *improvement* is through reaching out to people. Through this church. What you do at night is necessary, and it's good... but you're punishing the guilty. Putting murderers to death. That's not necessarily going to make things better. What you do here will."

Joe lowered his stare to her lap and his eyes moved back and forth. He took a deep breath before admitting, "You're right."

BANG! A massive gunshot sounded from somewhere in the near distance. It was loud enough to startle the average person but neither Joe nor Kana moved an inch. Their eyes found each other's and they exchanged a knowing glance. Joe frowned.

"You better get out there," she told him, pouting. "I'll eat your dinner and let you know how it was."

Joe stood up and kissed her on the forehead. "I might be hungry in the morning."

"I'll buy some cereal on the way home," Kana said, smirking.

"Funny." He turned and walked over to pick up the parts of his costume. Once he was in the doorway of the room he turned back to Kana. When he spoke this time, his voice had returned to the low, deep, monotone one of before. "I'll see you in the morning."

3

A young girl, maybe eighteen or nineteen, sat in the passenger's seat of an SUV screaming bloody murder. An older gentleman in a business suit occupied the driver's seat. He was slumped over in the other direction, his head leaned against the blood stained window. The liquid covered his entire upper body and the side of his head facing the girl was a mess. A small hole in the driver's side window was a few inches above, but perpendicular to, a hole in the glass on the passenger's side. The girl, Tara, pushed her car door open and tried to climb out.

In her panic, she fell on her side into the street. She landed hard and rolled onto her stomach, coughing and spitting. Light shone on her from the side at the same time a car horn blared in her ears. Tara lifted her gaze from the pavement to see a pick up truck speeding toward her. She shrieked and rolled out of the way so that her body hugged the side of the SUV.

The truck roared by, causing the earth underneath her to tremble as it went. She pushed up to her hands and knees with her entire body working against her. In addition to the trembling and the adrenaline coursing through her veins, her limbs seemed to weigh a thousand pounds each. Still she managed to lift her head and cry out, "HELP! I NEED HELP!"

Two young men appeared from near an alleyway ahead. The SUV had come to a halt in the middle of the road, hence her encounter with the pick up truck. A sign nearby announced that she was on "Lenola Road". The scarce lighting in the neighborhood was provided by a couple of yellow street lights, and a glowing neon sign in a liquor store's display window. One of the two men now walking toward her had a wine or beer bottle in his right hand enclosed in a brown paper bag. They both gazed around, seemingly checking for other signs of danger on the otherwise barren road. Neither of them even glanced at her for more than a few seconds.

Tara got a knee up underneath her and then she pushed up to her feet. She leaned on the truck with one hand to keep herself steady.

"What's the problem here?" A man called from behind.

Tara looked over her shoulder to see three of them, all dressed in hooded sweatshirts, approaching her. They were examining the vehicle, briefly checking her out, and eyeing the rest of the neighborhood. No concern in their expressions or in their voices.

"What happened? You get a flat tire?" One of the first young men asked.

Tara returned her eyes to them to see that two others had joined them. There were now seven men quickly moving in on her and the vehicle. Her hand moved slowly along the door of the SUV in the direction of the handle. She kept her eyes, however, on the men.

"I... something happened to him." She pointed at the man in the driver's seat. They followed her finger and briefly inspected the interior of the car. The dim lighting probably hindered them from observing the full extent of the grim scene, but they *had* to see the blood. If they did, it didn't bother them. Their attention was drawn back to Tara almost instantly. They drew within ten feet and the three behind her sounded as if they were closer.

"Really?" The young man who seemed to be the leader grinned without an ounce of humor in his cold, brown eyes. They were glued to her, with a violent obsession showing in the irises. "How about you step away from the car..."

THUNK! The vehicle beside her lurched underneath sudden weight applied to it and Tara jumped and backed away. All of the men who had been closing in also stopped in their tracks. Their eyes and Tara's went up to the roof of the SUV. A shadowy form was crouched there—humanoid but enveloped in a black cape hanging from wing-like fins on the shoulders. It rose, slowly, to stand at full height, displaying the medieval style uniform it wore. Dark eyes were visible through eye-socket shaped holes in the metallic mask, molded into a human skull crowned with horns.

One of the men, Reyes, reached into his sweatshirt pocket. The Avenger lifted his arm and thrust it in his direction. A silver star-shaped weapon flew from his grasp and struck the back of Reyes' hand as he brought it out. He cried out in pain and dropped the pistol to clutch his now bleeding hand in the other.

In an instant the Avenger dropped to support his weight on his hands before pushing off and extending his legs. His outstretched feet hit one of the other men in the chest and he was thrown back into two of the others. The Avenger landed on the pavement and stood in time to block a punch from Derek. He elbowed him across the face, then reverse elbowed him on the other side of the jaw. With Derek dazed, the Avenger hooked his head in the crook of his arm—a reverse chin lock—and spun around so they were back to back with Derek's head braced backward on the Avenger's shoulder.

Terrence was running forward only to be intercepted by a left boot to the face. One of the other guys, Hosea, was fifteen feet away reaching down for the dropped gun. The Avenger's foot was still in the air so he brought his knee into his chest. A knife with an eight-inched blade was tucked in a sheath strapped to the side of his boot. He slipped it out and brought the knife back over Derek's over exposed throat. In a fluid motion he swiped the blade across the flesh there and then tossed the knife at Hosea.

Hosea had the gun in hand by now and he fired once while evading the projectile. The knife sailed past him and embedded itself into the shoulder of Xavier. He screamed and staggered away. The stray bullet ricocheted harmlessly off a concrete building in close proximity.

The Avenger felt movement behind him and dipped to his left side, leaving his boot stretched out on the pavement. Damien had been lunging for him but now found himself moving toward empty space. He tripped over the Avenger's foot and fell face first to the pavement. The Avenger jumped forward and kicked Damien in the side of the head, knocking him out.

Then he continued to charge at Hosea who was beginning to take aim at his head. The Avenger dived under the line of fire with his body sailing horizontally above the asphalt. His arms were extended before him and he landed on his hands five feet from Hosea and ducked his head to perform a front roll. As he was coming up off the momentum he tiger palmed Hosea underneath the chin. His free hand grabbed Hosea's wrist, which he twisted, turning the muzzle of the gun aside. He kneed Hosea In the abdomen, doubling him over, and then aimed the gun at Ezekiel, who had a gun in his own hand. The Avenger clamped down on Hosea's knuckles and the gun fired. Ezekiel dropped. Jay ran toward the vigilante with Hosea between them.

The Avenger hopped onto Hosea's back and rolled over him onto his other side. Upon landing he lifted his knee up into Hosea's face, knocking him unconscious. Then he jumped off the ground with his back toward Jay and spun while in the air. His foot lashed out and his heel caught Jay right between his ear and the top of his jaw line. He grunted in pain as the power of the blow sent him twisting in the air before he landed hard on the ground.

Xavier, still struggling to pull the knife out of his shoulder, and another guy were running as fast as they could in opposite directions. That left the biggest of all the men, Ryan, as the last man standing. He glanced after his fleeing companions, his own eyes revealing that he probably wanted to follow them. Instead he focused his attention on the Avenger and raised two meaty fists. The Avenger stood at five foot nine and Ryan was six inches taller, with considerably more mass packed onto a powerful frame. Yet he was the one whose fists were trembling while the Avenger watched him calmly. His hands were at his sides.

Tara had her back pressed against the side of the SUV. She'd been frozen there since the fight started. Her mouth and eyes were stretched open at what she was witnessing.

Ryan made the first move, jerking his left shoulder forward in a threatening manner. When the Avenger flinched, Ryan immediately reversed his shoulders' positions and threw a right jab. The Avenger leaned to the side, narrowly avoiding the blow. Ryan followed up with a wild left hook that would've taken the head off of the average man. The Avenger ducked under it so that the hardened fist passed by overhead. Ryan raised his left knee, hoping to catch his foe with it before he could straighten up. The Avenger was too fast.

He arched his back while catching the crook of Ryan's knee in his left forearm. The back of the Avenger's head crashed into Ryan's chin, shattering teeth and drawing blood. Then he brought his right arm up and drove the elbow down into the center of Ryan's thigh. The bigger man cried out in pain. The Avenger lifted his right foot and stomped down on the inside of Ryan's other knee, driving it into the pavement. Ryan dropped to his knees, his face displaying even more anguish.

To finish him off, the Avenger dropped into a low crouch before him. He loaded his right fist at his own waist and unleashed it in an upward arch. The upper cut connected with the underside of Ryan's jaw and he fell over onto his back. Out cold. The Avenger rose to full height and embraced his gloved right fist in the left. He clamped down on his hand, cracking the knuckles, and then repeated it with the left fist. All the while his eyes surveyed the damage he had wrought upon the men. They were all either unconscious, dead, or in far too much pain to be a threat. Their enemy stood tall above them all.

His attention finally landed on Tara whose eyes had not left him since he'd arrived. She stared back at him, her chest heaving with each breath. The Avenger glanced over her shoulder to the body of the older man in the vehicle. He narrowed his eyes and stepped toward her. Tara retreated to the side, holding her hands up with the palms in his direction.

"I'm not going to hurt you," he said as he moved past and pulled open the passenger's door. He first observed the dead man and the blood covering his side of the car. Then his eyes moved to the hole in the glass near the top of the driver's side window. He turned to the open passenger's side door and scanned it until he found another hole in the window. It was considerably lower, maybe halfway down the glass. He pivoted on his right heel and peered over his shoulder.

Ten feet beyond the curb lined up with the vehicle was Sylvia's Nail Salon. A pink and green sign boasted the name of the establishment. A meter below it a darkened sign declared the store to be "CLOSED". The Avenger's eyes glossed over the bottom part of the small building. They landed on a dark indent in the glass, at the very bottom of the display wall. A cylindrical object had been lodged there, partly held up by the concrete floor. It was golden in color although part of it was smeared with blood. Roughly four inches long and closer to half an inch in diameter.

The Avenger dived to the side at the instant an explosion sounded from nearby. He turned his body to align it with the pavement and performed another front roll. At the conclusion of the maneuver he remained in a crouch and raised his eyes. The nearest rooftops were illuminated only by the moonlight seeping through clouds. It was enough to see that they appeared vacant. A tall hotel building a block in the distance was visible over the nearest roof. On its roof a man ran in the opposite direction, clutching a long object in his hands.

In an instant the Avenger tore around the vehicle and raced down an alleyway between buildings. The figure on the hotel had moved out of sight but he wouldn't get far. The Avenger ran as fast as he could and soon entered the next block. He tore across the street, ignoring an oncoming car. The driver, probably startled by the strange sight, slammed on the brakes. The Avenger cleared the road and headed into another alley between the hotel and a smaller building. He looked up at both rooftops but didn't see anything. *Which building to try first?*

As he considered his options a mechanical click came from behind and stopped him in his tracks. Something about the distinct sound, even above the noise of the city, was ominous. The Avenger began to turn when another explosion went off from half a block away.

WHAM! An immense force slammed into his left side. The impact lifted him off his feet and sent him sailing backward. He landed and rolled further away before coming to a stop on his side facing the street. It felt as if two hundred pounds of pressure had been applied to his torso. His ribs were literally throbbing with pain and his lungs had tightened. He struggled to take in air through the mask.

Under attack—can't stay here... Despite the pain, he forced his eyes open and looked up. Black had formed on the edges of his vision, which had also blurred. Through the annoyances he was able to make out someone walking toward him from the former alleyway. It was the young girl he'd rescued, Tara. The fear and panic in her face had subsided and been replaced by a surprising callousness. Her eyes were cold and locked on the Avenger. Her lips pressed tight together. She had a sniper rifle in her hands and she was in the process of chambering another round.

The Avenger got one of his palms on the ground and he pushed against it. What felt like a hot iron dug into his left side with the effort. He clenched his teeth together and fought through it. The pain increased to an almost unbearable level. It was so horrible that it was nauseating. The Avenger managed to get to his hands and knees but Tara was approaching fast. The other round had already been chambered and she shifted the butt of the weapon to her shoulder.

To the Avenger's right there was a window into the smaller building adjoining the hotel. *Move idiot—move!* He got one foot on the ground underneath him but the movement triggered the feeling of bone grating on bone inside him. Knowing his predicament, he focused on gathering as much strength as he could in his limbs. Tara lifted the muzzle of the massive weapon and pointed it in his direction.

"Hey—drop the weapon!" A voice called from somewhere nearby.

Tara removed her predatory gaze from the Avenger to glance to her left.

Now! He pushed with his foot and his hands and launched himself toward the window. He ducked his head as he hit and crashed through the glass. In midair he tried to turn to land on his back but instead fell on his right side. His body hit the marble floor with a thud and he growled in pain. The shock of the landing shot from his right side through to the left, further aggravating the point of injury. The Avenger hugged his sides with his arms and rolled over onto his knees, still hunched over.

Outside, Tara watched the police officer approaching from down the street. He was in his early twenties and had a pistol drawn, aimed at her chest. She glanced into the alley to see that the Avenger had disappeared. Her lips parted to reveal her teeth in a bitter scowl.

"Darn it," she whispered.

"I said drop the weapon!" The officer screamed as he neared. "NOW or I'll shoot!"

From inside the store, the Avenger raised his head and attempted a deep breath. He had to warn the officer who had inadvertently come to his rescue. His inhale went about halfway before the throbbing in his side became more intense. The air caught in his chest and he coughed.

Tara glared at the officer while lowering the muzzle of the rifle to the pavement. His stare matched hers in intensity and his grip on the gun was firm. Even for someone newer to the force he had gained the composure needed to deal with Minikin Capital's worst. Unfortunately for him, he was outnumbered this time around. Although sirens in close proximity alerted Tara to the presence of his backup.

BOOM! The officer was thrown to the ground. A bloody mist remained in the air where his head had been a split second before.

"Time to go!" A deep voice called from a block to her right, the direction the officer had come from. An old station wagon idled in the center of the road. A man in a ski mask sat in the driver's seat. He leaned over and pushed the passenger's door open. "Now!"

"Did you get him?" The man inquired.

"I hit him once in the side but he got away," Tara replied.

The Avenger could barely hear the voices above the approaching sirens. He sat on the floor with his back to the wall underneath the now empty window space. While his left arm remained pressed against his side, his right was extended in front of him. He clutched a sword in that hand with the blade stretched out on the floor. Ready to strike in case they had decided to come after him. Considering that he hadn't even been able to speak seconds ago—it was probably good that they hadn't.

With the threat gone, he took the opportunity to survey the room he'd thrown himself into. It was a rather large retail store filled with over a dozen rows of items. A smaller section off to the left was stocked with clothes and other apparel. Standing out amidst the darkness near the back wall, glowing red letters spelled out "EXIT". The shape of a door was visible underneath the sign. A mere twenty yards away but he had a feeling it wouldn't seem quite so short. Not when he'd barely been able to move a few feet a minute earlier.

4

In the living room of her apartment, Kana sat on one end of a plush white couch. Her back was against one of the armrests and her legs were stretched out across the other cushions. Due to her short stature significant space remained between her bare feet and the armrest on the far side. A bulky newspaper was propped atop her thighs and she held one section up in front of her face.

"Is There Really a Vigilante in Minikin Capital?" - was the inquiry posed by the headline of the article she read. Stephanie Morris had authored it. She also had a political and social commentary show that Kana watched from time to time. The current article examined some of the hard evidence found indicating the possibility of the vigilante's existence. Despite numerous reported sightings from civilians and criminals alike, many, including Stephanie, had their doubts.

"The idea of an individual surviving for two years while dealing with the underworld in a city like ours (God bless it) is ludicrous. Twenty police officers were murdered last year, and only ten of them have received any justice. Some have even pondered openly whether one or more of their fellow officers were somehow complicit in their deaths.

Despise Lieutenant Brooke's admirable attempts to persuade the citizens of Minikin Capital otherwise—the police do not have everything under control. They're not even fighting a winning battle at this point. And that is in spite of some hardworking women and men on the force. My problem with the so-called vigilante is this. If the police, working together and with some semblance of law backing them up, are barely surviving—how could a single man have lasted this long? I don't think it's possible."

A piano tune played in Kana's ears and she blinked twice before tearing her eyes away from Stephanie Morris's words. She glanced to her left then the right, trying to remember where she'd left her cell phone. To the left behind the couch the living room branched off into the kitchen. She hadn't been in there since she'd gotten home. On her right the coffee table surface was littered with magazines, old newspapers, and a Bible. No phone. She continued searching until her eyes landed on her jacket. It was hung on a rack beside the front door. Through the fabric she could see a dim light blinking on and off. She raised an eyebrow. *Do I really feel like getting up?* The answer to that was a resounding no. Especially not considering it was well after 10pm. Calls this time of night had to either be recorded messages selling some irrelevant nonsense, or a work emergency. Neither of which was compelling enough to rouse her.

When the tune continued, Kana sighed and shoved the paper off her lap. Then she stood and marched across the room to snatch the phone out of her pocket. She turned it around so she could read the caller's ID. "JOE". *Odd.* Pouting her lips in confusion, Kana pressed the talk button and raised the phone to her head.

"Hey honey," she said.

He didn't speak immediately but she heard him breathing. Wind and distant engines were audible as well with an occasional beeping horn. The sounds of the outdoors in the city. He exhaled sharply every few seconds. Almost grunting.

Kana frowned. "Joe?"

"I..." His voice was raspy, as it usually was when he was 'in character', but it was more forced. He was in pain. "I'm not sure..." His words trailed off as he took in a deep breath and spoke upon exhaling. "I can make it home."

"What?" Kana's free hand slipped into the matching sleeve of her jacket. She pulled it off the hook and let it fall around her shoulders. "Honey where are you?"

"I'm okay," he said. "I just...I need a ride."

"Where are you Joe?" Kana demanded. She switched the phone over to the other hand so she could finish putting her jacket on. "I'm on my way."

Twenty minutes later, they were together in the living room. The coffee table had been pushed aside and Kana kneeled in its place. Joe sat in the middle of the couch, only half dressed in the Avenger uniform. The cape and tunic were folded on the cushion next to him along with the mask. He wore only black pants, boots, and a black Kevlar vest. A golden logo decorated the chest underlined by Israeli lettering.

Kana leaned close to his left side and ran her index finger along the fabric covering the armor. In the area where he'd been shot the fabric had been destroyed, along with the top layer of the vest. A white and gray circle, about five inches in diameter, surrounded the point of impact. The shape of the bullet's tip had embedded itself in the armor, but hadn't been able to penetrate. Thank God.

"It was built to stop armor piercing rounds," Joe muttered.

"Did its job then. You said it was a sniper rifle?" Kana asked.

"Yeah... I didn't see the exact bullet that hit me," he said, wincing.

"But the ones her companion used were about five inches long, maybe a half thick."

"That about matches this one here." Kana eyed the impact point again. "That's a nasty round. Military grade. I've been shot with a handgun wearing a sturdy vest and *that* hurts..."

Joe narrowed his eyes. "When did that happen?"

"During training, Joe, but this isn't about me," she said, shaking her head. "You still in pain?"

"Every time I breathe."

Kana winced this time. She'd seen him sore after a long night of fights, including months ago when he'd fallen down the stairs. That bothered her even when he tried to hide his pain, which he always did. For him to actually call her to be picked up, she knew it had to be unbearable.

"You think the set up was for you?" She inquired.

"It had to be," he replied. "The only people who know for sure I'm out there are the thugs."

"Which outfit you think they were connected to?"

He paused and mulled it over. "Hard to say. They're probably hired guns. Although the gangs here usually don't like outsourcing..."

"It's not like you've given them a whole lot of choice, is it?" She shrugged. "You may be pushing them to extremes they wouldn't have considered otherwise."

"Maybe. I'll find out tomorrow night."

Kana sighed. "You can barely walk right now. You really think it's wise to go out a day after?"

"That's what pain killers are for."

Kana stared at him with her lips parted, not believing what she'd just heard. His own expression, determined as ever, let her know that he meant his words.

"Joe, you need to take it easy for at least one night." She said—her own determination evident in her voice and her eyes. "You run into them again and they get a shot off..."

"I'm going to be under the radar," Joe said. "And I won't be out long. Just long enough to set up our next meeting."

"Fine. But we're going to the hospital right now. We have to know in case it's something serious."

Joe brought a hand up to cover his face and sighed. The movement must have provoked his injury because he gritted his teeth immediately after. Kana noticed it despite his hand being in he way.

"We'll tell them..." She looked off to the side and mentally grasped for some explanation. "You fell at some point tonight?"

"Definitely."

Kana smirked. "We'll tell them you fell. That's all they need to know."

"And if it's not?" He raised his head to glance at her over his hand.

"I'm a cop—that's all they need to know," she smiled.

Joe grinned and lowered his head.

Kana placed her hand on his knee and squeezed. The anguish in her heart finally prompted her eyes to moisten with tears. She blinked them away and tightened her lips together, not wanting to upset him. Even if that meant she had to bear the pain alone. *He's in enough as it is.*

She visually roamed the body of the man who Stephanie Morris and others didn't believe could exist. Slender muscles, average sized hands, and a frame several inches shy of six feet. Whether he looked the part or not, Stephanie's disputed vigilante *did* exist. A man who had successfully fought assassins, hardened criminals, and street gangsters hand-to-hand. A man who had withstood the organized criminal elements that had run the city for years. Despite Stephanie's conclusions, it was possible for a human being to do all those things. But it did take a toll, as Kana could see. His bare arms had several old and fresh scars on them and his left elbow was wrapped in athletic tape. They were only a few of the many wounds and ailments he carried as a result of his 'work'. And before he stopped, if he ever did, Kana worried that they wouldn't be the worst of them.

5

The dark clouds in the sky that had dimmed the sun's light also kept Joe's office in the dark. A little light was visible from the hall through the narrow space under the door. Every once in a while the church secretary would walk by, shuffling papers or talking on the phone. She'd left him undisturbed as per his request. He had more than enough work to get to.

Most of that work was already prepared and waiting for him on his desk. They were spread out there in the form of books containing Greek and Hebrew lexicons, a notebook, and two bibles. They remained abandoned as his chair was facing in the opposite direction. His chin rested on one of his fists and he was staring out the window. The blinds were still down although they were angled open enough for him to be able to see the parking lot and the heavens overlooking the city. The bloody city of Minikin Capital.

The phone on the desk rang behind him. Without looking, Joe reached over his shoulder for it and groaned midway through the motion.

Pain shot through his ribs on the left side. *Idiot,* he chastised himself as he turned the chair to face the desk and answered the phone.

"Faith Bible Church, this is Joe's office. How can I help you?"

"Hi Joe," a girl responded from the other line. "Are you busy?"

"Rose?" He asked.

Twenty minutes passed before Joe reached the park where he had agreed to meet her. He parked along a wooden fence enclosing the designated area and climbed out. On the inside of the fence, an asphalt walking path had been built to encompass the entire park, which was half a mile in circumference. Joe scanned the area from left to right. His eyes passed over a fenced in tennis court that probably hadn't been used in years. A rusty padlock held the entrance gate closed. Next to it was an elaborate play set for children with multiple slides and gymnastic obstacle courses.

Beyond it were the swings, where a young woman in a pink hooded sweatshirt sat with her back to him. She was slowly moving back and forth with her ankles crossed and her feet above the earth. Otherwise the park was devoid of people. *Funny,* Joe thought. *One of the nicer places in the city and no one's here.* More sad than anything. He frowned and searched for an opening in the fence.

After finding it, Joe trekked across the field until he was within ten feet of her. As he cleared the remaining distance she must have heard his footsteps and peeked over her shoulder. She greeted him with a warm smile and said, "Hi pastor."

"Hey Rose." Joe nodded and came to a stop beside her.

Rose watched him for a moment with her eyes widened. Reading him, probably. He hoped his face wouldn't give away his discomfort. A Tylenol had taken the edge off of the pain but he was still more than aware of his injury. Bruised ribs according to the doctor at the hospital.

Rose tilted her head to one side, letting her hair fall to cover half of her face. "Have a seat. You'll make me nervous standing like that."

"A seat?" He raised an eyebrow.

She upturned one corner of her lips and nodded at the swing next to her.

"Uh..." Joe glanced to either side. He didn't see anyone out in the park or in the area surrounding it.

"Oh come on—you're not *that* old yet," Rose reminded him.

Joe grinned and lowered himself onto the swing. The motion caused a stabbing pain in his side so he turned his head away to hide his grimace. After pretending to survey the park again, he settled into the seat and returned his eyes to Rose.

"How are you, Joe?" She asked.

"I'm good." Joe shrugged. "Yourself?"

She lowered her eyes to the ground before her feet and kicked at the dust there. "Okay I guess. I've got school in a couple of hours but I wanted someone to talk to. I've been avoiding my friends the past couple of days. I didn't interrupt anything did I?"

"No. Anything in particular you want to talk about?"

She glanced up into the gray abyss overhead, blinking several times before she shook her head and responded, "No. Is that okay?"

"Sure..." He was almost at a loss for words. She called him out of the office just to talk? Not that he minded. Maybe it was a friend that she needed right now more than anything. "So... what're you studying in school?"

Rose grinned, apparently pleased with the question. "I'm taking prerequisites right now. I want to become either a veterinarian or a nurse. What do you think I should do?"

"Personally, I think it's more important to take care of people..."

"Yeah..." Her shoulders sagged a little.

"But I might be biased considering my profession," he said. "I couldn't imagine trying to preach to a dog... even though I feel like I'm doing it sometimes."

Rose laughed.

"But in the medical field, there may be a place for you. Don't take my word for it. Do what you think is best."

"I've got until next year to decide," she told him. Then she sat with her eyes narrowed for a moment, hesitating, before she asked, "Have you always wanted to be a pastor?"

"No," was his quick response. He hadn't even thought of it prior to Kana's suggestion.

"What else did you want to do?"

"No comment," he replied, trying unsuccessfully to hide a grin.

Rose put her hands on her hips. "Hey, that's not fair. Spit it out, man."

Joe winced. "Professional wrestling."

There was a pause. Then Rose doubled over and burst out laughing. Joe smiled. Even if it was at his expense he was pleased to see her amused.

"You in tights?" She managed to speak in between fits of laughter. "Pretending to beat up other guys in tights? Wow. I hate wrestling but I would pay to see that."

"That was when I was your age. Puroresu was pretty popular over there."

"Purrra - who?" She rolled her tongue on the R, almost getting Joe to laugh this time.

"It's the Japanese term for professional wrestling," he explained.

She raised an eyebrow and leaned in his direction, "You were in Japan?"

"Sure. I was born there. Lived there until I was 23."

"Huh." She appeared to mull that over. "Interesting. Is that where you met your wife?"

"No I met her here in the city," he replied. "About a year ago."

"Great place to meet," she said, dryly. "What made you come here, anyway?"

"It's kind of a long story, but..." He frowned and pondered a way to answer the question without lying. "I think God wanted me here."

"Hm." She turned to look at him again, a sad smile on her face. "I think so too. A lot of kids my age are looking for someone like you. Someone who can point them in the right direction and... be real with us at the same time. Ya know? I think maybe things wouldn't be as bad as they were on the streets if there were more of you around. And maybe it wouldn't be too late for me..."

Her voice cracked on the last word and she bowed her head, letting her hair fall into her face. It was Joe's turn to observe her now. The attractive and intelligent young woman who had sought refuge at the church even in the pouring rain. Whatever pain had driven her there had to be severe, and something told Joe he didn't know the half of it yet.

Regardless, she was trying, and she'd gone to the right place.

Joe reached up and put his hand on her shoulder to give it a comforting squeeze.

"I don't know exactly what's going on but I don't need to. It's not too late for you Rose. God hasn't given up on you... and I won't either. Okay?"

She nodded but didn't say anything. Probably couldn't. Her face was hidden but he could hear her attempting to refrain from crying. Quiet whimpering noises escaped her lips every few seconds and her stomach was visibly quivering. Her sorrow seemed to spread to Joe as his own heart began to ache for her. He gently pulled her in his direction and she complied, allowing her head to come to a rest on his shoulder.

6

"What are you waiting for?" Tara demanded.

She stood in the middle of a blue matted floor, wearing a black jogger's outfit and fingerless gloves. Three men, each of them over six feet tall and with massive frames, surrounded her. They moved in a slow circle, cross stepping so that they faced her at all times. Their fists were up and gloved like hers, their faces hardened with determination. Alone they would be formidable enough but with the three, they were as menacing as it got.

The coldness, and the confidence in Tara's blue eyes, somehow equaled the menace of the men. She made sure to look each of them in the eye as they circled, letting them know what to expect.

"Come on!" She ordered in a commanding voice.

Pete was the first to comply. He stepped forward and threw a right jab. Tara stepped to the inside of his strike's trajectory and chopped him on the bicep with her left hand. Her right elbow wasn't far behind and it pounded into his chest, reloaded, and then cracked him in the chin. Pete sank to the ground and Tara kicked him in the side. He didn't make budge or even make a sound. Out like a light.

Her eyes blazed with confidence as Tara spun around and raised her hands again. Tim and Alexander exchanged glances. Tara read the concern in their eyes. She could smell it in the air—their fear. It brought a smile to her face.

Tim lunged to try to grab her around her waist. She stepped back with her left leg and when he made contact, brought the knee up under his chin. Her right arm shot up in the air before coming down in an elbow to the back of his skull. She elbowed him twice more as Alexander closed in on her. Tara lifted her arms to protect her face but he punched her in the rib area instead. The blow stung and sent her staggering back.

Alexander charged and leapt into the air with his right knee aimed at her face. The speed along with his massive frame didn't leave her the option of side stepping him or ducking. She threw herself backward and arched her back to lean further away from his knee. When he passed by overhead she rammed her knee into his groin area. He curled into a ball in midair and she landed underneath him and grabbed a hold of his ankle. As soon as he hit the ground she stood and twisted his ankle up behind him. He screamed and tapped the mat.

"Nicely done," a man commented from nearby.

Tara released Alexander's ankle and headed toward the corner of the room where the speaker sat. The same man who had helped her escape two nights ago. He wore a navy blue business suit and dark sunglasses. A wry smile formed on his lips as he watched her approach. Once she was within five feet she lowered herself to her knees and bowed.

"Nicely done," he said again.

"Does it make up for two nights ago?" She inquired.

He held up a hand for her silence and leaned to one side, looking over her shoulder at the other men. "Go wait outside gentlemen, I'll have the rest of your money shortly."

"Thanks, Vincent," Alexander muttered. He was standing but hunched over with a hand near his groin. He helped the other two up to their feet and then limped out of the room himself with them in tow.

The man in the sunglasses, Vincent, smiled.

"You weren't completely responsible for that mishap, Tara," Vincent spoke after the door had closed behind the men. "In fact if it was anyone's fault—it was mine. I was too fascinated watching the vigilante work to pick him off when I had the chance. The way that man moves... his costume... it's quite compelling."

"It is."

"But you... you were on top of things. If not for that cop you would've had him."

"I didn't even see him coming," Tara spat, turning her head to the side. Her eyes burned with anger.

'I did," Vincent said. "I was curious to see how you'd handle it. And you didn't."

"I'm sorry."

"But you did have the vigilante dead in your sights." He held up an index finger. "That was impressive. Especially considering this man has been able to keep all the major players of this dump of a city on edge. And if not for an unfortunate... happenstance... *you*, not I, would have *killed* him. What better way to *bust your cherry* than to take out the invincible?"

"You think there's a chance he's already dead? I don't believe he was seen last night."

"He would've bled all over the alley if the bullet penetrated." Vincent further dismissed the notion with a wave of his hand. "He'll be back tonight, and he will *die* this time. As much as I do respect him."

"Are you going to let me... try again?" She asked, hopefully.

Vincent blinked behind the sunglasses. A ringing sound cut in before he could answer and he reached into his shirt pocket and procured a cell phone.

"Excuse me," he said before answering the call. "Yes?"

"Hey Vincent," a younger guy responded from the other line. "We just got word our boy's going to be meeting a street gang member tonight."

"What?"

"He wants to find out who tried to whack him a couple nights ago. Last night he made a deal with my boy Rex. Rex gets him info on you, he'll let Rex go. I can tell you *where* he'll be tonight and around *what* time. For the info, my informant wants 10 percent of your reward."

Vincent grinned. "Round two commences."

7

The man known to business associates as "Rex" paced back and forth near the window. As he walked his eyes were constantly scanning his forlorn surroundings. Searching the deep shadows in the recesses of the room. Spying the boxes and other piles of junk spread throughout.

The 'meeting place' was the upper floor of a long abandoned warehouse in Minikin Capital's West section. The section not even police dared to set foot in after dark. Being a man of reputation among the numerous 'street gangs' in the city, Rex frequented the area without fear of repercussion. Heck, he owned Minikin Capital West. While the Mafia and the Yakuza fought over the legal and more organized enterprises throughout the rest of the city, the lesser gangs settled for the drug trade. A booming business in Minikin Capital nonetheless. One that Rex had a good handle on.

And here I am… scared of some boogie-man. He shook his head in self-disgust. The floorboards creaked from somewhere in the room and he jumped and brought his fists up. Quiet squeaks in the darkness followed a scurrying sound as an unseen rodent hurried off in the distance. Rex sighed and continued pacing, but turned to glance out the window.

The neighborhood below was surprisingly docile. Voices called back and forth from blocks away and the occasional car sped down the street. Otherwise it almost seemed as if people were avoiding this block. This building. And likely for the same reason that Rex was a little jumpy. He wondered if word about his meeting had gotten out somehow. If so it appeared that instead of wanting to get a shot at the vigilante, the gang members had opted to stay out of his way. Considering the stories that went around about him, Rex didn't blame them.

He raised his eyes from the ground level to the three-story office building across the street. All of its windows, probably a hundred of them, were darkened. Rex's own reflection watched him from the glass directly across. He squinted his eyes and leaned closer to the window in front of him. His reflection had been joined by a shadowy, winged figure. He gasped and spun around to see the form of the Avenger. He stood six feet away at the edge of the room's shadows.

"You didn't have to sneak up on me," Rex complained. He reached up to straighten out his own shirt and run a hand through his hair. "Jeez, man."

"The couple that took a shot at me last night, you know who they were," the Avenger insisted in a gruff voice that sent shivers down Rex's spine. "*Talk.*"

Rex swallowed the fearful lump that had risen in his throat, not wanting to display any fear. If it wasn't too late. "Hey boss, I just hear things, know what I mean? Doing the deals I do, and with ladies workin' the streets for me, I know a lot about what goes on. So I got some ideas about who put the price on your head but for information like that—what're you going to give me?"

The Avenger didn't move but Rex could almost feel the glare coming through the skull's eyeholes. "How about your *life*?"

Rex took a step back and considered that, watching the Avenger's still frame.

"You know what I've done to the Mafia, the Yakuza, and even some of your lowlife friends. Do you really want to try to negotiate with me?"

Don't go for it. The Avenger was bluffing—had to be. If he really cared all that much about the identity and motive of the sniper, he wouldn't do a thing. That was Rex's only confidence in agreeing to the meeting. He was dismayed to find that one solace departing from him. *Relax man, he's bluffing.*

"Alright man, I'll talk, just stay off my back from now on alright?" Rex held his hands up to display his surrender. "It's an outside guy. Hired by the-"

BOOM! An explosion went off in Rex's ears at the same time glass shattered. Bigger shards and sprinkles of the material enveloped his head and torso from behind. He slapped his palms over his ears and dropped to his knees, landing hard on the unforgiving wooden floor.

Once the falling glass ceased, he slowly lifted his head to see what had happened. The Avenger was laid out on the floor with his cape covering most of his body. A puddle of blood, however, was visible surrounding his head.

"What the hell?" He jumped to his feet and crept toward the fallen vigilante. A large hole in the forehead of the skull mask also had specks of blood surrounding it.

"No way." He put his hands on his head in disbelief. Until he got close enough to see that something was amiss. There were wires visible underneath the "Avenger's" shirt and wrapped around his neck. An amplifier had been attached to the collar. Thick black wiring had been tied around the arms, pinning them to the sides of the individual.

In an office adjacent to the warehouse room window, Vincent leaned forward and took hold of the window top in front of him. He had the sniper rifle propped against his shoulder with the muzzle aimed at the ceiling. Its top was still smoking from the powerful explosion that had taken place inside it. Vincent grinned and pulled the window closed.

"It's not him," Rex's voice stammered from over a radio in the corner.

Vincent narrowed one eye and leaned closer to the glass to see Rex still hunched over the Avenger's body.

"He set me up..." Rex said.

At that moment a shadow appeared on the window directly above Vincent's head. He started to bring the gun down when a figure appeared before his face and the glass shattered. The Avenger kicked him in the face and in the hand. The rifle went sailing further into the room as Vincent staggered away, slammed back first into a desk, and fell over it.

He immediately pushed up to his hands and knees and looked up to see the Avenger standing in front of the window space. The Avenger swept his cape to the side, revealing a sword's sheath fastened to his belt. He took hold of the sheath to keep it in place as he drew the sword out by the hilt. Then he brandished the forty inches of steel blade before Vincent's eyes. Light from outside bounced off of the blade's sharpened edge, causing it to glisten.

Vincent pushed up until he was on his knees and gazed at the face of the vigilante. His eyes were widened and almost crazed in their intensity. He lifted his arm and wiped the blood that had spilled out of his nostrils away with the back of his hand. The liquid remained smeared between his nose and lips.

"That was a smart move—use a decoy similar to the one I almost killed you with," Vincent said, nodding his head. "Not bad. I was disappointed when you 'showed up' across the street. I had hoped you'd know better than that. I was right."

"Who hired you?" The Avenger swiped the sword's blade at Vincent's face, only stopping it a couple of inches short. "Start talking or I'll start cutting."

A smile broke out on Vincent's lips. Then he burst out in a hearty laugh. The Avenger, far from amused, narrowed his eyes in disgust.

"Does it really matter, vigilante?" Vincent asked, holding his arms out to his sides. "You know all the enemies you have in this city. Whoever did hire me is simply the most industrious. Or at least they were able to put out the right incentive. If you survive this night there will be others. Maybe sooner than you think."

Movement from further in the office drew the Avenger's attention. He removed his eyes from the assassin to glance up at the shadow-covered room. Vincent cocked his head upward and spat half a mouthful of blood toward the Avenger's eyes. He closed his eyes and turned his head aside. It was all Vincent needed to duck under the reach of the blade while kicking the Avenger in the chest. The Avenger went staggering back, holding both arms out to maintain his footing.

Tara appeared out of nowhere, five feet in the air, and kicked the Avenger in the shoulder. She pushed off of his body and snatched his sword, twisting around in midair to land in a crouch on her feet.

The Avenger had been knocked down to one knee but he stood and brushed dust from the top of his tunic, looking back and forth between his enemies. Then he brought his fists up and bent his knees, letting them know he was ready. Vincent stepped forward and assumed a similar posture with his hand closest to the Avenger open. His protégé, Tara, positioned the Avenger's sword horizontally before her own eyes. She glared at him from underneath the blade.

"Yield!" Vincent yelled as he charged. Upon his command Tara stepped back and dropped to one knee with her head bowed.

Vincent threw a left jab that the Avenger barely evaded, followed by a right hook which was ducked. When the Avenger rose Vincent brought his elbow back into his face. The Avenger latched onto the outstretched arm and drove his knee into Vincent's side. A pained growl escaped the assassin's mouth as he leaned sideways over the knee. Then he flipped upside down, landing on his hands, and punted the Avenger's head with both feet. The Avenger tripped, fell backward, and performed a back roll that landed him in a crouch.

Vincent stepped closer and threw a roundhouse kick at his foe's head. The Avenger dropped onto his side to allow the stiff leg to pass by. He swung his own leg and struck the assassin's base foot, sweeping it out from under him. Vincent crashed to the ground, landing face first.

The Avenger leapt into the air and came down on Vincent's back with both knees. Vincent roared in pain and anger. While his head remained arched upward, the Avenger slammed his fist into the back of his skull. Vincent's forehead was driven Into the floor with a solid thud.

The Avenger had barely taken a breath when his own sword flew at his face. He spun away but the very tip of the blade sliced through the cheek of the mask. After retreating five feet he turned to glare at the woman now wielding his own weapon. She stared back at him, holding the sword with the tip pointed at her enemy. Her eyes were every bit as fierce as his.

Next to her, Vincent was stirring, trying to lift himself on trembling arms. When she saw the Avenger glance down at him, Tara screamed and launched a diagonal cut at his head. He leaned back out of the way. The blade's tip passed a mere inch in front of his mask, whistling on its way.

Tara spun with the momentum of her strike and turned her back to him. The Avenger stepped forward, hoping to take advantage but she kept spinning and caught him in the stomach with the heel of her foot. The power behind the kick knocked him back toward the open window space. His foot landed on a piece of glass and he slipped and fell out into emptiness.

Instinctively the Avenger thrust his hands upward to grasp a strand of rope hanging down outside. His full weight threatened to drag him down but he held on tight, squeezing on the rope to maintain his grip. Momentum carried him four feet beyond the window, dangling over the street more than twenty feet below. Then it let up and he swung back toward the building. The rope ran up onto the roof where he'd tied it to a chimney before dropping in on Vincent. The bottom end extended several feet below the window space.

Inside, Tara ran across the floor with the sword's tip ready to be driven into his torso. The Avenger stretched out his foot and rested it on the bottom of the window space. That took the weight off his arms enough for him release the rope with one hand and reach down to his belt. Tara gave a great war cry and thrust the sword straight at him. The Avenger brought the sheath from his belt and held it horizontally between them so the opening faced Tara. She drove the blade harmlessly into its place in the sheath.

Twisting his wrist counterclockwise dragged Tara, who still had a grip on the sword's hilt, to his side. He elbowed her in the back and she was knocked forward through the window space. She plummeted toward the street twenty-five feet below, hands grasping at the air for something to break her fall.

The Avenger climbed into the office in time to see Vincent picking up the sniper rifle deep in the room. Roughly twenty feet away—far out of the Avenger's reach. Vincent turned toward the window with a wicked grin on his face, biting down into his bottom lip. He began to settle the rifle on his shoulder to take aim.

The Avenger held the sheath in both hands and tilted it downward so the blade slipped out about halfway. Then he swung it baseball-bat-style at Vincent. The sword ejected from its sheath and twirled in the air like a deadly boomerang, headed right for the assassin. He started to bring the gun up in the path of the weapon but wasn't fast enough. The sword spun around as it neared with the blade aimed at his neck.

Tara lied on the sidewalk, curled into a ball with her arms wrapped around one leg. Her teeth were clenched tight together, almost welded, in an attempt to muffle her sobs. They still escaped in the form of deep and pained moans in her throat. Her eyes were squeezed shut, preventing her from seeing two men creeping toward her. Despite her pitiful wails, their expressions were anything but sympathetic. One of them licked his lips while eyeing her shapely form.

"Poor little thing..." His partner cooed. The men drew within ten feet. She might not have heard them over her own noises, and continued to hold her knee, possibly oblivious to the approaching threat. They both grinned.

A flapping sound overhead prompted them to glance up at the sky. They looked in time to see the Avenger falling and landing on their shoulders. His knees dug in, driving them down hard. Their heads and bodies smacked against the concrete, knocking them unconscious. The Avenger pushed off of them and performed a front roll, tucking his sheathed sword into his body until he landed on his feet.

He put the weapon away under his belt and approached his fallen enemy. Once beside her he knelt down and slipped an arm under her knees, and the other under her shoulders. Being as gentle as possible, he stood while hugging her body into his chest. His teeth gnashed together as the extra weight seemed to bear directly on his ribs. Tensing his biceps so that they would take more of pressure, he turned and walked into a nearby alleyway.

Tara lifted her head and forced her tear-filled eyes open to gaze up at the Avenger. She scowled at him and growled through her teeth, "You..."

"Relax," he said. "You need medical attention, *now*."

"Why didn't..." she released another groan before she could speak again. "You just kill me?"

He narrowed his eyes. "I only kill those who take it upon themselves to shed innocent blood. Your decoy the other night only worked because of your innocence. Had you murdered someone before I would've killed you then."

"And if I shed innocent blood... in the future?" She asked, glaring at him. Her hatred, even through her obvious agony, was stunning. "Why not... stop me now?"

"I'll take my chances," the Avenger replied. "But surveillance video from a nearby store caught you holding the gun last night. The police will meet you at the hospital after you check in. I hope you take this as a warning and leave this lifestyle behind while you can... but if not..."

He lowered his eyes to peer into Tara's, giving her a firm look to assure her that he meant his next words. "I'll be waiting for you."

8

Rose sat on the side of her bed, staring into the mirror propped atop her dresser. A nervous, beautiful, and hopeful young woman was perfectly reflected in the glass. She was dressed according to her plans for the night. Joe's wife had told her to aim for casual if she preferred to. It wasn't until Rose searched through her wardrobe that she realized how suggestive the majority of her clothes were. She eventually selected a form fitting pink tee shirt and a snug pair of jeans. They weren't tight enough to offend anyone's sensibilities. At least she didn't think so. She wanted the Bible Study and the dinner afterwards to go off without a hitch.

Grinning, she took a brief look around her room. It had changed a bit since her meeting with Joe three nights ago. Some of the posters her mother had complained about in the past had been removed. That enabled the previously hidden pink wallpaper to surface. She'd also thrown out a few of the shirts, shorts, and skirts in her closet. The frame around her mirror was a brighter shade of pink. Behind her she could see the bathroom door. To her left was the door to the rest of the house, and a small wooden desk for her laptop.

A pink leather Bible she'd purchased yesterday sat atop the dresser next to her cellphone. She hadn't owned one, much less read one, in years. After buying it she'd read a chapter or two and to her surprise, she understood it. And as an extra plus, it wasn't as boring as she had expected. Which meant that either the pastor had cast a spell on her, or she was really changing. *Hm.* Rose tilted her head to one side.

Her cell phone rang and she scooped it up and answered it without checking the ID. "Yo."

"Yo yourself, Rose." It was Joe's voice.

She laughed. "Hi Joe. How are you?"

"I'm okay. Just been busy the past few days trying to prepare for tonight's Bible Study. I was a little worn out last week and I don't think I was too coherent. I want to do the best I can this time. Especially since I won't have my wife's support."

"Oh yeah, she is *really* nice. I honestly didn't know what to do with a Bible Study and I was too embarrassed to tell you. She hooked me up, though. Told me about what the Bible was, what to wear, and what to expect."

"Good. How have you been?"

"Awesome. I've felt great since we talked. Doing a lot of thinking, and making a lot of changes, too."

"So are you... you're a..."

"I'll tell you tonight during dinner. I want to talk to you about that and a lot of other stuff. You're not going to try to diss me, right?"

"I wouldn't do that. What kind of pastor turns down a free meal?"

"Yup," Rose said, giggling. "So are we going to Taco Bell or Olive Garden? And is your wife going to be coming tonight? I forgot to ask."

"Taco Bell is fine. And no, she's only able to make it to the studies every other week. She's a police detective and has long hours, sometimes."

"Ah, okay. So I can meet her next week. Or Sunday."

"Yeah. I went out to the store and bought a Bible for you. I don't usually care for them too much, but everyone told me I should get a study bible—since you're a beginner and all. It comes with notes."

"Oh, I thought Mrs. Mizaki would have told you," Rose winced. "I already went out and got one for myself. I hope you didn't spend too much."

"Only 95 dollars. Now, I could have gotten two gallons of gas with that..."

Rose laughed.

"That's okay, though."

"It wouldn't hurt to have two. Thank you, Joe. For the Bible and for everything."

"You're welcome. You've been an encouragement to me the past few days. It's not every day I get to meet new people. Nice people, anyway. Besides the groups at church and my wife, I really don't get out much. But... I'm glad I met you."

"Same here," She smiled.

"Anyway, I have some more work to get done before 8:30," He said. "Do you need a lift?"

"No, my Mom's going to bring me, it's okay. You take all the time you've got to study, because I'll have a LOT of questions, alright?"

"I'll be prepared." He laughed.

"See you, Joe."

"Later, Rose."

She held the phone to her ear for a moment. Somehow it seemed rude to be the first to hang up. She hadn't heard a click yet, and quiet background noise was audible. *I feel like such a nerd, but...* How did he feel? She was more surprised that he was still on the line than she was by her own reluctance. *Maybe he left his phone off the hook...*

"What are you waiting for?" Joe asked.

Rose laughed. "What are you?"

"I have work to do."

"I'm not stopping you, Uncle Joe."

"Uncle Joe?" He was holding in laughter.

A beep cut into the line and Rose groaned. "Saved by the bell."

"This time. See you at eight thirty. Call me if you need anything."

"I..." Rose started to say what came to her mind but she refrained. *He'll think you're nuts. What's wrong with you?* "I'll do that. Bye Joe."

"Bye."

Only when the beep repeated itself did she find the will to tap the Talk button. She sighed and said, "Hello?"

"Hi Rose." It was her best friend Amanda.

"Hi." Not her best friend today.

"Rosie, you've got to come to this party at my place tonight."

"What party?"

"You know how crazy my parents are. They decided to spend the weekend in one of the cabins up in Shabath. It's Anita's birthday on Sunday and since her parents make her go to mass, I figured we could just have her celebration tonight. Everyone is supposed to be there by eight thirty. So I'll swing by to scoop you up in about twenty minutes. Okay?"

"I can't," Rose said. "I can't."

"Why not?"

"I have plans, Amanda. I can't just skip out. Sorry."

"But girl, you can't miss this party. You know Anita will be upset if she doesn't get to see you."

"I know, but I have plans." Rose shrugged. "I don't feel like going to a party tonight, either."

"What plans?"

"I'm going to a Bible Study—not that it's any of your business. If I say I have plans it's as simple as that, okay? I'm not in the mood for parties tonight."

"Bible Study? Are you going to seriously miss out on a chance to spend time with Tony to read some boring old book? Come on Rose."

"Tony? He's going to be there?" Rose looked up to see the concern on her face in the mirror. That was an unexpected disclosure. She hadn't seen Tony in weeks and she had been interested in dating him for months. Her unwillingness to settle down had kept her from committing to him but now that might have changed.

"Yeah, he will, and he wants to see you," Amanda said. Her voice cracked on the last word. *Was she crying?*

"What's wrong, Amanda?"

"Nothing, I just... I really want you to come. I know how much you like Tony and it would *suck* for you to play him out over a Bible Study. You can just go next week, can't you?"

Rose sighed and her shoulders slumped. "Fine. Come get me when you're ready."

She pressed the talk button and tossed the phone onto the bed behind her. Then she leaned over and hid her face in her hands. *What are you thinking, Rose?* She and the assistant pastor had a connection—that was unmistakable. He had also exposed her to some things she'd needed to hear. How could she just leave him hanging? Perhaps because the connection she and Tony had was different. It was romantic. *But what will he think if he finds out about... what I have?*

She was also worried that Joe wouldn't forgive her if she skipped out on him. Even if he did, she might permanently damage whatever it was they'd felt. *Then again... I could just go next week. Everyone goes home happy that way.* Besides, Joe was much more likely to be there for her than Tony was. No matter what.

Joe stood outside the church with his eyes surveying the streets around the parking lot. He didn't see anyone and there weren't any approaching vehicles. A few had come and gone in the last eight minutes. The streetlights would have allowed him to see if *she* was inside any of them. She hadn't been thus far. Joe frowned and raised his left arm to look at his watch. 8:43.

He considered going inside and calling her on the church phone. *No, no. Don't want to push it.* She'd agreed to call him if she needed anything, especially a ride. *So where is she?* When they'd spoken on the phone an hour ago she'd sounded positive that she was going to be there on time. She also struck him as the type to call if she'd changed her mind.

Unless he had misjudged her. Maybe he had been a little too hopeful after all.

The door behind him opened and he reluctantly turned to see Lizzy stepping outside. She pushed her glasses closer to her face and crossed her arms over her chest. It was a little cold out. Joe's concern for Rose's whereabouts had distracted him from the weather.

"Hey Pastor, right after this song is the opening prayer," Lizzy told him.

He nodded and turned to continue looking over the area surrounding the church. Still no signs of anyone. No Rose.

"I know we usually sing 5 songs before we begin, after the doxology, so I wanted to give you a heads up," she explained. "The worship leaders were looking around nervously when they started the last one, so…"

"I'm coming," he said. A jolt of pain, like electricity, shot through his heart at the words. Had she really decided not to come without at least telling him? As much as he wanted to call her, and wait for her if necessary, he had to tend to the rest. They were waiting on him.

"Are you okay pastor?" Lizzy took a step closer and peered into his face. "You waiting for someone else?"

"I…" He glanced back at her, seeing the eagerness in her large eyes. She was worried, and unlike Rose she had shown up tonight. There were twenty five to thirty others in the sanctuary depending on him as well. He couldn't let them down. He managed to smile at her before he permitted himself a final scan of the area. She wasn't coming.

"I guess not." He sighed. Then he turned to Lizzy, put his hand on her shoulder and led her toward the door. "Thanks for getting me."

9

Detective Kana Miyoshi stood beside Lieutenant Brooke Morgan, less than a foot away from the two-way mirror. Both women had their arms crossed over their chests, and wore grim expressions on their faces. A single uniformed officer, Andy Doyle, and three plain-clothes officers waited quietly behind them.

On the other side of the glass, in the interrogation room, sat Angel Gonzales. He reclined in a wooden chair on the far side of a round wooden table. His hands were folded behind his head and his feet rested atop the table. He sneered through the glass, although he could only see his own reflection. Every few seconds he'd roll his eyes, and shake his head. Mutter something under his breath. For a young punk being considered for murder charges he was unusually relaxed. Irritated yes, but he wasn't sweating the situation. *Not yet,* Kana said to herself.

Brooke sighed, heavily, and spoke, "We have all of the evidence but it won't be concrete enough until we get a confession. He's not changing his story. I don't want to press him too hard because at least he's talking. Not waiting for a lawyer."

"I'll do my best," Kana replied. "I owe it to that girl's mother. She wants to know the truth."

She approached the door to the interrogation room and grabbed the knob.

The door on the opposite side of the room opened and Kana turned, along with everyone else, to see who it was. A young woman of average height stepped in the doorway wearing a police uniform. Officer Patricia Miles. She had shoulder length red hair, neatly tied behind her head in a bun, and larger eyes set on a thin face. Her most compelling feature to most was her southern accent.

"Hey," She said, looking between the Lieutenant and Kana. "I thought I should let you know. His mother hired a lawyer and he or she is on the way. Ought to be here within ten to fifteen minutes."

"Oh boy." Brooke rolled her eyes. "Kana, you think you can do it in that time? It could aggravate the situation if the lawyer shows up in the middle of it."

"I've got an idea." Kana opened the door and moved inside the twelve by twelve room. The suspect, a Hispanic muscular young man with a mustache and intense eyes, stared holes through her. The venom and hatred inside him seemed to seethe out of his irises. It permeated the already thin air in the interrogation room.

He continued to watch Kana as she closed the door and approached the table. She was every bit as annoyed as he was, if not more. Yet she remained careful to hide her feelings under a cool, calculating exterior. He smirked and, once she paused beside the seat across from him, looked her up and down. Sizing her up, it seemed.

Kana brought the sole of her foot up to the edge of the table. She pushed it three inches forward, which tipped him over backwards with his arms flailing. The shock in his eyes brought a smile to the detective's face. She watched him drop his legs off the table and stand up, furious. "What the hell's your problem, lady?"

Kana ignored his question and pulled her own chair three feet back from the table. She kept her eyes on him while lowering herself into the seat.

"You're going to be in deep trouble soon, Mr. Gonzales," Kana said. "I hope you're able to make yourself as comfortable in prison as you are now."

"Don't try to play me," He replied with a scowl. "I'm not going to prison because I didn't *do* nothing."

"Keep telling yourself that if you want." Kana shrugged. "You must have some intelligence in that tiny brain of yours. If you do, you know that it's just a matter of time before we gather the little bit of evidence we need to put you away. And if that doesn't happen Anthony will confess. He's not nearly as stern as you are. Or as loyal."

"You're wasting your time." He sat down and folded his hands on the table. "The real killers are getting away while you're messing around with us. Has to be a serial killer or something. Tony and I aren't as crazy as whoever did that to her."

"No, you see... the murderers *knew* Rose. What they did to her wasn't a random act of violence. She was beaten and abused for nearly five hours. Sodomized with a broom handle, and left to die in an alley. Her face was barely recognizable. Also, some of the weapons used during the assault have been found. Washing them off and throwing them in a dumpster the block over from where the body was dumped off—not smart."

The rage in Angel's eyes briefly softened with recognition. He lifted his head and breathed out hard through his nostrils. Unfortunately, facial expressions weren't admissible in a court of law.

"So what," Angel snapped. His voice wasn't as confident as it had been seconds ago.

"A frying pan was used to bash her in the skull. As were two cans of food, and a nearly three pound glass jar of spaghetti sauce. You guys tried to clean up but glass fragments were left in Rose's hair and skin. We found traces of her blood on the glass taken from Amanda's apartment."

Angel's eyes widened and he opened his mouth to speak.

"Oh yeah," Kana cut him off. "I forgot to mention—we know she was attacked there. There was a dent in the wall that is the exact size and shape of the back of Rose's head. Amanda's parents complained about it and it turned out to come in handy. Rose did receive serious trauma to the back of her head."

"Maybe Amanda killed her, then. Why aren't you bothering her? Because she's white?"

"Detectives are picking her up as we speak. She may have been involved but she's not the main suspect. She went to a friend's house that night about forty minutes after she picked Rose up for the *party.* She stayed until the next morning when her parents came home and called her about the hole in the wall. So she wasn't there for the last four and a half hours at least. But you and Tony were. Two independent witnesses saw you two go in, and we have a text message from Amanda's phone to yours asking when you'd be there on that day. Your response was, 'In twenty minutes,' which was right before she went to get Rose."

"We left early. Before Amanda even came back. We told you Rose was drunk and acting all weird."

"One of several fabrications you guys used to cover up the truth. There was no alcohol in her system. She wasn't drunk."

"But…" He was groping now, breathing heavy and shaking his head in frustration. "She—"

"You and Anthony beat her almost to death in Amanda's living room. You did a poor job of cleaning up, and you left evidence behind. The only question is why. What did she do to deserve that?"

"Rose was our friend!" Angel pounded the table with his fists and stood up. He leaned over the wooden surface toward her. His teary eyes were ablaze and his hands trembled. "You don't know nothing! We wouldn't do that to her."

"Whoever did needs to be checked for HIV. Her blood was all over the place and I have no doubt it got on the murderers. Unless it was one of them who gave it to her. Your friends and the usual party crew say you get around, you know?"

"No!" Angel cried. "That dirty slut had HIV!"

Kana rose from her chair. "Don't lie."

"I'm not! She messed around with me and Tony and she didn't even bother to tell us about it. That was disgusting! She could have warned us."

"So she got what she deserved," Kana said, her voice getting louder as she grew sick to her stomach. "You and Anthony were angry that she exposed you to HIV without saying anything, so you set her up that night and beat her to death. Then you went as far as to rape her with a broom to get even. She violated you, so you violated her. Is that right?"

"She took our lives away from us," He argued as a single tear ran down his cheek. "She didn't care, either. I've got a daughter and a girlfriend to take care of, man. And now thanks to her, I might not be around so see my girl grow up. It's all her fault. She brought it on herself. She could have told us, but we had to find out from her friend, instead."

"Huh." Kana shook her head and wrinkled her nose in disgust. She was either going to rush around the table and beat him to a pulp, or leave. Considering that the former would impede progress in the case, she backed away toward the door. "Did you bother to get tested before you killed her? Have you since?"

He appeared to mull that over for a second. Then he spat, "Doesn't matter. She was running around spreading her legs like a diseased, filthy, rat. We just put her out of her misery."

Lord, please give me control, Kana asked before responding. "You two were the filthy animals, Mr. Gonzales. And you either need to be locked in a cage or put to sleep."

Kana yanked the door open, fighting against every fiber of her being screaming for her to hurt him. She stormed through the next room as the law enforcement agents cleared a path for her. They all, except for Brooke, continued to stare at Angel, dumbstruck.

"I have to get out of here before I break his face," Kana said.

"I'll call you later," Brooke replied.

Kana opened the door Patricia had entered earlier and stepped into the lobby of the Minikin Capital Police Department. She came face to face with Leslie Walsh outside the doorway. The surprise of seeing the lawyer briefly covered the anger welling up inside her. Leslie nodded to her and uttered a quiet, "Hi, Kana."

Kana leaned close and whispered, "Please, do your best." Then she brushed past her to head to the exit.

10

"Today is the birthday of Rose Gwen Arturo, who would have turned 20 if not for her unfortunate and brutal murder," Reporter Julia Newman spoke, staring solemnly into the camera.

Leslie Walsh, a woman in her late twenties with reddish blonde hair and sharp green eyes, sat in her apartment watching the Television. She was in her homemade office, reclining in a comfortable chair behind her desk. The TV sat atop a thin table against the far wall. An accompanying VCR was set up on one side of it, with a pile of VHS tapes on the other.

"It was just over seven months ago that her body was found in an alley between Eighth and Orchard. Autopsy reports confirmed that she suffered several broken bones, a dislocated jaw, lacerations, and some evidences of abuse too brutal to mention on air. A brief investigation revealed that her murderers were Anthony Jones and Angel R. Gonzales.

A mutual friend of Anthony and Rose's, Amanda Young, escaped a conspiracy charge because of her testimony.

"It was less than a month ago, however, that Anthony and Angel were charged with a misdemeanor thanks to their Defense Attorney Leslie Walsh. Here is footage of her explaining her defense after the jury found her clients not guilty of first degree murder."

The screen split it into two. One showed Julia sitting in the studio, and Leslie appeared on the other in the midst of reporters, cameramen, and others. She stood at the top of a concrete staircase just outside the courthouse's entrance. From the black trench coat and dark sunglasses she wore, it was obvious that she had attempted to disguise herself. Her efforts were vain because the media had recognized her immediately.

"Listen, as I explained to the judge and jury," Leslie snapped, "my clients were only guilty of falling prey to Rose's recklessness, and malicious plotting. She had sexual intercourse with Anthony and Angel with full knowledge that she was HIV positive. In the process she endangered both of their lives. It was her jealousy of Anthony's relationship with Amanda that drove her to expose them to the virus. To charge these young men whose whole lives are ahead of them, with murder, conspiracy to commit murder, or anything else—that—*that* would be the real crime!"

The second screen was overtaken by the one showing Julia and she continued her report. "Although Mrs. Walsh, known as the female Johnny Cochran, received a huge backlash from law enforcement agents, the Arturo family, and the media, she proved her case well enough for the jury to agree with her. Judge Fayden later said that he was very disappointed in the jury's choice, and that if he had any say, Angel and Anthony would be serving multiple life sentences. Mrs. Walsh is known for defending the worst criminals that Minikin Capital has to offer, and many are calling for her resignation. We here at M.C. West News, certainly hope she has to answer one day, for her crimes against the victims of the murderers she has set free."

Leslie shook her head and muttered, "Thanks Avenger. Thank you very much."

"Good evening, Leslie," A hoarse voice replied.

She jumped, startled, and took a deep breath. "You... are going to give me a heart attack one day." Leslie turned to see that the Avenger stood in front of her double windows. They had been closed behind him. *Man is he quiet.* The lights in the room were dim, so she was only able to see his outline. She was thankful for that much. The mask wasn't pleasant to look at.

"I need a little information on Jim Persiano," He said.

The short reply meant that he wasn't in a talkative mood tonight. He hadn't been the last few times she'd seen him. "I'll need a few days to give you something concrete. He just came to me last week with a generous offer and I haven't had time to review his case. Honestly, of all the people I've defended... I think he's the one I'd want to pass on."

"What do you know?" The Avenger stepped toward her.

"He was arrested and convicted for rape, sodomy, and murder," Leslie explained, peering up into the shadows covering his mask. "His supposed victim was a ten year old girl. Celeste something or other. Cute kid, bright future. The jury deemed him guilty after a ten minute deliberation. There was evidence that was considered solid at the time. Thanks to some new discoveries that have turned up, and technology, he is appealing the court decision."

"Do you think he's guilty?"

"From what I've heard, the evidence may very well clear him. Tests have shown that DNA samples collected didn't match him. Beyond that, I do think he's guilty. I remember the case when it happened. He was involved in a pretty sick group that was into all that child abuse filth. Like I said, give me a month and I'll have more for you."

"Thanks." He began to turn.

"Avenger," Leslie called. When he paused, she stood and leaned back against her desk, palms on the surface. "I haven't asked you until now, and I think I've been very patient. But I have to know... when are you going to do something about those losers who murdered Rose Arturo?"

He stood his ground. Though his face was concealed, Leslie could tell that he'd been caught off guard by the question. He blinked several times. "I never asked you to take that case, Leslie."

"Ha." Leslie couldn't believe it. She raised her eyebrows and gave him a humorless smile. "You're kidding me, right? Those *punks* were among the most disgusting, evil, and heartless humans I've ever met. And I've met *a lot* of jerks. It is true that Rose had HIV, and was aware of it, but the fact is—she hadn't had sex with either of them since she found out. They couldn't tell me when the last time they'd slept with her was. I had to ask them a million times, in a million different ways before they came up with an answer. My defense was an absolute lie.

"And although the jury was convinced, Mrs. Arturo's mother and her supporters never bought it. The people that *knew* Rose knew she wouldn't intentionally try to hurt anyone. Not like that. I had to really go after the character of her witnesses to discredit them. You want to know what that's like? Especially knowing that they were telling the truth?"

She reached down by her ankle and pulled open the bottom drawer. The Avenger watched her, silently. Her eyes remained on him the entire time as well. *Not letting you sneak away this time.* It wasn't like she had the ability to stop him from leaving. Perhaps her words were getting through to him.

Leslie reached into the drawer, felt around, and scooped up envelopes from the top of a pile. She rose and held them out to him. There were at least eight envelopes clutched in her hand. They were still sealed, and came in various sizes and shapes.

"This isn't it, either," Leslie said. "Only a handful of the 40 pieces of mail I've gotten calling me a devil, and some other choice words I won't even repeat to you. Only six of them are from Rose's family members. They hate me. And quite frankly, knowing that those boys are out there free—and that *I* set them free—I almost hate myself. I wanted to go to visit her grave. I was going to do that today but when I drove past, I couldn't bring myself to step foot in the cemetery. I'm too ashamed."

"You did it for the right reasons," He replied. "You were just misinformed. Let it go. It's not your concern."

She tossed the envelopes at his feet and marched toward him. Once she was maybe a foot away, she stopped and put her hands on her hips. "Don't you tell me that! It is my concern, and it's my fault they're out there on the streets. They showed no remorse for killing Rose. If anyone has ever deserved to die, they do! And if you refuse to act, then what makes you think I'll defend anyone for you again? I don't need this, you know?"

The bodies of two women lied side by side in the center of a living room floor. The room around them was a disaster. Expensive looking furniture had been overturned; a vase had been shattered into pieces. Blood was mingled with the remains next to the wooden stand the vase had been removed from. The crimson liquid had soaked the white sheets used to cover the abused bodies. Leslie stood, her hands on her face, staring down at her victims. Dead because of her greed.

"No." Leslie shook the visual from her head. "I took this job for you so that I could escape my guilt. So that I could help you rid scum like Tony and Angel from the earth and the legal system. I would have said no if I'd known I had to be put through this. It's not fair. You're using me because you know that... that I..."

"Leslie," He spoke softly. "I don't hold that over your head. Your client was the one who went out and murdered his sisters. Not you."

"I helped him," Leslie muttered as a tear ran down her cheek. She wiped it away. "I set him free to go do it."

"Angel and Tony won't hurt anyone else. And... I'm not using you. Nor did I ever intend to use your guilt to get you to help. I understand what I've asked you to do isn't easy. If you think it's better for you if we end our deal, then that's fine. I appreciate your help and all that you've done but I don't want to add to your pain."

"You don't, maybe I'm just really emotional about this one or something." Leslie shook her head. "It's just that those two talked as if they'd killed a rabid animal, not an innocent girl. She didn't deserve what happened to her."

"I've got a lot of rounds to make tonight," He told her, turning and approaching the windows. "I'll see you soon."

"About Rose..."

"Later." He pulled the windows inward, stepped up onto the frame, and then he was gone.

11

Harvey Brown leaned back against the wall, folded his hands on his lap, and smiled. He could almost feel the proud twinkle in his eyes as he surveyed the setting before him. He sat on a stool at the back of a spacious store and café, behind a large marble counter. A couple of young ladies walked among the five aisles to his left, browsing through the assortment of cards, supplies, and knick-knacks. Six tables occupied the center of the floor with four white plastic chairs pulled up to each of them.

Ten feet past the last table to the right, a glass door led to the café. On either side of it were machines containing soft drinks, and a variety of foods and snacks arrayed on booths. Beyond the door, additional tables were spread throughout the cafeteria. A cursory glance over his shoulder at the clock on the wall revealed that it was ten minutes until closing time.

Harvey took in a deep breath and released it with a contented sigh. His eyes returned to the store in time to catch his daughter walking through the café door. One of the three cops who'd entered earlier held it open for her—a tall redheaded man. She thanked him and headed toward her father carrying a sturdy looking register drawer. It was loaded with paper money and change, each coin type and bill separated into their slots.

Does it get any better than this? What more could a man ask for than the opportunity to sit back, relax, and observe the proceeds of his hard work? Four years ago, he'd been making $40,000 a year selling drugs and ripping off casinos. His home life had been a mess and deep down he knew he had nothing to be proud of. Currently, with Christmas season approaching, his year's income would near $60,000. His daughter Mia, eighteen years old, worked alongside him while attending Nursing School. She was intelligent, caring, and every bit as beautiful as her mother. Harvey was black and his wife, light-skinned Hispanic, which left Mia with an appealing olive skin tone. She had also inherited her mother's stunning brown eyes and curly black hair.

"Things are winding down in there, huh?" He asked, leaning forward.

"Just the police left," Mia replied. She set the drawer on the counter next to the main register and rested her hands on her hips. "Lieutenant Morgan really likes what you've done. She said It's not everyday someone who was in as deep as you were is able to turn it around."

"Yeah." He nodded, slowly. "I like it, too. They don't look at me as suspiciously as they used to. Maybe I'm starting to rub off on them. You know, when they first started coming in frequently, I was uncomfortable, but..."

"They're proud of you, Dad," She said, smiling. "Not as much as I am, though. Or as Mom would be."

He returned the smile.

At that moment, two men burst in through the glass double doors across from the counter. Both wore ski masks, black baggy jeans, and white tee shirts. They were of Hispanic descent, judging from their skin color, though one was slightly lighter than the other. They rushed toward the counter and the lighter skinned one raised a pistol. He aimed it right at Harvey's chest.

"Don't move, don't do anything," The one wielding the gun ordered, his voice as callous and hate filled as his eyes.

Harvey peeked at the café door out of the corner of his eyes. He couldn't see anything but empty tables from his position. The cops must have been seated further in the room. He rolled his eyes back to the intruders to see that the unarmed one was watching him, intently.

"We saw the cops out front, and we *know* they're in there," He said. "We don't want to be bothered with them, so don't raise your voice—and don't scream. You do anything stupid and we'll shoot your little girl right in front of you. Alright?"

"What do you want?" Harvey stood and stared back into his eyes, showing no fear or concern. His own life meant nothing to him. It was his daughter he was worried about. She was shivering with her back pressed against the counter. Harvey swallowed his emotions. He hated seeing her in fear but he couldn't afford to show them that he was bothered by their threats. That would almost ensure his daughter's death. He reached over and patted her on the shoulder. "It's okay, Mia."

"First, your daughter empties the register into my bag," The man said. He pointed behind his back to the black satchel strapped on over one shoulder. "And then you tell us where that stash is hidden." He glared at Harvey's daughter, who watched him with panic stricken eyes and a quivering bottom lip. "Now idiot, we don't got all day."

She turned and picked up the register drawer from the counter. Her eyes met her father's and she appeared to ask him a question. He sensed what his often reckless daughter was thinking. If this had happened two years ago, he might have let her do something. But now, her life and not his, was most important to him. He shook his head.

The gunman aimed his weapon directly at Mia's head. She lowered her eyes, turned to them, and stepped behind the main speaker. The bag was already unzipped and open, so she raised the drawer above it and shifted it right side up. Nearly a hundred bills floated inside along with hundreds of silver and copper coins. Some began to spill onto the floor, but a stern look prompted Mia to adjust her aim.

Harvey cringed each time a coin hit the floor. He knew that these punks were only a heartbeat away from shooting him and his girl. Mia glanced up at him with wide eyes, blinking in distress. It was as if she was asking for his approval like she had so many times throughout her life. He nodded reassuringly and said, "You're doing fine."

The last of the money disappeared in the bag's mouth. "Good, now put the register back where you got it. Nice and easy. Then, we need to get down to business with your Dad."

She obeyed him and the man holding the gun kept the muzzle trained on her head the entire time. He wouldn't hesitate to blow her away if she gave him a problem.

"Who are you punks?" Harvey asked, bitterly.

"I'm Fernando, and this is Reyes," The unarmed man told him, adjusting the bag so he could zip it up. "Why?"

"I don't suppose it'll help to tell you boys that you're going about things the wrong way? Not even from someone like me."

"Where is the money?" Fernando demanded, raising his voice. "Reyes, if I have to ask him a second time blow her brains all over his register."

His partner stepped closer to Mia and held the gun to her head. He pressed the cold muzzle against her temple hard enough to hurt. She groaned, closed her eyes, and clenched her teeth. Unfazed by her angst, Reyes glared into her father's eyes with rage. Harvey couldn't keep his promise. Not at the cost of his baby's life. The money, in the hands of these heartless, brutal, animals, would reenter the cycle of death. More young gangsters, innocent bystanders, and cops would be slaughtered over it.

"The Methodist Church on Union—in the nursery in the west wing," Harvey relented. He didn't want his daughter murdered because of it. *God forgive me.* "It's buried in a bag under the floor."

"You better not be lying to us," Fernando warned, reaching behind him for something in a back pocket. "Otherwise your daughter will join you in heaven."

"What?" Harvey's eyes widened in alarm.

Before he could take another breath, Fernando brought out a gun, aimed at Harvey, and fired three times. Each gunshot sounded like mini explosions. The first two slugs tore into the older man's torso, knocking him down below the counter. Blood splattered onto the wall behind the spot where he'd stood and the third bullet punched a hole into it as well.

"Daddy!" Mia cried and ran around the counter.

Reyes began to aim at her when she ducked down over her father, out of sight. He spotted movement through the café door to his left and swore. No time for her, but he couldn't afford to let her go. He paused, his eyes darting between the counter and the door.

"Reyes, come on!" Fernando urged. "Forget her!"

He reluctantly turned and fled after Fernando, who had already gone out the front doors. He reached them as they were closing and rammed into them. At the same time he heard the café door open over Mia's screams.

Lieutenant Brooke rushed though the café door into the main shop. She stopped five feet inside and held her pistol straight ahead. The officers that had accompanied her to Harvey's place, Patricia Bennett, and Andy Doyle, stepped up on either side of her. The three took a quick inventory of the area. Two teenaged girls stared at them in shock from the aisles across the room.

Harvey lied on his back behind the counter. A blood-covered stool had been tipped over beside him. His daughter was hunched over him on her knees on the other side. She held one of his limp hands in hers, now soaked with his blood, and cried, "Daddy," in between sobs. He didn't respond. His eyes were closed and his mouth open.

"There!" Andy yelled and pointed across from the counter. The double doors came back into place and two men, identically dressed, were visible running across the street.

"Hold it!" Brooke called.

She and her officers raced for the doors. The retreating men reached the other side of the street where a six and a half foot fence awaited them. They jumped up onto it, clambered over the top, and leapt down on the other side. A busy street stopped up with traffic awaited them twenty feet beyond the fence. *Can't let them disappear.*

Brooke pushed through the doors and ran to the center of the street. Her unmarked car was parked on the side of the road near the fence and the patrol car Andy and Patricia had brought was in front of the store. She began to head for her car when she noticed how low to the ground the body was. Frowning, she lowered her eyes to the wheels and muttered under her breath. The bottoms of the front tires were almost nonexistent. They'd been slashed.

"They slashed our tires!" Patricia complained.

"Okay." Brooke glanced up to see the culprits nearing traffic. "Patricia get on the radio, call for an ambulance and back up."

"Right." Patricia nodded and jogged toward the patrol unit.

Andy stood beside Brooke with his hands on his hips. He glanced back at the store, and then glared after the men. They were running along with traffic on the left side of the street. He turned to the Lieutenant and asked, "What are we going to do? Wait for back up?"

"You can wait," Brooke said.

She charged toward the fence and jumped to catch hold of the bar at the top.

"Lieutenant." Andy stepped toward her.

She thrust her feet into the wiring, and the toes of her left foot wedged into a hole. She swung her right leg up and onto the top of the fence. *I should practice this more often*, Brooke said to herself as she brought her left foot out and shifted her weight onto the other side. She immediately hopped down, landed on her feet and staggered. Once she regained her footing she raced for the street.

Patricia was already on the radio, and Andy had seen their vehicle's condition. The fleeing suspects had at least one gun on them, and a bladed object sharp enough to shred rubber. General police policy in these situations was to wait for backup rather than put an officer or two in harm's way. Yet, he couldn't let the Lieutenant go after the murderers by herself. *That's just not an option.* He shook his head and ran for the fence.

"Move to the side—police!" Brooke hollered.

A tall blonde woman rushing down a sidewalk in plain clothes wasn't apt to alert citizens to the severity of the situation. The men who'd shot Harvey were shoving their way through the crowd thirty-five feet ahead. Some pedestrians yelled after them but no one bothered trying to get in the way or putting up a fight. That was for the best. Brooke didn't want any more innocents hurt tonight.

Upon reaching the traffic lights, a block ahead of Brooke, the men cut right into the street. One lifted a gun in the air and fired twice. The vehicles that had been inching forward stopped abruptly. Screams and panicked cries rang out as those traveling on the sidewalk ducked for cover and ran. Brooke peered around them to see her targets heading across the street toward an empty parking lot. It was a large space between a series of connected stores and apartment buildings.

A tall man with broad shoulders passed Brooke, fleeing in the opposite direction. His lowered left shoulder struck her arm hard. She stumbled, nearly fell, but managed to stay upright.

Thirty feet to the Lieutenant's rear, Andy Doyle watched the murderers head for cover in the Meadowbrook Shopping Center parking lot. Brooke continued fighting through the throng of pedestrians on her way to the traffic light. Andy knew that their quarry wasn't running endlessly or attempting to lose them. There had to be a getaway vehicle nearby. If they reached it, the chances of ever finding them were slim to none.

Andy drew his pistol and stepped into the street. Traffic was inching forward so he retrieved his flashlight with his other hand, pressed a button to turn it on, and aimed it ahead. Several drivers saw the light, recognized the uniform, and stepped on the brakes. Andy slipped through the open spaces provided and into the path of a moving jeep. A young woman behind the wheel swore and stopped inches away. He glanced at her, saw the cell phone in her hand, and rolled his eyes. No time for that now.

Andy rushed past and came to two cars idling practically bumper to bumper. At most there were five or six inches between them. He pushed off the asphalt on his left leg and landed on the rear bumper of the first. It sunk a little under his weight but he scampered across the surface and dropped onto the sidewalk. He lifted his eyes in time to catch the thieves run out of sight into the parking lot. *Keep it up.* After a deep breath, he dashed after them.

"Lieutenant Morgan and Andy are in pursuit of the suspects—headed east on Andover across from Harvey's Café. Backup needed, and send an ambulance to the café." Patricia sat in the passenger's seat of her patrol car. Her legs hung over the side of the chair outside the vehicle. The tips of her toes barely touched the ground. She watched Andy move beyond her view while holding the radio to her lips. A shotgun was propped up in the driver's seat.

A station wagon slammed into the back of a pickup truck right before her eyes. She gasped and said, "I'm going Carla—just hurry it up."

"Patricia, wait!" The dispatcher called.

"No time," Patricia replied. She grabbed the shotgun's lengthy barrel and climbed out of the car.

Andy burst around the corner, tossed the flashlight aside, and scanned the area. Darting across the street had gained him some ground. The suspects were running about twenty yards ahead. Close to two football fields in front of them, a row of vehicles were parked. Headlights illuminated the path from one minivan facing in their direction. *There's the getaway.* It appeared that they had backup to cover them as well.

The cop slowed to a halt and dropped into a textbook shooting posture. His feet were shoulder's width apart, knees slightly bent, and arms extended forward. He held the gun in both hands and aimed it at the suspects. His finger began to tighten on the trigger.

BOOM! A jolt of fiery pain pierced Doyle's left thigh. He dropped the gun and collapsed.

Brooke entered the parking lot in time to hear the gunshot and see Andy fall on his side. He lied there, writing in anguish, holding his leg above the knee. A cry of pain sent shivers down Brooke's spine as she jogged toward him. The suspects hadn't lost a step after presumably taking the officer out of the chase. They were still running into the distance at full speed. *They must be good shots,* Brooke grimaced. She considered chasing them but couldn't leave one of her cops behind.

Unbeknownst to the Lieutenant, a thin black man crouched three feet from the edge of one of the rooftops overlooking the vast parking lot. His black tee shirt and sweatpants helped him blend in with the shadows. Giant letters, each a foot and a half tall, lined the outskirts of the roof and further concealed his frame. His partner, Jamal, watched the action on the ground from ten feet away. He whispered, "Easy, Chris. Go for a headshot this time."

Chris rose a little and lifted the large rifle to rest its butt on his shoulder. He leaned closer to the barrel, closed one eye, and peered through the scope. His target came into view immediately, rushing to the side of the first cop. She dropped to one knee and placed a hand on his shoulder. The sniper began to take aim when the bottom of his screen was obstructed by the top of an oversized M. He muttered and rose to full height for a clearer shot. He got it. The woman remained oblivious. Chris zoomed in on her pretty blonde head.

Brooke avoided looking at Doyle's leg and trained her gaze on his face. It wasn't much more pleasant to look at. His eyes were squeezed shut and his teeth ground into each other. He'd ceased screaming but pained groans escaped his throat. Blood was all over the pavement and his leg practically swam in it. *Please have missed the artery.* Brooke ripped her jacket off and began to slip one end under his leg.

"This is going to hurt," She warned. "But we need to do it, okay?"

"Brooke," He said through clenched teeth, breathing heavily. "It wasn't them… they didn't shoot…"

"What?" She shook her head.

The sniper's finger settled calmly on the trigger as the woman scanned the area—her face filled with fear. He started to clamp down when a palm struck the gun's barrel from below, shoving it to the side.

BOOM! The rifle fired with the muzzle pointed harmlessly at the clouds. Eyes wide, the sniper turned to see the Avenger of Blood. He stood, facing Chris, holding the barrel with his left hand. The right appeared suddenly and a fist slammed into his jaw. The force of the blow knocked him back a half step. He shook it off and tried to bring the gun between them, forcing the tip toward the shadowy figure.

The Avenger gripped the barrel with his other hand and stepped from the line of fire. That left the muzzle pointed to where he been a second before. With Chris using his full strength to gain control of the weapon, the Avenger brought his foot up and kicked him directly on the right kneecap. Chris cried out and leaned on the good leg. His fingers loosened on the weapon so the Avenger drove the butt into his abdomen, thrusting the air from his lungs.

Jamal hadn't made a move yet but his mouth, which had been hanging open in horror, closed in a scowl. Noting the threat, the Avenger wrenched the rifle from the sniper's grasp and jabbed the butt into his face. It struck his nose and blood spurted from his nostrils. He had no time to react before the Avenger pulled the weapon back to his own chest, holding it horizontally, and lashed out. The barrel hit Chris in the side of the head and he collapsed. The Avenger tossed the gun aside to approach Jamal, who already had a pistol in his right hand.

On the street, Brooke and Andy gazed up at the monstrous silhouette gliding toward a bulky man with a gun. Andy's face was still contorted in pain while Brooke's eyes stretched as wide as her mouth.

The Avenger brought his right forearm down forcefully on Jamal's outstretched hand. The gun dropped and the Avenger pivoted counter clockwise on the ball of his right foot. That sent him into a spin and briefly left his back open to his enemy. There was no time to take advantage because he immediately raised his left elbow at the conclusion of the turn, ramming it into Jamal's head. His arms went up as he began to reel backward.

The Avenger seized his left wrist in his left hand, and stepped closer to deliver an uppercut to Jamal's underarm region. He struck the nerve he'd aimed for, producing a cry of pain. Then he pulled Jamal forward and lifted his knee into his stomach, doubling him over. His right fist rose above his own head and he paused, gathering strength in the limb. Half a second later he swung it down in an arc and opened it into a knife-edge hand as it bore down on Jamal's neck. The gangster dropped and the Avenger hurried past him.

"Who…" Brooke stammered. It looked like a monster with wings but its movements were human. Sort of. They were much smoother and more precise than an average person's. It flowed gracefully from one motion to the next without hesitation. "What *is* that?"

Andy didn't answer. He seemed momentarily too stricken to even notice his pain.

Fernando and Reyes ran across the parking lot, their eyes locked on the four vehicles parked sixty yards ahead. They heard the gunshots loud and clear yet ignored them. Nothing behind mattered—only the van idling ten feet past the gathering of smaller vehicles. Once they reached it, their mission was accomplished.

The young men were unaware of the figure racing atop the roofs of the nearby stores. It resembled an opaque shadow, outlined by the moon perched high in the black sky. In seconds it caught up so it would've been running side by side with them if not for the fifteen foot height difference.

As he ran, the Avenger reveled in the adrenaline coursing through his veins. He felt lighter than ever, his feet barely touching the ground upon each step. The wind blew against him but failed to remotely affect his speed. It cut around his torso and held his cape up vertically in the air behind him. The leathery, yet silent fabric whipped about in the current like a flag.

The Avenger chanced a glance down to his left where he saw the runners falling behind. Perhaps they had grown tired. They seemed to have been going for quite a distance. He'd heard the gunshots that aroused his attention two to three minutes ago. Either the run was wearing on them or he really was moving as fast as he thought. He returned his gaze to the oncoming obstacles.

Two additional men waited on a rooftop in front of a chimney, thirty yards ahead. The sniper, oblivious to his presence, stared through the scope of his gun, which was aimed in the direction of Fernando and Reyes. His companion appeared to be talking on a cell phone with his back to them.

Beyond them he spotted the top of a white semi-trailer truck close to the edge of the roof. On the street, three cars and an SUV formed a makeshift barricade for a van. Several men, dressed in dark clothes, crouched on the other side of the vehicles, their backs to the van. Three of them brandished shotguns. Whatever gang had arranged the affair had covered all bases. Except one.

Patricia reached her fellow law enforcers and slowed to a jog. Her brown eyes widened at the blood under Andy's body. Lieutenant Brooke's jacket was wrapped and bound securely around his thigh. She kneeled on one knee beside him, both watching the scene a hundred yards in the distance. Brooke turned to see her as she drew near.

"What happened?" Patricia asked.

"They had snipers covering their tracks," Brooke told her. "Almost got me, too."

"I'll be careful." Patricia charged past them.

"Patricia, you…

"I can't let them get away," She called over her shoulder.

Hose turned, still holding the phone to his ear, and saw a creature hastening toward him and his partner.

"What the—" He dropped the phone. "Eric! Shoot it!"

Too late. The Avenger stepped in the midst of the men and used both hands to shove the barrel into Eric's face. Jose started to throw a punch. The Avenger held onto the gun with his right hand and turned over his left shoulder to deflect the blow with his elbow. His bone smacked Jose's hand aside, then he released his fist and struck him in the temple. As Hose went down, the Avenger pivoted clockwise to turn back to Eric and punch over the barrel and into his face. Eric dropped and left the gun in his assailant's hands.

The Avenger adjusted the rifle and lowered it to aim at the barricade. He fired. The recoil almost tore the weapon from his grasp but he clung to it. An SUV's rear windows shattered, eliciting curses and yells of surprise. One gunman fell to the ground. The Avenger re-aimed, eyeing the car two gunmen hid behind. He pulled the trigger and one of them dropped. The other juggled with his gun. The bullet ended up embedded in the front bumper of another car. Once the last gunman regained his grip, the Avenger zoomed in close. A single shot broke the shotgun in half and its contents caused an explosion of gunpowder and light. The weapon's possessor staggered back.

"It's gotta be the cops, let's roll!" Another thug called.

While the gang was disoriented, he searched the rooftop for a way down. The men had to have used something to climb up there. *Got it.* The fourteen foot high truck was parked along the front of the next store, facing away from him. He ran to the roof's edge and dropped down onto the truck's cargo trailer roof. He landed on his feet and crouched to absorb the impact. Then he stood and headed to the front of the truck.

Two cars pulled off, exposing the remaining gangsters who'd hid behind them. When the men realized they were no longer concealed, and that their cover was gone, they stood and hollered after the departing vehicles. The drivers paid them no mind and sped into the street past the van.

"Come on, man!" One of the gangsters, Jack, shook his head and turned to check on Fernando and Reyes. They had paused, ten feet from him, to scan the environment. Like everyone else should have been doing, they were looking for the source of the hostile gunfire. It appeared, to Jack's alarm, to be standing right behind them.

"Nando," He stammered, pointing.

Fernando and Reyes looked at each other first, and out of the corners of their eyes, noticed something over their shoulders. A horned, winged, yet humanoid creature stood there. They began to turn to it when it reached out and grabbed the backs of their skulls in each hand. Their foreheads and faces collided with a *crash* and they fell over backwards.

Jack backed away and reached into his jeans pocket for a pistol. His hand closed around the handle but it became trapped inside the folds of his denim. He frantically tugged at the weapon, trying to pull it loose. The creature was closing in. "Stay back, freak!"

The Avenger lowered his shoulders and ran toward him. Eric took his hand out of his pocket and threw a wild punch to ward him off. The Avenger read the attack, ducked under it, and plowed right into him. He kept his feet moving until Eric crashed back into the SUV. Then he pulled away and jammed his elbow in his stomach. Before Eric could blink, he stood erect and raised his elbow. His hand snapped out in a hammer fist which struck the thug in the face.

The rest of the group scampered around the vehicles to surround their attacker. A stocky light skinned Hispanic kid approached first with his hands up. The Avenger stepped closer and kicked him in the stomach, bending him over. Without letting his foot touch the pavement, he grabbed the kid's hair to hold him still, and drove his knee up into his face. A sickening noise was made on impact and he staggered away, holding his nose.

Chavo jumped in his place and hit the Avenger with a right hook to the jaw powerful enough to turn him sideways. Using the momentum, the Avenger spun the rest of the way and extended his arm. The back of his fist caught Chavo in the head. As he reeled, the Avenger slipped his thumb up and braced it against the side of his index finger, tip pointed upward. He brought it down to his side, and jabbed it into Chavo's throat. Gurgled noises escaped his lips as he held his neck and fell down.

"Get him Hulio!" Someone behind him called.

At the same time, a baseball bat wielding thug, probably Hulio, moved toward the Avenger with the weapon's tip prepared to be driven into his torso. A strong hand grabbed his shoulder to hold him in place. He turned to the attacker and threw his left arm in a circle over the gangster's arm, trapping the elbow between his forearm and bicep. He punched him in the face with his free hand, then braced his elbow against the man's triceps. He stepped sideways and hauled him into Hulio's path.

The bat slammed into his stomach and he doubled over it in pain. When he leaned forward, his hand latched onto the bat and he pulled Hulio down over him. The Avenger brought the sole of his right foot up to Hulio's shoulder and shoved them both down.

Another thug was already throwing a front kick at his face. He dodged to the left, leaving his hand out to catch the kicker's calf in the crook of his arm. He immediately hammered down on the thigh with his left hand and lowered his legs. The kicker was dragged to the ground where the Avenger raised a foot and stomped on his crotch.

The one kid who'd managed to hit the Avenger earlier had recovered. He stepped forward and held his fists up in a boxing stance. The backs of his fists faced his opponent. Judging by the hook he'd thrown earlier he knew how to use his hands. Someone behind the Avenger began moving and he saw Nando and Reyes climbing to their feet. *No time for you, kid.* The Avenger thrust his palms into Chavo's forearms, sending his fists into his own face. He stepped to Chavo's side and punched him in the jaw to take him out.

Reyes sprang toward the cloaked warrior, eyes mad with desperation. He swung at his head with a big fist which missed by miles, and continued to run past him. The Avenger wrenched back and elbowed him between the shoulder blades. Then he kicked back without turning and sent Reyes staggering. Nando was coming as well so he brought his leg forward and booted him in the chest, throwing him back to the ground.

The Avenger turned in time to see Hulio on his feet wielding the bat again. This time it was braced on his right shoulder and he held it as if he were about to hit a homerun. He swung, but the Avenger moved forward into the attack and jabbed his left arm toward his face. His elbow struck Hulio's fingers as he flinched to avoid the Avenger's outstretched fingertips. Small bones were smashed between elbow and aluminum. As he growled, the Avenger dipped his arm through Hulio's and brought it to his side. With his right hand he reached underneath and snatched the weapon from Hulio's grasp. He lifted it and belted Hulio across the back of his neck.

Jack had made it to his knees when Hulio collapsed. He looked up and swore as the Avenger drove the butt of the bat into his chest.

Tossing the weapon aside, he took a moment to press a button on the gauntlet covering his right arm from the elbow down to the wrist. A thin piece of plastic stretched out under his wrist with a circular pad attacked to the end of it. The pad, the size of quarter, stopped in the center of his palm. Satisfied, the Avenger returned his attention to Reyes. The masked thug crawled toward the van, only three feet away. He dragged himself along the asphalt on his elbows, his back arched in discomfort. The Avenger rushed to his side and reached down to seize his collar.

Reyes was unable to fend him off as he yanked him to his feet and shoved him back first into the van. He grasped Reyes' throat in his left hand and pinned him to the side of the vehicle. The criminal stared back, his eyes filled with anger and disbelief. Suddenly, his irises turned red. Blood red. *He's a murderer.*

The Avenger raised his right forearm and held it straight up. He closed the hand into a fist and when his fingers pressed on the pad, two wrist blades shot out of the top of the gauntlet. The murderer's eyes widened at the sight of the serrated blades. Anger abandoned him to complete dread. The Avenger posed the blades to be driven into Reyes' face. Then he released his throat to grab the top of the mask. He ripped it off.

The young, mustached, and clean shaven face was familiar. *It can't be...* It was Angel Reyes Gonzales. One of the two young men who'd murdered the girl. Rose. He gazed into the Avenger's eyes, his expression mirroring the Avenger's emotions.

An image of Rose sitting on the floor with her back to a wall forced itself before the Avenger's eyes. It first melded with reality and then completely overtook his vision. Rose sat with her hand covering her bloody forehead, staring up at people he couldn't see. Her brown eyes seemed to search their faces for compassion as she pleaded for her life. Tears streamed down her reddened cheeks. "Please don't do this!" She broke into sobs. "Please, I have a family, and I—"

A young man in jeans rushed forward and rammed his knee into her face. The back of her head was driven into the plaster behind her. Before she could recover he reared back and kneed her again. Blood flowed from her nostrils as she slid to the floor, revealing a dent in the wall where her head had been. Her dazed eyes lifted to the face of her assailant who glared down at her. It was Angel. He spat on her head and kicked her in the stomach. She helplessly curled around his leg and gagged.

No, not now! The Avenger fought to clear his head of the hallucination. He caught a glimpse of Angel's baffled face. The kid was probably wondering why he wasn't dead yet. Another picture forced itself before the Avenger's eyes at the same time a sharp pain stabbed through his chest. Rose lied in the fetal position with her arms draped over her head. She was attempting to protect herself but left the rest of her body exposed. Angel and Tony took turns kicking and punching her stomach and sides. Her body lurched and twitched with each brutal blow.

Why is this happening now? Rose's thoughts were loud and clear in the Avenger's ears. Her emotional pain also infiltrated his being to suck the power from him. She was obviously hurt by the body shots and the knees had left her head ringing. Still, the torment of knowing that she was at the mercy of these cruel men overwhelmed her. A young woman watched the beating from a couch a few yards away. Rose's best friend. Their eyes briefly met and she shook her head, her own face stained with tears. Yet, she didn't attempt to stop Tony and Angel or call for help. She just watched.

Rose's sadness and fear for her life dragged the Avenger to his knees. He released Angel and tried to regain control of his senses. Something slammed across his back, causing him to collapse in a heap. The only pain he felt was the anguish Rose was enduring.

"What the hell's wrong with him?" Nando asked. He stared at the prone form of the winged 'creature' on the ground, holding a baseball bat in one hand.

Angel rubbed his sore throat and glared at the fallen being with contempt. "Who cares," he said through the pain. "Just crack his skull open."

"Gladly." Nando raised the bat above his head.

"Drop it!" An authoritative female voiced commanded.

The men looked up to see a short redheaded woman in a police uniform. She stood beside one of the cars with a shotgun in her hands. Though she was breathing heavily and appeared exhausted, her grip was firm. Her eyes were steady and every bit as unyielding as her voice. "Now!" She ordered.

Nando tossed the weapon aside and sneered at the officer. She took a step closer only to have one of the men lying on the ground grab her ankle with both hands. When she lowered her gaze to him, Nando turned to the van and yanked the door open. He dove in and scrambled to the passenger's seat while Angel hopped in after him.

"Are you crazy?" Patricia asked the kid on the ground who clung to her. He already had a bloody nose as it was. She raised her eyes to see the van already rolling forward. Her first thought was to take aim and get off a shot or two but she shook her head. The shells could scatter and hit someone else. Like the strange winged creature lying on its stomach close to the curb. It brought its arms out from underneath its body and braced its hands on the ground. Then it gingerly pushed upward. *What the...* It wasn't a monster. Or at least she hoped it wasn't.

"That's enough." Patricia kicked at the hands wrapped around her ankle. They released her immediately and she jogged toward the street. The creature had one knee up and was leaning on it heavily with its elbows. It raised its head to watch the departing vehicle. Patricia stopped six feet away and glanced after the van. Too far down the road to read the plate, although she saw that it began with "6M." Police sirens were audible in the near distance. Hopefully someone would spot the van and pull it over before the fugitives disappeared into the night.

Patricia sighed and turned to the *thing* as he climbed to his feet. *It is human*, she assured herself. Quite a getup he wore, though. She lowered the shotgun and took in the details of the outfit, eyes wide in awe. The wing-like apparatuses on which the cape hung, the bold silver cross displayed on its chest, the belt and the loin cloth. It resembled a medieval soldier mixed with something more terrifying. A man in the guise of an ancient, perhaps mythological being.

"Can I—" Patricia began. *Help you?* Didn't sound right. "Uh, are you— what are you?"

The masked man turned his attention from the road to Patricia. Her breath caught in her throat as their eyes met. His were dark and peered out at her from the sockets in the metallic skull. She let the air out of her lungs and tilted her head to the side.

"Thank you," He said in a hoarse voice.

"Huh?" She scratched her head. *You did save his life.* "Oh, yeah. You're welcome."

Tires screeched up the road and the two turned to see a police cruiser zoom past the street. A second followed close behind while a third turned in their direction. The headlights illuminated the area. Patricia lifted a hand to shield her face and looked back to the medieval warrior. "I'm going to have to..."

Patricia gasped. *No way.* She scanned the area, eyes passing over the buildings, parked vehicles, and dark alleyways. She slowly spun in a circle to scan the rest of her surroundings. A few gangsters were rousing near the parked cars and she could see the flashing red and blue lights across the parking lot. *He* was nowhere to be seen.

12

A soothing breeze met Kana Miyoshi as she climbed out of her car. The wind cooled her face and swept through her ravenous, shoulder length hair. She lingered in the doorway to enjoy it, and watched the white BMW pull up and park across the street. The engine cut off and the driver's door swung open. Leslie exited the vehicle, closed the door behind her, and started toward the detective.

I suppose that's one of the perks to being the most hated lawyer in the world. Kana raised an eyebrow. The car appeared to be a perfectly maintained year old model. More impressive was the black leather trench coat enclosing Leslie's shapely form. It was the type that claimed—if you have to ask the price, you probably can't afford it. Kana shoved her own car door shut and extended a hand.

Leslie glanced to both sides before allowing her green eyes to settle on the detective's. She flashed a polite smile and firmly shook her hand.

"Still worried about people seeing us together in public?" Kana asked.

"A little," Leslie replied. "It would raise some questions don't you think? The good cop who puts criminals behind bars casually meeting with the bad lawyer who sets them free."

Kana shrugged, an oblivious expression on her face. She walked around her car toward two benches facing each other, six feet apart. They guarded the entrance to a trail through a park. "I don't see any harm in that. I hear some opposing lawyers can be pretty chummy."

"Usually the corrupt ones." Leslie followed, her high heels clicking on the pavement. "In some circles, the prosecutor, defense attorney, and the judge are all the best of pals. They flip a coin or take bets to determine who will win the case. It's all a game to them regardless of the circumstances. Haven't you ever wondered why so many innocent people get convicted?"

"Because criminals aren't honest?"

"Besides that."

"You're not kidding are you?" Kana frowned. She sat on the bench to the left and turned to see Leslie adjust her coat while staring down at the plastic white surface. The lawyer narrowed her eyes and fretted. Kana grinned. "Too good to sit with the common, dirty, detective?"

"You know what teenagers use these benches for when they don't think anyone's around?"

"I've heard." Kana's disgust was evident in her voice.

Leslie sighed and settled on the bench next to the detective. She put her hands in her lap and sat up rigidly, surveying the surrounding area. They were in a nicer part of town but nowhere was safe in Minikin Capital. A murder had been committed a mile along the trail last week.

The victim was a notorious drug dealer who probably had it coming. Still, Kana kept that incident to herself.

"They cleaned the park this afternoon," Kana said. "Benches, too."

"Okay." Leslie relaxed.

"So, who will be joining us?"

"I tried to get in touch with all of them, including Amanda. She didn't want to talk. Angel I wasn't able to find, but I did get in touch with Anthony. He said he would show up but couldn't vouch for the others. He claims he hasn't been in contact with Angel and didn't know where Amanda was either."

"I believe it. Angel was picked up for fighting in a store three weeks ago. Did a good number on the other guy, too. I'm sure we'll be seeing more of him in the near future. Anthony hasn't shown himself to be a nuisance yet."

"Angel had no prior record."

"You know how it works, though. You get a taste for blood, forget the value of human life, you typically come back for more."

"Yeah." Leslie nodded, lowering her eyes to her hands. She notably blinked back tears before turning toward the street.

Kana felt her pain in the pit of her own stomach. Prior to learning about Leslie's arrangement with the Avenger, she'd added to that grief. She recalled reminding her at every turn that she had blood on her hands. Now she admired the tough defense attorney as much as anyone. Leslie had put aside her guilt to aide the Avenger's cause. She was obviously still hurt.

"So," Leslie said with a sigh. "Any word on when our mutual friend plans to meet these guys himself?"

"He hasn't said anything to you?" Kana shifted, uneasily.

"No, he seems intent on changing the subject, if not ignoring it completely, whenever I bring it up."

"Hm."

"Look." Leslie sat forward and made eye contact with Kana. "There's no one else I can talk to about this. It's driving me crazy. I've been holding my breath, even praying that neither of those animals kills again. It's not fair. I want them off the streets whether it means jail time or death. Do you know how hard it is to sleep at night? Worrying that someone innocent will die because of me again."

"You're not responsible for their choices," Kana said.

"Unless my choice gives them the opportunity."

"No. You may have gotten them off the hook but you have not given them a license to kill. They should just be happy not to be in prison and take advantage of their undeserved freedom. Plenty of people turn their lives around, and so can they."

"We both know that doesn't happen nearly as often as we'd like. Typically, when these losers go free they think they'll be able to beat the system the next time around. Why change your ways if you won't be punished for it?"

"That's where conscience comes in. They—"

"These two don't have consciences, Miyoshi," Leslie snapped. "They never once said they were sorry for what they did. And my suggestion that they apologize to Mrs. Arturo? They refused. In their eyes they did no wrong. Rose deserved it." She paused for a moment. Winced. "Is that what he thinks, too?"

"I doubt that," Kana replied. She doubted it, but she really wasn't sure. She wondered why he hadn't gone after the boys herself.

"He doesn't talk to you about it?" Leslie pressed. "You have to know who he is. And it's convenient that you were unmarried until two months after you met him. So you must know something."

Kana followed Leslie's eyes to the ring on the appropriate finger of her left hand. She took a deep breath and let it out, slowly. "I'll ask him again. For you."

Leslie raised an eyebrow.

"No promises, though. He doesn't have to tell me anything. But I'll see what I can do."

"Thanks, Kana." Leslie smiled.

"You're welcome. I understand how you feel—trust me. I want them dealt with as badly as you do. But perhaps, tonight, we can dissuade Anthony from doing something stupid again. Angel I'll get to another way if I have to."

"Thank you."

"Of course." Kana gripped Leslie's nearest hand in hers and squeezed. "I've got your back, Leslie. I still feel bad about the hard time I gave you before I met *him*. I am sorry…"

"Don't be." Leslie squeezed back. "All is forgiven. As long as you don't charge me for your counseling services."

"I won't. You are buying me some pizza when we're done with his jerk. I'm starving."

"Fair enough."

Leslie returned her hands to her lap and turned to watch the road. A few cars passed every minute or so but the night was quiet. Still. No sign of their *guest* yet. Kana glanced down at her watch. He had eight minutes. The women had arrived a bit early. She reclined on the bench and looked to the trail that led through the forest. It was lit by lampposts on either side of the path, set up every ten yards.

So why aren't you avenging Rose' death, Joe? Where's her justice? Kana refused to believe her husband sided with the murderers. He sometimes did things she didn't understand or agree with, but not to that extent. Even if Rose had known of her sickness prior to having sex with Anthony and Angel, torturing her wasn't excusable.

They'd unleashed a level of brutality on her that Kana rarely witnessed. The worse of criminals didn't go as far as they did. Seeing her body and reading the autopsy report had driven her during the investigation. She became so involved that she'd asked to be removed from the case. But how could she not be upset and desire justice? And what on earth was holding Joe back from meting it out?

Fifteen minutes after Kana's interrogation with Angel

"I'm going to get fat eating this," Kana said. She sat in the passenger's seat of a tan 2005 Toyota Corolla, holding a double whopper before her eyes in both hands. Compared to her petite frame it was ridiculously hefty. "Is that what you want?"

"Doesn't matter to me." Joe shrugged. He was behind the wheel and halfway finished his own sandwich.

The car was parked alone at the back of a Burger King parking lot, facing away from the restaurant. An almost barren road afforded them a clear view of a wide grassy field across the street. Several toddlers ran about chasing a ball and each other while a woman in her late twenties watched from a bench. She gently rocked an occupied stroller back and forth with one hand.

"Besides," Joe continued, "you grew up eating General Tsao's Chicken and pork fried rice. If that greasy mess didn't put pounds on you…"

"Those are Chinese dishes, Joe," Kana said, grinning. "My mom only wanted us to eat Korean food. Dad didn't care for that too much, of course."

"I wouldn't either if I had to eat kimchee all the time. It burns your taste buds for a week and it's barely worth it."

"It's good for you!" Kana insisted. "And it's how we stay skinny."

"That's because you didn't want to eat it, either."

They both laughed.

"No, kimchee is a masterpiece, Joe. It takes three days to prepare."

"And you'll eat anything after going without food that long, I know."

Kana giggled. She wasn't winning that one today.

"Lizzy did like it when you made some for the get together last Saturday," Joe admitted.

"Yah. She has better taste than you. I was surprised she came. It's very brave for an Atheist to come to a Christian event like that. I like her. She's a nice girl."

"It is encouraging to have her there. She's very attentive and she throws some tough questions at me. Keeps me on my toes. I just wish some of our Christian youth would show half the interest she does. I used to wonder why I bothered before she started coming. Still do."

"Joe." Kana swallowed a mouthful of beef, bread, cheese, and lettuce. "Hang in there. If Lizzy is the only one paying attention then I think she's worth it. And maybe her example will bring the others around. You are a good teacher. I mean, you had *no* life when I met you—outside of God and the Bible—which was fine for a while but, still. Now you can put all your knowledge to good use. Save some souls instead of killing them, for once."

"Thanks," Joe muttered, smirking.

"By the way, what happened with that girl who was supposed to come to the Bible Study last week? Um... what was her name again? I don't think she mentioned it on the phone."

Joe's eyes lowered to the dashboard and he shook his head. "She... uh, she didn't show."

"Huh." Kana furrowed her brow and cocked her head to one side. "She sounded like she was definitely going to go when I talked to her. Maybe something came up, you know?"

"She was into a lot of sin so... I presume she didn't want to give that up. It's her choice and her problem. Not ours."

"You're really disappointed."

"It's a sore subject."

"Okay, sorry." Kana took another bite of the whopper, and eyed the kids running around in the grass. Three of them chased a five year old girl fleeing with the ball held high, giggling. Kana smiled and turned to her husband. He was staring off into space, chewing the last bits of his sandwich. None of it has spilled on his white dress shirt or the black tie. Why he had dressed up to take her out to lunch at Burger King, she'd probably never know. It caused her smile to widen, however.

He caught her gaze out of the corners of his eyes and turned to her. She set her whopper on the dashboard, leaned over and rested her head on his chest. His arms encircled her and held her in place.

"I wish you could pick me up for lunch everyday," Kana said as she stared up into the sky above and beyond the field. "Or at least three days a week. Even if it's just for fifteen minutes, and if you insist on making me chubby... I would love that. To be with you out here in peace. It's nice."

"Maybe I could—"

"No." She looked up at him, sadly. "You have three jobs now. Pastor—"

"Assistant pastor."

"Same difference. Then there's your paper job, and of course—cleansing the city. The last two keep you up during the most of the night, and the pastoral duties take a few hours during the day. I don't want you to be overburdened because of little old me. You don't get enough sleep as it is and I know you're hurting."

"That stuff doesn't matter. I want to be around more and I plan to try my best. I didn't marry you so you could be lonely and sitting at home by yourself..."

"Joe—"

"When things settle down a little more, maybe we could get away for a while."

"Can you actually take a vacation?" Kana asked. *Would be great, but I doubt it.*

"I may have some overtime to put in afterwards but sure. Once I've caught up with all the leads I have, and when the city is quieter, I'll set aside a few days or a week. That might not be for some months, though."

"I understand, and I'm sure Mrs. Arturo and Leslie would appreciate it," Kana said, rolling her eyes. "I interviewed one of the losers who killed her today. We got the confession out but I'm assuming you already knew who it was?"

"I, uh..." He looked out the window to his left. "I don't want to talk about that."

Kana blinked several times, eyes stretched. "Huh?"

"I'm not going to get involved. I... it's not... I'm leaving it alone for now. And I would appreciate it if you didn't bring it up again. Sorry."

"Okay." Kana nodded. She went against her curiosity and kept the dozens of questions that sprang up to herself. Perhaps he was really upset about how things were progressing at the church. He didn't say it, but the prospect of the girl attending the bible study had excited him. That had to be a major letdown. On the other hand, his night job had the tendency to take a toll on him. *There are more pleasant things to talk about in your free time, I guess.*

"You'd better eat the rest of that burger." Joe returned his eyes to her. "You asked for it and it wasn't cheap."

"But I'm so full," Kana whined, rubbing her stomach. "It reminds me of kimchee."

Joe laughed. Kana picked the whopper up and took another bite.

The vacation hadn't come yet. Joe was always vigilant to keep his word so she was confident that the time was near. She hadn't mentioned it again afterwards and to respect his wishes—she'd left the issue of Rose alone as well. Kana narrowed her eyes. It was odd that the girl Joe met had failed to show up the same night Rose died. He'd been reluctant to say much on either topic. *Come to think of it, he's never told me that girl's name.*

"Here's our guest of honor," Leslie announced under her breath.

Stirred from her memories, Kana turned to the street to see Anthony striding toward them. His hands were tucked in his jean pockets and his frame hidden under a large camouflage jacket. He watched the ground in front of his feet, only occasionally glancing up at the women awaiting him. It had been months since the murder, but his demeanor wasn't nearly as confident as his partner's.

"Hello Anthony." Leslie gestured to the bench on the other side of the trail. "Have a seat."

"Sure," He said, eyeing them curiously as he followed her directions. "What's up?"

"The case is over with, and you're not going to be retried," Leslie told him. "But we… want to set a few things straight."

"First, you didn't fool anyone," Kana spoke up. "Regardless of her having HIV, you were *wrong* to take Rose's life. It was a cowardly, sick, and evil thing to do."

"She tried to get us infected—on purpose." He looked to his former defender for support. "It was her fault, right?"

"No, it wasn't," Leslie cut in. "She received the results of the test two days after she was last intimate with you or Angel. Other than that she had no way of knowing. None of the symptoms had shown up. We're not in court anymore so you can drop the lies, okay? Kana and I both know the truth."

"I'm out of here." Tony leaned forward to stand.

"You leave before we're finished and I'll see to it that the case is reopened," Leslie warned, sternly.

Tony sat back with an exasperated sigh and crossed his arms over his chest. "What do you want from me?"

"We want to make sure that you keep your hands clean," Kana replied. "You can't get away with murdering innocent people. Leslie may have gotten you out of a little jail time, but you *did not* win."

He rolled his eyes.

"Listen to me, scumbag," Kana said, leaning forward herself. "She may not have meant much to you but that was a human being you slaughtered. And I can assure you that you'll have to answer for it one day. I don't know if you're going to go out and get involved in the gangs like your pal did, but I would advise you not to. If we don't bust him one of his own will take him out, eventually."

"Man, I'm not joining some stupid gang. I don't even talk to Angel, anymore. I'm not like him."

"No?" Leslie raised her eyebrows and crossed her arms over her chest. "Have you gone to apologize to Mrs. Arturo like I said? To give her some relief?"

"I can't do that..."

"Which shows you don't have any remorse at all for what you did."

"It's your choice, Anthony." Kana shrugged. "But I can assure you of one thing—you won't escape punishment for what you did forever. Even if you live a long, supposedly happy life. When you die you're going to face God and good luck trying to appease him with your defense. Leslie certainly won't be there to cover for you, and your excuses won't matter to Him."

"I'm not worried about that. I don't believe in no—"

"Hell? Trust me, five minutes after you die you'll believe in it. You can fool yourself into thinking it doesn't exist all you want. It's there, and that's where you're headed. To burn forever like the filthy, wicked, disgusting, loser that you are. You think what you guys did to Rose was bad, huh?"

Leslie sat back with a smile on her face, enjoying Kana's tongue lashing as much as she would if she was the one dishing it out.

Kana reached into her inside jacket pocket and pulled out a thin piece of paper. She stood and tossed it at his feet. He looked to see that it was an image of Rose printed on a sheet of eight by eleven photo paper. Her face and hair were smeared with blood. The liquid couldn't conceal the knots on her forehead or her swollen face. Her nose was contorted as well from the abuse she'd suffered. Kana had been shocked at how beautiful Rose was prior to the beating. Tony tore his eyes away from the picture.

"Don't like your own handiwork? Imagine how her mother felt when she saw what you monsters did to her child. I can promise you this, though—what she went through for five hours will be nothing compared to the hell you're going to face. So live and be happy while you can Anthony. Death will come for you. Might not be for forty years. Could be tomorrow. I hope you're ready."

Leslie rose and the two headed toward the street. Once they were out of earshot Leslie leaned close and said, "I owe you one."

"Huh?" Kana paused beside her car. "What for?"

"You have any idea how long I've wanted to let one of my clients know what I really think of them?" Leslie smiled, holding onto the smaller woman's arm. "Man that felt good to watch. You sure do know how to make a guy feel like dirt and a woman like a queen at the same time."

"Glad I could be of some use to you."

"You would make an awesome prosecutor, you know?"

"I prefer detective so I can actually make good on some of my threats." Kana paused beside her car door and pulled it open. "Ready to buy my dinner, Mrs. Walsh?"

"You've earned it."

13

An hour later, Kana lied in her bed with her head and shoulders elevated on four pillows. Her hands were clasped over her stomach and her legs crossed at the ankles. The television six feet from the foot of the bed was the lone source of light in the spacious room. A bronze lamp propped atop the nightstand on the left side of the bed had stayed off since she arrived home. In front of its base sat a small frame containing a photo of Joe and Kana on their wedding day.

To the far left, a closet door next to a window was cracked open. The closet was dedicated entirely to her husband's uniforms and an impressive arsenal of weapons. A second walk-in closet directly across the room held their regular clothes, jackets, and shoes. Another nightstand was positioned to the right of the bed. Two Bibles occupied its oak surface.

The detective watched the opening credits of the Julia Newman Hour, content to finally be home after a day that seemed to drag on for centuries. Hopefully Joe hadn't already gone to work. She hated not seeing him at night and waking up to find him knocked out beside her in the morning. Guilt advised her not to bother him while he rested, and she seldom did.

"Tonight, Jennifer Arturo, mother of Rose Arturo—speaks out for the first time since Angel Gonzales and Anthony Jones were acquitted of all charges," Julia Newman announced. She sat on one end of a plush white couch with the camera zoomed in on her upper body. Behind her, a wooden wall and an out of focus painting indicated a setting outside the studio.

"I'll be speaking with her live in a moment to get her thoughts on the verdict and the defense. And more importantly I want her to provide us with insight into the life of the young woman whose life was tragically cut short in March earlier this year. Afterwards we'll talk with a prestigious prosecutor in Minikin Capital, Michael Haines. And in the second portion we'll take an intricate look at the child prostitution industry on the rise in Minikin Capital, and what that means for the rest of us. This certainly has some implications for the parents out there, so stay tuned to learn how to properly protect your children."

The camera panned out to reveal a massive living room. On the other end of the couch sat a distraught looking Mrs. Arturo. She took in deep breaths with her eyes closed before turning to the journalist.

"Thank you for joining us first of all, Jennifer Arturo," Julia said, smiling.

"Thank you for having me," Jennifer replied.

"How are you holding up?"

"Well." Jennifer sighed. "I've had worse days. It's my family that's helping me to stay sane. They're all busy today but I've hardly been by myself since it happened. My sisters, brothers, neighbors, and some of Rose's real friends... I thank God for them."

"What did you think of the verdict?"

Jennifer shook her head and rolled her eyes. "I couldn't believe it. First that they tried to make my daughter out to be some kind of a monster, and that everyone actually bought it. I don't know what was going through the minds of the jury. And Leslie Walsh… I think she's just as responsible as those boys were. The way she talked about my daughter…"

"So, you say there's no weight to the defense's case? In a poll of 3,000 of our viewers, only thirty eight percent said they agreed with the judgment. It was claimed that Rose purposely tried to spread the virus to get back at Amanda and Tony."

"It's a lie, Julia," Jennifer said. "I know my daughter better than anyone else did. She was *my* best friend and I—I know she would never intentionally hurt anyone. And she loved Tony and Amanda. They were supposed to be her friends. She wouldn't risk their lives. I mean, in school Rosie would walk away from fights all the time. There were a lot of girls jealous of her who tried to pick fights. She was suspended only once, and that was for self defense. My daughter *hated* the thought of harming another human being."

A photograph appeared on top of the living room scene. In it, Rose and her mother's faces were pressed together, cheek to cheek, as they stared into the camera. Jennifer looked surprised and was in the middle of a nervous laugh. The tip of Rose's tongue stuck out between her lips, her eyes bright. They both had clear beautiful skin of roughly the same shade.

"She is *not* a vindictive person," Jennifer went on. "Rosie would kill me if I told you this, but she still had stuffed animals in her room. And when she had a nightmare the week before…" Mrs. Arturo's voice cracked and she paused and closed her eyes. She took a long, slow, deep breath. "She came in my room to sleep with me for the night. Read the Bible to calm us down… she was no monster. She was a beautiful person.

"The partying and drinking and sex she used to do—that's what most kids her age experience with. It's a normal teenaged thing, you know what I mean?"

No, Kana frowned. *She shouldn't have been messing with that stuff in the first place. Doesn't excuse Anthony and Angel's actions, but...* Her eyelids began to grow heavy and her thoughts trailed off.

"Rose didn't tell you that she had HIV?" Julia asked. "She stopped partying two weeks before her death and the test results came in around the same time."

"I knew she had something on her mind..." The next thing Kana heard was, "And she had plans to open her own vet clinic once she graduated. She was only twelve credits away from finishing her prerequisites."

Wow. Kana yawned. She closed her eyes to rest them for a few seconds. When she opened them, the closing credits of the Julia Newman Hour were rolling on top of different images of Rose. Some were baby pictures, and the rest spanned from her as a toddler to her last year. At the conclusion of the credits, a message appeared in bold letters over the photo of Rose and her mother. "HAPPY BIRTHDAY ROSE."

The screen went blank for five seconds and then a commercial came on. The lamp next to the bed clicked and a dim light shone in the room. Startled, Kana looked up to see the fins and cape of the Avenger costume beside her. She put her hand over her heart and sat up groggily. "Hey. You're in for the night?"

"For now," The Avenger replied in a gruff voice. He turned to the television, remote in hand, and switched it off.

"I was watching that."

"You were watching your eyelids." He dropped the remote on the nightstand and turned to her.

"You're home, babe, you can drop the voice," Kana said, grinning. "And what did I tell you about wearing that ugly thing in the house? I don't want to have to repeat myself."

Chuckling, the Avenger reached up to the back of his neck with both hands, undid the black strings there, and pulled off the mask. He headed toward the closet and said, "Sorry, ma'am."

"I talked to Patricia, one of the cops, earlier." Kana watched him, tiredly. "You're starting to become popular among the force. Brooke said you probably saved her and Andy's hides."

"I heard gunshots while I was patrolling the area," Joe explained, lifting the cap and shoulder pads over his head. He opened the closet door and stepped inside, out of Kana's sight. "I started to take the high ground and apparently they beat me to it. There were snipers on the rooftops."

"Patricia was pretty wound up—said she felt like she was meeting some celebrity," Kana told him. "Brooke was glad to see that you were on their side. Oh, and they passed a private order to arrest you on sight. As a token of appreciation, of course."

"Of course. I guess I couldn't stay the myth I wanted to be forever. It'll make working a pain with them looking out for me. More risks. But it was worth it to save their lives. I do prefer prevention to avenging when it's possible."

"I know. You did well, too. Even if they got away. Sad what happened to Harvey, though. His daughter is still missing last I heard. I don't suppose you know where she is?"

"No." Joe emerged from behind the door wearing a thin black tee shirt and shorts. The shirt was rolled up with the front of it tucked between his chin and chest. His entire torso from the waist to just under his chest was wrapped in an ace bandage. One end of it had come undone and hung down to his thigh. He approached and sat on the bed's edge, facing the window. "I'm hoping I don't see her. She might be tempted to follow in her father's footsteps."

Kana scooted closer and took the free end of the bandage to secure it around him. As she worked, she noticed a large black bruise under his right shoulder blade. "She was born into it and her father died in it, so we'll see." She hesitated. "Leslie wanted me to talk to you."

"That's great," He muttered.

"She does have a point, Joe." Kana pulled on the gauze to tighten it around him. He groaned. "Sorry."

"Yeah." His voice was almost a whisper.

"I would be very upset if I was in her shoes. Defending those kids, and expecting you to do what you always do. You don't, and now that poor girl is all over the news. You have to try to imagine what you're putting her through."

"I can imagine, and it's not what I want, but... I can't do anything. I won't."

"Is it because Rose didn't come to the Bible Study that night?" Kana asked. She finished with the bandage and held her palm over his bruise. He flinched at the contact but didn't pull away or rebuke her. She carefully applied pressure and massaged the point of injury.

"How do you..." He sounded surprised. "Doesn't matter. She made up her mind. She chose her sin over God and she suffered the consequences."

"So that *is* the problem." Kana paused to consider a way to approach the topic. "You liked her a lot, huh?"

He lowered his head and said nothing for a moment. That was enough of an answer as far as Kana was concerned but she remained quiet.

"She was..." He began, his tone solemn. "There was something about her. I hadn't met anyone like that before. Funny, blunt, smart... and she seemed to be headed the right way."

"She really liked you." Kana vividly recalled the conversation she'd had with Rose. "It's hard to keep up with the new lingo these days but she found you pretty neat. I don't know how you managed to get along considering your personality differences."

"I was 'Uncle Joe' to her," He said, smiling. "Or at least I thought I was. Like I said, she made her choice."

"Can I tell you what I think?"

"Sure."

"I think you're letting your personal feelings get in the way of doing what's right," Kana said. "I remember the right of avenging was taken from family members for similar reasons. In their anger they'd go blind and hurt anyone who was in the way. The Avenger of Blood had to be impartial. And it seems that you aren't thinking of God's will when it comes to Rose. Just yours.

"If she did reject salvation to stay in her sinful life then ultimately that's an offense against the Lord. So if you're acting, or not acting, because of her lesser offense against you—you're missing the point. I mean, everyone who you avenge is a sinner. Unless you think that Rose was somehow to the worst of them?"

"No, she wasn't," He admitted.

"And I know you don't buy their defense. I hope not."

"I don't. I just..." He covered his face with one hand and tiredly rubbed his eyes. "I'm not ready to confront this... not yet. I'm sorry if that disappoints you."

"Uh, uh." Kana stopped the massage and scooted forward to join him on the edge of the bed. She gently wrapped her arms around him and rested her head on his chest. "I'm not disappointed. I can understand how you feel. But I want you to do what's best so you don't regret it later. Just keep in mind that God is kind to the unthankful and evil. It sucks that she didn't take to heart what you talked about—"

"She lied to me. I called to check on her and she said she was still coming. She could have just told me, 'No thanks, I changed my mind,' but she lied. That's what bothers me. Why didn't she just tell me the truth?"

"Maybe she didn't want to disappoint her Uncle Joe," Kana offered.

Joe winced in pain and lowered his eyes to the floor. Kana sighed, feeling his anguish in her own heart. She was upset to learn that she had talked to the girl on the phone days before her brutal death. Would Rose have lived if she had said something more than she did? Kana might've persuaded her not to attend the party. *It's all hindsight, and you probably wouldn't have changed anything.* Still, it hurt. And she could only imagine how much it bothered her husband.

"I need a vacation," Joe muttered.

"I'll be ready when you are," Kana said. "Whenever you are."

"I owe you one." He turned to stare into his wife's eyes, the admiration in his own unmistakable. "I don't deserve you. And I'm grateful that you put up with my nonsense."

"Well…" Kana tilted her head to one side. "I married you to make you happy. I'll take what you think is fair."

Joe smiled.

14

Joe had lain in bed for what seemed like hours under a snug blanket, cradling the warm, smaller form of his wife. The massage had soothed his cramps enough for him to lie comfortably on his back. Yet for an hour sleep fled from him, refused to grant him the solace he sought. Biologically, he was overdue, having woken up shortly before eight a.m. A quick glance down at his watch revealed that it was 11:23.

Despite the time, he was surprised to find that he wasn't remotely tired. He felt more awake than he had while engaging the gang in the parking lot. It was the knowledge that he would pay for staying up late that had kept him in bed as long as he stayed. About twenty minutes ago he'd grown tired of lying around, being tormented by his thoughts. He threw on a pale blue work shirt and black slacks and went out into the night.

Currently, he walked along a sidewalk with his hands tucked in his pockets. There wasn't a whole lot of activity in this part of town, tonight. The gangs that usually roamed the streets were absent or fewer in number than usual. Citizens rushed past Joe every few minutes, hurrying to get home before the night creatures showed themselves in full power. He nodded to those who looked in his direction and continued his stroll.

Joe shook his head clear and gazed around to take in his surroundings. He was walking along the outside of a large clothing store called Teen Style. *How'd I get here?* The alley between Joe's Pizza Place and Teen Style was twenty yards ahead. Though he'd left the house without a destination, somehow he'd ended up here. The alley, known to locals as a popular haven for runaway teens and young people experimenting with drugs, was also where Rose had been found around 2 a.m. on March 27.

It was her who had kept him from sleeping. He assumed that his mind had led him here in search of peace. As he neared the alley his heart grew heavier and the streetlights seemed to dim. *No.* Avoiding it... avoiding the plain truth of what had happened to Rose Arturo had brought nothing but grief. Joe balled his hands into fists and pressed on.

Ever since the conversation with Kana, all that he had held in the last seven months came to the surface. The suppressed emotions, the pain, and the memories demanded his attention. His acceptance. He tried to swallow them again to no avail. When he closed his eyes Rose's face appeared. Her voice and her laughter replayed as if she was standing beside him.

Joe had concealed his sorrow over her demise by focusing on his anger at her betrayal. Whether she brought the attack upon herself or not, it wasn't justified. And he had come to consider her a friend. He seldom enjoyed being in a person's presence, and much less younger folks. She had been different. The playful banter, her sarcasm, and her depth had allured him. She was fun to talk to. Not that any of that mattered now. Rose was dead. Gone. Probably forever.

"I remember that night, too," A woman's voice from the alley became audible as Joe neared. "Your eighteenth birthday. We got stuck at your house because of the big thunderstorm. All the partying and drinking we wanted to do that night and we were trapped. It was still a lot of fun, though. I mean, I thought I knew all about you up until then. Even though I picked on you for the stuffed animals, and for crying during both of the movies we watched that night... it was probably the best time we all had together, you know?"

Joe reached the alley and paused just inside. It was illuminated by a lamppost a quarter of the way down the wide, fifty-foot passage. There were two dumpsters and three gray metal trash cans spread further along the way. Other than that, the alley was relatively clean. On the lamppost, a picture of Rose hung on a nail seven feet above the ground in a glass case. An inscription was written on a card over the bottom right corner of the photo.

A young woman with dirty blonde hair stood before the lamppost, gazing into the sky with her back to him. She held something in front of her body in both hands. Another item was hidden in a silver gift bag by her feet. He took a step toward her as she continued speaking.

"You showed me that night who you really were. And I never told you before now but that was really special to me. I'll always remember it. The last... the last night is something I'm still trying to forget. I don't think you deserve to be remembered that way. You're one of the nicest, sweetest human beings I've ever met. So... well, I wanted to eat this here in front of you. Leaving it here just seems weird. I'm not Hindu, so—anyway, I brought a present, too. I didn't know what else to do with it, and..."

The woman must have sensed a foreign presence and she turned to see Joe standing ten feet away. There was no fear on her face, only curiosity. In her hands was a plate boasting a miniature cake coated in vanilla icing, and the name, "Rose," written on its top in pink. The woman glanced down at the cake in her hands and back up at him.

"Hey," She said.

"Good evening." He wasn't sure what to say.

"I came here to spend a few minutes with Rose on her birthday," The woman told him, smiling sadly. "I couldn't do anything else, really, and it seemed like the right thing. Hey, you… you look familiar. You're that new pastor from the old Baptist church, right?"

"Assistant Pastor. You can call me, Joe."

"I'm Amanda." She nodded. "I used to be Rose's best friend. I was supposed to be, anyway."

Joe narrowed his eyes in thought. After a few seconds it occurred to him that Amanda was the one who picked Rose up the night of the murder. He'd seen her on the Television earlier that evening while Kana slept.

"She was a nice kid," Joe said, raising his eyes to the picture.

"She was the best friend you could ask for," Amanda concurred. "I met her in high school when we were both Freshmen. I was kind of a dork back then but she stuck up for me. I appreciated that, so… we were attached at the hip after that."

"Hm."

"You… you're kind of a priest, right?"

"Not exactly. A priest typically refers to the leaders who serve in the Roman Catholic Church. In the Bible, anyone who's a Christian is called a priest of God."

"Okay." Amanda paused and bit her bottom lip. Her eyes darted back and forth along the ground before her feet. "Um, so if you're a pastor do you still have to be confidential or what?"

"Well…" Joe grinned. "That depends. If the person you're talking to asks for you not to share their information then it's best to oblige."

"I was raised Roman Catholic," Amanda told him. "Of course I haven't been to mass in a really long time. I've wanted to go to confession since Rose died, though."

"You don't need to go through anyone except Christ for forgiveness. I can listen and give you counsel but ultimately you have to—"

"Can I tell you, then? I mean, I haven't talked to anyone about it. Angel and Anthony got angry when I brought it up and... there's no one else I can trust."

"I'll listen."

"Promise me you won't tell anyone? Not a word?"

Joe nodded. "I promise. You have my word as a Christian."

"Thank you." Amanda closed her eyes and let out a sigh of relief. She opened them a few seconds later to scan the area. Joe followed her example and affirmed that they were still alone.

"Okay," Amanda said, looking at him. "I thought you might like to know some of this, anyway. Rose and I were having a little friendly competition—starting in like, November of last year. We were both messing with Tony back then. Neither of us was really interested in dating at first, it was just for fun, you know what I mean? We drank together, smoked pot, and played with the same guys."

"That's not really my idea of fun."

"Yeah, and I know I need to straighten my life up. I haven't smoked pot since April."

"Good."

"But that's what we all used to do. Then in January I told Tony that I wanted to be in a serious relationship. I hadn't dated anyone in a year and I wanted to know what it was like to be committed to someone again. To be treated out to dinner and to cuddle without it all being about sex. And Tony was such a nice guy. He wanted a girlfriend too but he said he had to consider all of his options. Rose was one of them. She kinda liked him that way so he had to make a choice…"

Joe began to feel tired for the first time that night. He detested what he considered to be the vanity most teenagers and young adults considered normal.

"We had a friendly competition that got a little catty at times. We wanted to see who could make Tony the happiest and please him the best. It was really stupid but, I even provoked her into a fist fight. In February he told me he was going to pick Rose because they were more… compatible. So I told him about the one night stand she had with his cousin when he visited back in November. He changed his mind and we dated for like two weeks.

"After that Rose and I started patching our relationship back together. It was going great, although she was acting a little different—like more quiet. She asked me about where I used to go to mass, and stopped messing with boys. So one night she's over and she goes into the bathroom for twenty minutes. Her purse fell off the table and all her stuff spilled out. The radio was on too loud for her to hear it so I started picking it all up. Then I noticed a strange looking letter from a hospital. I don't know why, but I opened it. I wish I hadn't."

She paused. After a couple of deep breaths, she continued.

"There was a test… and it said she had tested positive for HIV," Amanda said with tears streaming down her cheeks.

Joe winced.

"I didn't know how to react so I just put it back and didn't say anything. I was sad for Rose, but… we'd had sex with the same people all along so I was scared that I caught it, too. She left and turned down a ride in the rain. It was coming down pretty hard that night. I called Tony crying and told him that we might have gotten AIDS from Rose. She hadn't mentioned it so we thought maybe she purposely kept it secret to get me for telling Tony about what she did with his cousin.

"Angel and Tony came over and they were ticked. They wanted to confront her. But I knew she'd never agree to seeing us if she found out that we knew. So I made up the party and told her that Tony would be there and I'd pick her up."

Joe nodded.

"I went and got her and tried to act casual, like everything was fine. I don't think she suspected a thing, but…"

The air inside the red Ferrari was permeated by a smothering tension. Amanda felt it and she was sure that Rose did as well. She had picked her up from her house ten minutes ago, and the majority of the car ride had been spent in silence. Rose sat in the passenger's seat with her hands cradling the purse in her lap. She stared blankly out the window on her side, her plush pink lips seemingly plastered in a frown.

Does she know something is up? Amanda glanced at her out of the corner of her eyes to avoid arousing suspicion. Her best friend had been quieter than usual the past few weeks, but nothing like this. Something seemed to be going on. However, it was unlikely that Rose would have consented to come along if she knew the whole truth. Amanda took a deep breath, returned her eyes to the road and asked, "You okay?"

Rose didn't speak or move. She continued to watch the buildings, pedestrians, and vehicles passing her side of the car.

A large knot tightened in Amanda's stomach. *What's with her?* She kept herself from sounding overly concerned as she asked again, "Rose, what's up with you?"

"I..." Rose shook her head, as if snapping out of a daze, and looked down at her purse. "I did have other plans tonight."

"Rose, come on," Amanda fought the urge to vomit. It felt like the knot had tripled in size. She breathed in deep once more and reminded herself that she couldn't let on. *Act natural.* "You can go to the Bible Study any other time. Friday night is supposed to be for fun. Church is just on Sundays."

"I don't know if he's going to be there on Sunday," Rose replied.

"Who?"

"The assistant pastor."

"That black dude? What does it matter if he's there?"

"Because he invited me, and he's supposed to be teaching tonight. I didn't want to just no show—that's really rude."

"What are you, trying to date a pastor?"

"It's not like that." Rose glared at her, then rolled her eyes and looked out the windshield. "He was really nice, and... he was honest, but he wasn't judgmental. That's the reason I stopped going to church with Mom when I was little. I couldn't stand the way they looked at me like I was *dirt*. He told me I was wrong, but he wasn't a jerk about it."

"Well, you can pick Tony and Anita and have fun on Friday night. Or you can pick the Pastor and be bored sitting in church, listening to someone talk about a guy who died 2,000 years ago."

Rose seemed to consider that. She lowered her eyes to her purse and gently caressed the larger leather pocket. It was impossible to tell what she was thinking, but Amanda hoped she would see reason. Rose lifted her head and turned to face her best friend.

"Pull over and let me out," She demanded in a firm voice.

"What?"

"We're only seven blocks from the church and I *know* you won't take me there. But I am *not* going to miss the Bible Study. The pastor was counting on me coming, and I told him I was. Besides, I'm trying to get out of this *stupid* lifestyle. I'm sick of getting drunk every weekend, letting guys treat me like a piece of meat, and wasting my life away. I'm worth more than that."

"But... Rose..." Amanda fumbled for the right words but they escaped her at the moment. She stared at Rose, incredulously. "Rose..."

"I'm done with it," Rose said. "Pull over and let me out."

"Rose..." Amanda couldn't do that. Tony and Angel were counting on her, and Rose *had* exposed them to AIDS. *Have to stay strong.* "No." She put on a calm exterior and looked out the windshield. "You'll regret it later. All that fighting we did over Tony and you'd give him up for church. I can't let you do that, sorry."

"Excuse me." Rose's eyes were ablaze as she returned her gaze to Amanda. "Do you remember what happened the last time we got into a fight? You let me out of this car, and you let me out *now.* Because if you don't, I'm either going to call the police, or I'm punching you in the face. Stop the car!"

Amanda stepped on the brakes in the middle of the road. Tires screeched fifteen feet behind them as a trailing vehicle struggled to keep from plowing into them. By the tone in Rose's voice, Amanda knew she was deadly serious. The last time they'd fought Amanda walked out of it with a black eye and a bloody nose.

"Fine, get out!" Amanda cried. "Don't ever talk to me again, don't ever call me or ask me for nothing!"

"I won't, I have a better friend than you now." Rose opened her door and climbed out. She closed it gently, to Amanda's surprise, and hurried to the sidewalk.

The drivers behind Amanda started beeping. She snapped herself out of her daze and began forward, slowly. *What do I do?* Her cell phone, which sat inside one of the empty cup holders between the driver and passenger seats, caught her eyes. She snatched it up and dialed a number with one thumb.

"Yo, where you at?" Tony answered.

"I'm on…" Amanda searched for a street sign. "Union and Park. But Rose… Rose got out the car. She's not coming."

"What?" Tony asked. "Why isn't she?"

"She's going to some Bible Study, I don't know…" Amanda was crying.

"Nah, we can't let her do that. We need to talk to her. How long ago did she get out?"

"Like ten seconds ago."

"She's going to that crazy, strict church, right? The one on Royal?"

"Yeah…"

"Alright, Angel and I are going to pick her up before she gets there. You just go to your house and make sure no one's there, alright?"

"You're not… you're not going to hurt her, right?" Amanda didn't like the desperate measures Tony was willing to take.

"She's coming to the house. It's up to her if she wants to fight us or not."

He hung up.

Rose walked through the alleyway with her Bible in hand, head held high. She pressed her lips tightly together to keep from weeping or laughing, unsure of which would come out of her. Though she was upset to have threatened one of her best friends, someone she loved dearly, she couldn't help but be proud of how she'd stood up for herself. She also couldn't wait to tell the pastor what she had turned down to join his study tonight. God already knew, and she imagined the smile on His face. *Alright, you don't know if he's smiling, don't get all goofy.* It was a nice thought, though.

A few seconds later, Rose reached the end of the alley and came to a pause. Across the street, with its entrance facing her left, was the Faith Independent Bible Church. The parking lot was occupied by fourteen vehicles—mostly cars, a van, three SUVs and one jeep. Someone stood outside the front door, staring across the parking lot. Rose couldn't see his face because he was turned sideways but she recognized his shape and height. It was Pastor Joe. *Waiting for me?* The prospect warmed her heart and brought a big smile to her face. *Who needs Amanda when you've got friends like this?*

She stepped forward and was immediately struck on the back of the head. The last thing she saw as she fell was the pastor surveying the area beyond the parking lot. Then her vision was overtaken by black.

"Angel knocked her out, and they brought her to my house, unconscious, and carried her inside," Amanda said, wiping the tears from her face.

Joe's own heart was broken as he stood quietly, listening to her account. He wasn't crying nor did any tears come to his eyes, but inside he was crushed.

"I was shocked that they actually *hit* her." Amanda went on. "She had a big welt on the back of her head. And when she woke up, they…"

"You should have just told us told us in the first place, Rose," Tony told her, shaking his head in disgust.

Rose sat in the center of the couch in Amanda's living room. Her hands were folded in her lap and her chin was buried in her chest, eyes on the floor. Tony stood a few feet in front of her with his fists at his sides. Angel paced behind him, walking between the living room and the kitchen. He muttered to himself as he went, occasionally glancing at Rose in spite. He was reminiscent of a caged bull, waiting for an opportunity to lash out.

"I've got a daughter and she's going to go and give me freaking AIDS—" Angel was saying under his breath.

"Why did you keep it from us?" Tony asked.

"I wasn't trying to," Rose replied. "I was going to tell you guys soon—I really was. I was scared."

"You should have been," Tony said through clenched teeth. "You probably got it from my cousin. I warned you about how nasty he was and you went and did it with him, anyway."

"I'm sorry—"

"No you're not." Tony stepped closer and slapped her across the face. The force of his strike knocked her onto her side. She brought a hand up to her cheek, where his hand left a red print, and gazed up at him. Her eyes were wide in fear and disbelief. She must have realized, at the same time that Amanda did, that they weren't looking for an apology.

"I'm leaving, I have somewhere to go," Rose said, climbing to her feet.

She stepped toward the door only to have Tony shove her from behind. She had barely landed when he was on top of her, dragging her away from her exit. Rose fought with him, punching and screaming to no avail. He pulled her behind the couch and dragged her up.

"Hold her still," Angel charged in from the kitchen doorway, wielding a sturdy frying pan in his right hand. He headed around the couch to join them. "You want to play around and try to give somebody AIDS, right?"

"No, it wasn't like that!" Rose cried. Tony had her pressed against the wall driving his nearest elbow into her chest, and holding her wrists in place in front of her with the other hand. She visibly struggled to get loose but his grip was like iron. "Angel, I promise you I didn't mean to. I just found out... I swear, Angel..."

"My little girl might have to grow up without me because of *you*," He jabbed the index finger of his free hand into her forehead. "You dirty slut."

"Please don't hurt me," She pleaded. "I don't want to be here..."

"Should have thought about that sooner."

He reared back with the pan as far as his arm would stretch, and swung it at her head. It connected with a sickening *thud*. Rose groaned and collapsed on the wall, still held there by Tony. Angel pulled his arm back again and struck her harder this time. Amanda cringed as he continued to assault Rose. The fourth time he brought his arm back there was blood on the bottom of the pan.

"They beat her up pretty bad," Amanda said. "I just left after a while because I couldn't stand to watch anymore. But I swear to God I didn't think they would kill her. When I got back, they told me what had happened and asked me to help them cover it up. I went to the place where they caught her and this was still lying there..."

She stooped over to reach into the bag at her feet with one hand. After digging around inside for a moment, she withdrew a six by nine book with pink leather covers. It was thinner and more compact than most Bibles, and seemed to be Rose's style. On the front it was identified in silver letters as the "NKJV Study Bible." The front was blank, with the exception of a black petal in the bottom right corner.

"I was going to leave it here but I think she would have wanted you to have it." Amanda held it out to him.

Joe, stunned, reached up with both hands to accept the gift. A surge of emotions flowed through him when his fingers enclosed the cool leather. He wasn't a mystic, or particularly sentimental, but touching Rose's Bible was overwhelming.

"You still won't tell anyone, right?" Amanda asked.

"I gave you my word and I'm going to keep it," He replied, tearing his eyes away from the Bible to look to her. "I won't tell anyone. But I do have something to ask of you."

"What?"

"Eating that here by yourself would be pointless." He gestured with his eyes to the photo of Rose. "Take it to her mom's house and eat with her."

"At this time of night? I think tomorrow would be better."

"She's awake and trust me, she would enjoy the company. Especially from her daughter's best friend."

"I think that title is yours, but I'll go," Amanda said. "Maybe I'll… see you at the church or something."

"I'll keep an eye out for you." He turned to leave.

"You sure you don't want to go tonight, too?"

He paused and glanced over his shoulder. Though Amanda's face was eager and he looked forward to eventually meeting Mrs. Arturo, tonight wasn't a good night. He told her why, "Maybe another time. I have work to do."

"Goodnight!" She called as he exited the alley.

15

Joe stood in his spacious closet wearing a long sleeved black shirt, matching pants, and boots. Several copies of the various pieces needed to complete his apparel surrounded him. Shelves were built in six feet above the ground, and his masks, belts, and other items occupied them. A dozen gauntlets sat in a box to his right, five pairs of capes rested on hangers before him, and six aprons were hung up behind him. The seventh was in his hands.

Joe slipped the apron on over his head and pulled it down as far as it would go. The loin cloth unfolded from the rest of the clothing and the bottom dropped to his knees. In the mirror between the capes in front of him, the silver trim of the cloth stood out with the bold cross on his chest. They were the lone parts of his outfit besides the mask that weren't black. He considered them the light in the darkness—his personal reminder that Christ was his righteousness and his sole strength.

He took a black sash from a hanger next to the capes and held it before his eyes. He measured with his hands to the center of the belt and wrapped it around his waist from the front. After crossing both ends behind him, he brought them to his front and tied the sash securely. Then he reached for one of the two gauntlet types in a box to his right. He slipped it onto his left arm and pressed a button to open the top. Six silver throwing stars were aligned in a single row of three, two in each slot. He clamped down on the lid to shut it and it blended in with the rest of the gauntlet.

Joe put on the next gauntlet and immediately used the switch to bring the pad out over his palm. He made a fist, pressing on the pad, and the wrist blades shout out with a metallic *shing*. When he released the pad the blades retracted into the gauntlet. His weapons were functioning. Satisfied, he brought the shoulders pads with the fins and cape attached off of their hanger and down over his head. He straightened the shoulder pads out, nodded, and finally reached for one of the masks.

The Avenger of Blood emerged from the closet and paused outside the door. Kana was lying on her side in the bed, in the closet's direction. She'd heard him moving around inside there and the light showing through the doorway had awakened her. Tiredly, she lifted her head and sat up. "Not finished tonight after all?"

"They've gotten away with their crimes long enough," The Avenger replied. "Tell Leslie to stay up. I won't be long."

"See you in the morning." Kana smiled and dropped her head back onto her pillow.

"Hey baby," Isabel called from the porch door.

Her "baby", Brandon Duran, sat on the railing on the opposite side of the porch with his back to her. The porch, roughly four feet above the ground, overlooked the backs of similar apartments on the block. A space of fifteen by ten feet was allotted to each building. Some had plants growing, and others stored various tools and appliances there. Besides freshly cut grass and two white lawn chairs in the center, Brandon's was clear.

"I heard that you guys knocked off Old Harv," Isabel said.

Brandon glanced over his shoulder to see her standing in the doorway with one hand on the doorknob. The other was brushing through her long reddish brown hair. She wore one of his black tee shirts, which nearly came down to her knees. Her legs had the same milky white complexion of her face. Though her statement annoyed him, he couldn't be too angry with her. *How can you get mad at something so hot?*

"I bet you hear a lot of nonsense. You and your girlfriends don't do nothing but gossip, anyway."

"Hey, you can tell me." Isabel approached him, her bare feet barely making a sound on the wooden platform. "Nobody here but you and me, right?"

The windows of the surrounding apartments were dark and void of activity. Their porches were unoccupied as well. They were alone, but he still shifted uncomfortably.

"Why you worried about it?" Brandon asked.

Isabel wrapped her arms around him and rested her hands on his chest. She leaned close to his ear, filling his nostrils with her scent, and said, "Because if it's true, my man should be getting a nice cut. Especially since you've been so loyal to the gang. And after all, it was your idea to hit up Old Harv in the first place."

"Yeah well, we'll see." Brandon shrugged. "Me and Hector peeled out when the cops started shooting. So Jones is talking crap about us almost blowing the whole thing. Like we were supposed to sit around and get shot at or something."

"They busted Eric, Luis and them. You don't think they've talked do you?"

"Of course they haven't—and they're not going to. They don't even know where the stash is."

"How soon are you guys going after it?"

"We have to meet up in twenty minutes."

"Who all is going?"

"Fernando, Jose, Ramses, Trevor, that new guy Angel... and a few others," Brandon told her. "There's only supposed to be nine or ten of us, though. Everyone who's there takes home a bigger cut. We'll still have to split it about sixty different ways."

"From fifty million?" Isabel grinned. "That's not bad."

"I told you about nonsense. It's thirty five mil."

"Hm." Isabel lowered her chin to his shoulder. "If only nine or ten of you are going, though, then you ought to get a million each at least."

"Probably."

"You know if that happens I can actually afford to move in here for good. And I can finally leave that slob and afford the divorce lawyer. If you're as serious about us as I am."

"Of course."

"Good." Isabel kissed him on the cheek and backed away. "I need to get a shower. I'll be nice and clean for you when you get back, okay?"

"Nice and sleep you mean."

She laughed as she stepped inside. "You could always wake me up."

"Yeah, yeah," He muttered under his breath, a sly smirk on his face.

His mother wouldn't leave him alone if she found out that his girlfriend was a married woman. She had to wonder why Isabel only slept over half the week. Mrs. Duran had invited her to stay there permanently free of rent. The reason was, her husband Bill thought she was helping her parents a few days a week. Him knowing that she was committing adultery would spell trouble for both Brandon and Isabel. It would also stop him from paying off the bills she couldn't afford on her own. Brandon hadn't been able to afford them either until now. He breathed a contented sigh and closed his eyes.

A hand wrapped around his ankle in a vice-like grip. Before he could even open his eyes it pulled down on him with force. Brandon was yanked off of the railing and fell into the grass. He landed on his hands and knees and immediately tried climbing to his feet. Something dark and misshapen stood beside him. One hand grabbed his curly hair and hauled him into an upright position. He gazed up in horror into the face that Angel had described earlier that night. A metallic version of the face of Death.

The creature raised his right hand with the fingers spread and tightened them into a fist. Twin silver blades or claws sprung out of the back of his wrist. Their tips and the serrated edges appeared to glisten in the moonlight. The creature lowered the arm and held the blades inches from Brandon's face.

"What do you want, man?" Brandon held his hands up in surrender.

"Where's Harvey's money?" It demanded in a throaty growl.

"Harvey..." Brandon stammered. He'd momentarily forgotten about Harvey and the money. He barely remembered his own name. A glance at the razor sharp blades brought his memory back. "Union Avenue—the Methodist Church!"

"What time?" It asked.

"One a.m."

"If I find out you're lying..."

"I'm not—I swear!" Brandon pleaded.

The creature leaned forward and shoved him back into the wooden porch. His head collided with the unforgiving surface and darkness clouded his vision.

16

A loud sound reverberated through empty halls of the Minikin Capital United Methodist Church. Mia, who sat in the pews of the sanctuary, lifted her head. The sound repeated itself, a clashing of two sturdy materials. Then she heard the doors open and the regular noises of the street seeped in. *It's time.* She stood and rushed toward the altar at the head of the room. Two windows high above the floor provided her with enough light to avoid running into something.

She stepped up onto the stage, slipped around the altar, and hurried to the door at the back of the platform. Rough and hurried voices could be heard in the distance. The main entrance to the church was beyond the back of the sanctuary. From there, those visiting could either enter the large room where services were held, or walk around it to reach the numerous offices and passageways. It was doubtful that the robbers would bother with the sanctuary but there was always a chance.

Mia quietly opened the door, moved across the threshold, and closed it behind her. She was in the interior hall, where the majority of the building was accessible from. It was lined on the opposite side by doors and a large gray water fountain. A wide doorway was visible to the far right and led into the cafeteria. To her left, twenty feet away, was a medium sized lounge. If her memory served her correctly, it contained two staircases. One would take visitors to the second floor and the other to the basement. The gang had to pass the opening to the hallway to reach either of them.

Lowering herself, Mia crept toward the water fountain while drawing a pistol from the holster around her waist. She held it in her left hand and turned to face the lounge once she reached the fountain. Then she dropped to her right knee behind it and pressed herself against the wall. Her thin frame allowed her to be concealed by it for the most part. She wore an all black outfit consisting of a long sleeved shirt and sweatpants, both made of thin, almost noiseless fabrics.

Mia leaned forward and aimed the gun straight ahead of her. She braced her other hand on the foundation and prepared herself. In a few seconds, she'd have the option to push off on it or hold on as she took aim around it. All of her toes remained on the ground to enable her to spring to her feet. The cafeteria would provide a sufficient amount of cover if she had to run for it. She took a deep, quiet breath to relax the butterflies in her stomach. It relieved her a little but didn't quench the voice in the back of her head telling her that she was making the wrong decision. She ignored it. *Can't let them get away with what they did to Dad.* They'd murdered him in cold blood. That gave her the right to exact revenge—an eye for an eye, in the gang world.

"You sure we shouldn't have checked on Brandon?" Fernando asked.

He was one of the nine men walking through the narrow hallway alongside the sanctuary. The width forced them to move in twos with Angel beside Fernando at the head of the group. Hector and Trevor walked a few feet behind, followed by Jose and Manny. All of the six carried a black duffle bag on one shoulder, and an AK-47 in the opposite hand.

The last couple consisted of Rameses, the enforcer of the group, and Jones, the current leader. Rameses, like the others except Trevor, was Hispanic. His role of enforcer was given to him due to his tank like build, and his fighting abilities. He'd only had to show them off to the gang once. Since then it had only taken a look to correct unruly behavior. Jones, a black man who shared Rameses' height of 6'1", was thinner but no less feared. He'd fought hard to attain his position and had gone unchallenged thus far. Behind the two, Xavier brought up the rear, walking backward to thwart an ambush.

"Brandon knew what time to be here," Jones said, flatly. "He'll have to take a smaller cut like the rest of the crew. Simple as that."

"What if the cops got to him?" Angel glanced back.

"He won't talk, and they don't have anything on him," Jones replied. "Besides, they won't be able to offer him as much as we'll have. He's smart. And personally, I'm more worried about your and Nando's imaginary demon showing up."

The others chuckled, but Fernando and Angel exchanged a wide eyed glance as the hallway opened up into a room. It was roughly twenty feet by twenty-five. To the far left in the corner was a single door with a red glowing EXIT sign above it. Seven round white tables with steel chairs pulled up to them occupied the floor's center. Against the far wall was another larger table next to a tan, grand piano. Several piles of hymns laid atop the table and one was propped up and open on the piano.

To the right of the piano a staircase, divided by a white guardrail in the center, led to the second floor. The steps above the first two were swallowed by darkness. Fernando glanced to the left and saw an opening in the wall further down from the EXIT. It appeared to lead to another set of steps going down, as he could see nothing past the large doorway. He tucked his gun into his duffle bag and fetched a flashlight from his pants pocket. After switching it on, he pointed the beam into the darkness at the peak of the stairs.

"Wasn't our imagination, man," Fernando said, searching the second floor for anything out of the ordinary. He saw a wall a few feet past the top step, which led to a hallway. Nothing up there as far as he could see. "It was *something* freaky."

"Maybe it was Bigfoot," Trevor suggested, deriving more laughter from his peers.

"We'll be alright," Jones said. "With the guys watching the cars outside, he won't be able to get near the place without us knowing. So chill out."

The voices sounded clearer, which probably meant that they had come into the line of fire. Mia recognized one of them from the two men who robbed and murdered her Father. He seemed to be the closest so she tightened her grip on the gun and slipped her index finger into the trigger guard.

"Wait there, let me get the flashlight," Jones called.

"Alright, but I don't see—" Fernando began.

Mia pushed herself from behind the water fountain and brought her right hand up to balance the gun. Four men stood at the end of the hallway, three of them looking back over their shoulders. The one at the front of the group had a flashlight pointed ahead. She aimed as best as she could and pulled the trigger.

The first gunshot caused all of them to jump and they retreated. Mia fired a second and a third time and the man wielding the flashlight dropped it and collapsed, crying out in pain.

"Over there!" Angel pointed in her direction.

Mia took a final shot to thwart them, and then spun on her heels and darted toward the cafeteria opening. The half a dozen doors between the fountain and the cafeteria were to offices and classrooms. Dead ends.

"Shoot him!" Angel cried.

Gunfire erupted behind her as Mia reached the doorway. She ducked her head and pushed off with her legs, diving through the open space. She landed on her side and slid further into the massive room along the icy tiles. The wall in the hallway was ripped apart by a myriad of bullets. It sounded like automatic gunfire. Mia rolled onto her hands and knees, and scampered to her feet. The moderately lit cafeteria was filled with dozens of tables separated by several rows. There were also pillars set up throughout, six on the sides of the room, and three along the center. Across the room, about thirty yards, she spied an exit on either side, both doors facing each other.

She ran down the center of the floor to avoid the tables. There was no time to try to maneuver through them. She estimated fifteen seconds before the gangsters put dozens of bullets in her back. The thought of being literally torn to pieces by the automatics pushed her to run faster than she ever had. Her legs and arms pumped together to propel her toward the end of the room where she'd have to choose one of the exits. She neared the last pillar

"There!" A voice behind her announced.

Mia took three more running steps and threw herself to the ground. A single gun fired, sprinkling bullets into the wall where her torso had been a split second ago. She dragged herself along the floor and crawled behind the last pillar. Once she was completely hidden, she sat up and pressed her back against the sheetrock. Three other guns joined the fray and they sprayed the area around the pillar with bullets. A hundred holes were punched into the wall ahead of Mia as someone hollered above the commotion.

"Stop, you idiots!"

The gunfire died down and another person asked, "What, man?"

"She's behind that pillar. The more noise we make, the quicker the cops get here."

"So?"

"We play chicken," Hector said. "We walk closer to the pillar, keep our guns ready, and blast her when we reach it. If she tries to run, she dies, anyway. UNLESS, she comes out with her hands up and tells us what she's doing here."

"I think that was Harvey's daughter, man," One of his comrades said. "Who else would be here with a gun trying to off us?"

"Well, Harvey's daughter better make a choice, and quick.'

She heard their footsteps begin across the floor in her direction. That left her with twenty seconds to decide what course of action to take. Unfortunately, none of the three that came to mind were promising. If she stayed low and ran or crawled, they might not be able to see her. By the time she reached one of the doors, however, she'd have to open it, which would alert them to her location. They'd already made it clear that staying put was a last option. And one lesson she'd learned from her father was not to trust anyone. Especially not if that person had a gun.

Mia lifted her own gun and held it before her eyes. The weapon suddenly seemed so weak and trivial in her trembling hand. There was a fourth option. She could stand up and fire. Try to take out one or two of them before their superior guns destroyed her. She remembered the stories she'd heard her father and his friends tell about gun wounds. How some people were loaded with bullets and still lived for minutes, sometimes even hours in horrible pain. The hot rounds in their flesh torturing them the entire time.

Stop it, Mia told herself. She brought her heels back close to her butt, and slowly pushed herself up. Her back dragged on the pillar as she went, and kept her steady. Once on her feet, she held the gun up in front of her face again. Her last way out was to shoot herself in the head and get it over with. That was the way least likely to result in a slower more painful demise. *Why did it come to this?* Those vermin had murdered her father in cold blood. He'd already given them the information they wanted and they still shot him. They deserved to die. And yet here she was, seconds from death herself for trying to carry out justice. She forced the muzzle of the gun toward her head and closed her eyes.

A loud metallic sound startled the five gangsters. They paused, twenty feet from the pillar their future victim was concealed behind. Hector gazed around for the source of the sound. It was too close to be something the girl had caused. He narrowed his eyes and raised his head to look at the ceiling. The chandelier a few feet above them rocked gently back and forth. It hadn't been moving when they entered the cafeteria. "Guys, something…"

A small dark object, the size of a man's palm, flew into the light source. The chandelier shattered into pieces, which came raining down to the floor. Hector covered his head and backed away as the others followed his example.

The Avenger of Blood launched himself from the doorway and charged toward Harvey's daughter. She stood with her back to a pillar in the middle of the floor, wielding a pistol in her trembling hands. The wall was on his right and to his left the gangsters were recovering.

He reached Mia, who turned to see him and screamed. The Avenger kept his feet moving as he scatted the gun aside, lowered his torso and scooped her up across his right shoulder. That left most of her body between him and the wall—out of the line of fire. He raced for the closed door now twenty-five feet away. To his surprise, even with Mia's extra hundred pounds he seemed to devour the distance.

"What the?" One of the men had seen him.

Gunfire rang out. The Avenger ran to the exit, being chased the whole way by a steady stream of bullets hitting the wall behind him. Once he was within five feet, he jumped forward and thrust his foot into the barrier. The sole of his foot slammed into the wood and the door crashed open. He lowered Mia, held her around the waist, and spun both of them through the doorway. On the other side, he dropped her to her feet and fell down to one knee. Momentum carried her back into the wall six feet beyond the door. She spread her hands out to the sides and absorbed some of the impact with her arms.

The Avenger stood and stepped closer to her. "Stay quiet, and do as I say," He ordered.

Angry and panicked voices in the cafeteria prompted Mia to nod quickly. "Yes, sir."

He took her hand and glanced in both directions.

"That's a dead end," Mia said, pointing to her left. The hall ended at a large framed window not far from their position. Then she gestured with her head in the opposite direction. "That way leads back to the staircase."

"Let's go." The Avenger pulled her down the hallway to the right.

"Man, what the *hell* was that?" Trevor asked, scratching his head and looking back to the others.

Hector, Jose, Manny, and Xavier stood motionless with their guns lowered, eyes concentrated on the empty doorway.

"You shot at it and don't even know what it was?" Manny asked.

"I shoot first and ask questions later," Trevor replied over his shoulder as he inched toward the doorway. While his buddies stared in shock at its appearance, he had instinctively charged and fired at the phantom. Once it disappeared into the hallway his rational thought process returned. Now he was ten feet from the doorway and steadily advancing, both hands on his weapon. "You know what I think it was?"

"Fernando's boogeyman, it looked like," Hector said. He slowly began forward and motioned for the others to follow. "Wait up, Trevor."

"I ain't afraid of no weirdo." Trevor paused a couple of steps from the threshold. Despite his brave words, he wasn't anxious to draw any closer. The hall on the other side was poorly lit by dim fluorescent lights lining the ceiling. The floor and a large part of the area seemed to be bathed in shadows. "Can't let them get away, can we?"

"Trevor, that *weirdo* jacked up eleven of our boys earlier."

"Whatever." Trevor smirked, glancing back at them. "They didn't have automatics so I'm not—"

Two hands shot through the darkness of the doorway. One turned Trevor's AK-47 aside and the other latched onto the front of his shirt. Before he could finish his sentence he was hauled forward across the threshold. His comrades watched him vanish into the darkness beyond the doorframe.

"Hey, what the—" Trevor cried out, but was abruptly cut off.

"Idiot," Hector muttered, fear filling his own heart. He swallowed, trying to force it down, then rushed forward. "Come on!"

Hector ducked through the doorway, staying low to avoid an ambush, and paused a couple of steps into the hall. He held up his free hand to signal the others to slow down. Jose, Manny, and Xavier practically skidded on their heels to stop short of crashing into him. Hector lowered his hand and scanned the darkened passage. To the right, it came to a dead end twenty feet away. Five closed doors were on each side between the gang and a window overlooking the city. He turned left to see even more doors along a thirty five foot stretch. The hallway continued around a left corner. The door across from the opening appeared to be the only one cracked open. It was almost too obvious. Hector wrinkled his nose.

"Should we split up?" Manny whispered.

Jose and Xavier shot him dirty looks and Hector glanced back at him in disgust.

"What?" Manny shrugged.

A barrage of gunfire interrupted the silence, startling all of them. Hector turned left where the noise seemed to be coming from. The darkness around the corner was broken up by bright flashes of white. It was one of their own AK-47's.

Hector ran down the hallway, tightening his grip on the gun to steady his trembling hands. The others ran right behind him.

They reached the corner the moment the gunfire ceased. Hector jogged to the center of the new passage.

"Trevor?" He called. Movement three fourths of the way down the thirty-foot corridor caught his eyes. Someone, it was too dark to see who, moved through a doorway and slammed the door shut. He took a cautious step forward, searching the floor for one of three bodies he expected to see. It appeared barren, through parts of it were splintered.

More gunfire sounded and prompted Manny and Jose to charge ahead. "That thing's playing with him!" Hector and Xavier followed, hesitantly. Manny's foot came down hard, halfway to the door. The floor underneath him cracked, creaked, and groaned. Jose stopped next to him and they both grabbed each other's nearest arm to balance themselves. They held their outside arms up as they teetered back and forth. Manny and Jose exchanged a dread-filled look. With a deafening crack, the wood under them gave way. They cried out as gravity sucked them into the dark.

"Shoot!" Hector started toward the hole when the Avenger appeared, seizing his gun with both hands. The masked man brought his foot up to Hector's forearms and kicked as hard as he could. Hector staggered back, leaving the weapon in his grasp.

Xavier swung his AK-47 around to aim it in their attacker's direction. The Avenger brought the butt of Hector's gun down forcefully on Xavier's hands. He released the weapon with a cry of pained frustration. The Avenger quickly adjusted his grip on the gun and drove it into his chest. Xavier bounced off of the wall and threw a front kick at his groin. The Avenger's left leg shot out in a counter clockwise circle. His foot caught Xavier's calf and swept it aside, leaving him hopping on one leg. The Avenger pivoted further and brought his foot to the ground, causing Xavier to keel over.

As he turned to find the other gangster, Hector grabbed his shoulder with his left hand and threw a wild punch with the right. The Avenger stepped toward him and raised both hands. His left palm struck Hector under the chin, knocking his head back. His right arm hooked Hector's left elbow and he cupped his face in the left. He pulled on the arm, shoved the face, and dropped to one knee simultaneously. Hector was thrown down hard and the back of his head crashed into the hard wooden surface.

Xavier saw that and rolled onto his stomach. He scanned the area and located his gun lying three feet away. He crawled for it on his elbows and reached out with one hand. It was an inch or two beyond his fingertips. Cursing, he maneuvered himself a little closer and extended his arm again. A heavy black boot stomped on the back of his hand. Xavier screamed and raised his eyes to the Avenger who stood tall above him, pinning his hand between the sole of his boot and the wood.

The Avenger stooped over to seize Xavier by the lapels of his jacket. He moved his foot off of the young man's hand while dragging him up to his knees. Xavier stared into the frightening, metallic mask, his hands raised in surrender. The Avenger leaned back, then head butted Xavier in the face. The gangster fell limp and hung in his captor's grasp.

A door opened ahead, on the other side of the hole. Mia stepped into the hallway holding an AK-47 in front of her hips, aimed at the ground. Her chest heaved with each heavy breath. Strands of her curly hair hung in her face as her eyes met the Avenger's. She nodded and gave him an exhausted half smile.

"Good shooting," He said.

"Good fighting." Mia gestured toward the unconscious men.

"I'm going up."

"So am I," Mia stepped toward him. "One of those losers up there murdered my Father in cold blood. I have to finish the job I started. I have to."

"It's not your place."

"But it's yours?" Mia narrowed her eyes.

The Avenger stared at her for a moment. "I understand your pain. But people out for revenge are likely to hurt innocents to get what they want. If you kill him now, you'll never escape the gang life that led to Harvey's death. And one day it'll lead to yours."

"I'm not worried about my life."

"Your father would be. He spent the last part of his life making an honest living. Do you think he'd want you to undo that?"

Mia lowered her gaze to the floor as tears came to her brown eyes. She blinked in thought.

"Where are you parked?"

"A couple of blocks away."

"Go and wait for me."

"Yes, sir." Mia dropped the gun and turned to jog down the hall. The Avenger watched her momentarily, frowning under the mask. Then he spun around and rushed off.

The Avenger of Blood stepped into the Nursery Room doorway. Inside Angel was down on one knee next to a three by three foot hole in the wooden floor. The dim hallway light behind the Avenger and the moonlight pouring in through the window on the other side of the room, couldn't penetrate the opening's darkness. Two flashlights, both off, were among many tools scattered throughout the floor. Seven black duffle bags, packed full lied behind Angel. He was frantically stuffing stacks of 20 dollar bills into the mouth of an eighth bag, taking them from a trash bag next to the hole.

The kid looked up when he noticed the winged shadow cast over the room. His eyes widened and he shot to his feet.

"You again," Angel stammered. "You following us around too, huh? What are you, some sort of a crime fighter?"

"No," The Avenger replied. "I'm here for you. The blood you've spilled needs to be accounted for."

"How do you know Fernando didn't kill old Harvey?"

"Rose Arturo," The Avenger said, taking a step closer.

Surprise covered Angel's face and his lips moved, obviously trying to formulate the words for a response. After a few seconds he clenched his teeth and his eyes burned with hatred. "No. That whore got what she had coming to her."

Anger rose in the Avenger's heart. Months removed from Rose's death and Angel still clung to his defense. It seemed he honestly believed that he had the right to beat her to death and walk away as if he'd done no wrong. They'd come up behind her, knocked her unconscious, and carried her away. She'd been thirty yards from the church entrance.

"You're about to get what you have coming to you." The Avenger began toward him. "It's written, 'Whosoever sheds man's—'"

A second shadow appeared on the wall next to the Avenger's. Through his cape he felt the muzzle of an AK-47 press into his back. He spun counterclockwise on his heels and deflected the aim of the weapon with his left elbow. Using the turn's momentum he struck the tall black man's jaw with a sideways palm strike. Then he snatched the weapon and kicked him through the doorway.

Movement came from Angel's direction and the Avenger started to turn to him. Another larger man, who'd had a running start, rammed into him shoulder first. The force of the blow tore the AK-47 from his hands. The aggressor kept running, shoving the Avenger into the hallway toward the wall. His right side, inches above his oblique, crashed against the railing along the wall. He groaned in pain and grabbed the back of the man's shirt.

Jones, the tall black man, had already recovered. He pulled his right arm back to his side and launched his giant, bony fist into the Avenger's back. Rameses continued pressing his full weight into him, using the railing for leverage. It was almost as if they knew of his injury. Jones cocked his arm back and punched him again, this time on the covered bruise. The Avenger growled and his eyes rolled up in his head. His ribs and his back felt like they were on fire. Jones repeatedly unloaded his fist into the Avenger's torso, sending shockwaves through his body.

Get a grip, Joe, he warned himself. His mind was too consumed with pain to even consider defense. Yet, he knew he couldn't withstand much more of the assault without suffering serious damage or passing out. As Jones drew back to prepare for another punch, the Avenger raised his left arm. Moving it away from his body caused a cold, wet, pain to shoot through his ribs. He brought the elbow down between Rameses' shoulder blades. The big man grunted but the blow wasn't nearly as powerful as it should have been. It also left the Avenger open to a bone shattering blow from Jones. His upper body curled around the big fist.

"Watch out, watch out!" Rameses warned. Jones moved away as Rameses stepped back, pulling the Avenger with him. The Avenger tried to turn toward him to bring his right hand into the fight. He'd only managed to rotate slightly when the larger man speared him into the wall. A roar of pain escaped his lips as his ribs were crushed between the railing and Rameses' two hundred and sixty pounds. Jones delivered a blow to his back before he had time to draw in a breath.

Rameses stepped back again, clutching the Avenger's shirt and cape in his hands to haul him along. The Avenger shifted himself toward Rameses with the split second he had. As Rameses began to push he wrapped his arm around his head, tucking it under his underarm. They hit the wall hard and his head slammed into the hard surface. The big man fell backwards and collapsed.

Immediately, Jones rattled the Avenger with another punch to the side. The Avenger turned to throw a right hook. Due to his deceased speed it traveled half the distance before Jones blocked it with his left hand, and decked him across the face with a right hook of his own. He staggered away. *Punching hurts me more than it does them.* Jones seemed to sense the weakness, and stalked his prey, fists up and ready.

As he threw a left hook the Avenger ducked and stepped forward. He lifted his elbow under Jones' chin, ignoring the intense pain in his side. Then he kneed the inner part of Jones' right thigh, midway between his hip and knee. Something cracked inside and Jones cried out. The Avenger dropped to one knee and drove his elbow diagonally down into Jones' thigh close to the pelvis. The tall man keeled over, grasping his injured leg.

The Avenger climbed to his feet, stumbled, and turned to see that Rameses hadn't moved. The hard wooden floor seemed to welcome him as well. His body craved the rest and minimal comfort that it would provide. Even thirty seconds would be blissful. *Not yet.* He hugged his throbbing ribs between both arms and walked to the Nursery doorway. Angel was gone and he'd left only three bags behind. The Avenger rolled his eyes and looked toward the steps leading to the first floor. *My night isn't finished.*

Angel scampered down the church steps, pulled by the weight of three bags on his shoulders and one in each hand. He hadn't expected paper money to weigh so much. The gang's vehicles, three SUVs, were stationed across the street in a parking lot that matched the width and length of the building. A large white church van at the front was parked closest to the street. Behind it the SUVs were almost concealed from his angle.

He gazed around while jogging across the street. An old woman stood on the front steps of her home in a nightgown to his left, across a bigger road. She had a cell phone in her hands and upon noticing hlm, turned to hurry inside. He briefly contemplated whether he should let her go. *No need to add to my crimes, tonight.* He could already hear police sirens in the distance.

They'd probably been summoned by a neighbor who heard the gunshots. Jones had wanted to bring silenced weapons instead of the AK-47s but Fernando and Angel pressed for the automatic guns. They didn't want anything less than the best in case the masked man showed up.

Angel reached the single row of vehicles and ducked between the van and the first SUV. He dropped one of the bags and reached up to try the back door handle. Locked.

"Miles, open the door," He ordered.

Nothing.

"We don't have all night, man." Angel moved closer to the driver's door. Miles was there slumped over the right side of the steering wheel. His eyes were shut and his mouth open. "Shoot!" Angel lifted his hand to try to handle when another dilemma snared his attention. The underside of the vehicle was closer to the asphalt than it should have been. The rubber on the bottom of the tire had melted into the concrete. Slashed.

With his own mouth open and dread overtaking every fiber of his being, he staggered to the grass median separating the lot from the larger street. He looked at the other two SUVs. Both of them had flat tires and the drivers were unconscious in their seats. *He* did it. It had to have been him. As tough as Rameses and Jones were, they wouldn't be able to hold him off for long. The only question on Angel's mind was if the police would get to him first.

Rather than stick around and find out, he dropped the bag in his hand and ran across the median. On the other side of the street an alleyway seemed like the safest route. The sirens were bearing down on him from all sides and far up the road to the right, blue and red lights danced.

Angel lowered his head and raced for the alley entrance.

17

"How was she?" Tony asked, his eyes on the floor.

"She was grateful for the company," Amanda replied.

They were alone in the finished basement of the home Tony and his parents shared. The concrete floor was covered by a thick gray carpet that nearly matched the wall paint. A bed was pushed against one wall across from an entertainment center complete with a TV, a DVD selection, and a Game Cube. Behind the center a staircase, also covered with carpet, led up to the second floor. Tony sat on a footrest near the middle of the floor with his fingers interlocked on his lap and his head down. Amanda was on the edge of the couch three feet in front of him. She examined her palms and fingers as they talked.

"And she liked the cake, too," She added with a half smile. "She asked about you and Tony."

Pain showed on Tony's face and he closed his eyes.

"Maybe next time I go you can come with me?" She offered.

Tony nodded, biting his bottom lip. "Soon. I don't know if I'm ready for that step yet. But I do want to apologize to her. I need to."

"I'm curious. You seemed to have an abrupt change of heart. Last time you cursed me out for bringing it up."

"I have had a change of heart." He looked up into her eyes. "A big one. I've... I feel horrible about what I've done. But, I know I'm forgiven."

Amanda grinned. "You sound like a Catholic now, Tony. Don't tell me..."

He smiled. "Yep, I got saved."

"You went to a mass?"

"No." He shook his head. "Right in my own bedroom."

"What happened?" Amanda leaned forward even more. She appeared captivated by the news.

"Well, I don't want to get into all of it just yet," He said. "But, one of the police detectives who worked on the case visited me. My defense attorney was there, too, but she didn't do a whole lot of talking. She just made it clear that she believed I was guilty. The detective though—some Asian woman—she ripped me a new one. I mean, if they had a job for like... the opposite of a motivational speaker, she would have it."

"Man..." Amanda rubbed the back of her neck.

"She told me that I was evil."

"No way, Tony, you're not—"

"I am. And I was then, especially. She made me realize that for the first time, you know? That I was wrong. And she told me I was going to burn in hell forever. Now, I'd been in church before but there all I heard was, 'accept Jesus into your heart, and He'll bless you, and you'll live a happy life, blah blah blah.' But she laid it on me. Bad enough so that I practically ran home and dug out my Mom's old Bible."

Amanda laughed and clapped her hands. "No way, man."

Tony snickered himself. "I started reading through it and saw what Jesus did for us so... I apologized for my sins, all of them, and asked Him to save me."

"All of them? That's quite a list, Mr. Duran."

"Yeah, it was."

"Maybe you ought to come with me to that church on Friday. The assistant pastor personally invited me."

"Don't you feel special?"

Amanda giggled before loud knocks interrupted their playful banter. They exchanged looks, and then turned to the door to Tony's left. On the side of his house a set of concrete stairs led down to the basement. Anyone who used that entrance had to open the tall wooden fence surrounding the property to reach it. No one besides his closest friends and family members had permission to access it alone. His parents were sound asleep upstairs.

"Who is it?" Tony called, standing up.

A pause. Then, "It's Angel!"

"I haven't heard from him in two months," Tony said to Amanda over his shoulder. He approached the door, unlocked it and pulled it open.

A blast of cool air seeped in with Angel as he stepped across the threshold. He was sweating and out of breath, his shoulders slumped under the weight of three black bags which hung from sturdy straps. Once he reached the couch he dumped them on the floor and plopped down on the cushion beside Amanda. He reclined in the seat and brought his hands up to cover his face.

Tony closed the door and shared another confused glance with Amanda. They both read the alarm through the bewilderment mirrored on the other's face.

"Uh… you okay, Angel?" Tony reclaimed in seat on the stool. "Haven't heard from you in ages, man."

Angel sighed and shook his head. "Yeah it has been a while, man. I'm good. You?"

"Haven't been better in a long time," Tony admitted. "What do you have in the bags? You planning on moving in or something? I could have used a couple of days' notice you know?"

Angel snorted, and a tiny hint of a smile showed on his face. "Nah, man. Not yet. I might be getting out of town for a while, though." He glanced at Amanda out of the corners of his eyes. "What are you two up to down here? Did I interrupt something?"

"No," Tony replied. "Just talking, man."

"What about?"

"Catching up mostly."

"And talking about church," Amanda lifted her index finger.

"Let me find out…" Angel rolled his eyes and sat forward. "What are you guys, Jesus Freaks now?"

"Tony is." Amanda grinned. "I don't know about me. I've still got some partying to do. A little bit. It's been almost a year since I've actually gone out."

"What made you suddenly get in touch, Angel?" Tony asked.

"Well, I was in the area and remembered that you lived here," Angel told him, solemnly. "I'm not sure where I'm going after this but... I needed to see you again, I guess. We were boys for years. Was supposed to be for life."

"We're still young. Plenty of time to catch up."

"But we could die at any time. And when you're doing the dumb things that I've been involved in... you're likely to go a lot sooner."

"I heard you were in a gang, or something."

"Yeah." Angel pulled up his left sleeve to reveal a black tattoo on his bicep. It was an image of a skull, with sharp features, and fire in its eyes. Two horns protruded from the front of the head, both decorated with the Puerto Rican flag. The words "Thugz 4-Life" were inked in underneath it. "Got a new family."

"Why'd you do it? You're smarter than me, you don't need a gang to get somewhere."

"It's a little easier for you than me."

"Garbage, Angel."

"Try being Hispanic and getting a job, or enrolling in school, when you have blood on your hands." Angel held his hands up in front of his face and stared at them, as if he expected to see blood. "That whore ruined me even after she was dead."

"Angel..." Amanda glared at him. "How can you talk about her like that? We all know she didn't do it on purpose."

"Doesn't matter. I still say she got exactly what she deserved."

Tony and Amanda lowered their heads and said nothing.

Angel looked between them, realization settling in on his face. "You guys don't agree?"

"I don't, at all," Amanda said.

Angel shook his head and turned to his old friend. "Tony?"

"What we did that night was wrong, Angel," Tony replied, softly. "Rose wasn't trying to give us HIV and she's no lesser than us because she caught it. All of us were stupid back then. Messing around and having sex when and with whoever we felt like. Doing what we were it's a wonder we didn't catch anything from someone else. And… we all tested negative."

"Whatever."

"Angel, you really don't care?" Amanda asked, leaning toward him, her eyes searching his face. "Rose was as good of a friend as any of us ever had. Even though she and I had our problems, I still loved her. Some of my fondest memories are the days we all hung out down here."

"And that time she beat the crap out of you?"

"I started it. And afterwards, she called me to apologize. I ignored her for weeks and she didn't give up on our friendship. She was there for me when I needed her. And you know she would have done just about anything for us. I wish I had realized that before we… before we did what we did. I haven't had peace since that night. I know Tony hasn't, either."

"She's right," Tony said. "I tried to tell myself that we were justified but deep down I knew we'd done something rotten. I just didn't think about it until recently."

"And now what?" Angel frowned. "You going to turn yourself in?"

Tony hesitated. "It's the right thing to do. I won't say a word against you or Amanda, but I have to tell the truth. Even if there is no retrial… for Rose's sake, I have to speak out. I can't let people go on thinking things about her that weren't true. She wasn't trying to hurt us,

Angel. She was just scared. And we overreacted. We murdered an innocent girl."

Angel stared at Tony for a long moment. The anger in his eyes slowly peeled away and was replaced by painful recognition. Tony returned his gaze with a sad, hopeful expression. It was apparent that he wanted his friend to see the same light that he had. Angel appeared to be on the verge of that breakthrough. He swallowed and shut his eyes tight.

"I've found peace, man, and I think the way you're going to get there is by facing the facts," Tony explained. Angel nodded his head. "You don't have to turn yourself in and I'll cover for you. But I think the reason you got into the gangs was to escape the pain of what we did. She barely looked like herself after we finished. We were like animals. She pleaded and begged us to stop…" Tony's voice cracked and he paused to compose himself.

"And we stopped our ears. After that, I think we all needed something to hang onto. We lied to ourselves, told us we did the right thing and pushed it deep inside. But you can't hide that kind of guilt. It comes out, eventually. One way or another. Otherwise it'll destroy you. And I think… I hate to say it, but I think it's brought you to that point. You never would've thought about joining a gang before. You thought that lifestyle was for losers. And don't give me that trash about having a hard time finding a job. You got into it because of your guilt. I don't know what you've done since then, but I do know it won't help in the long run."

"I know what I have to do." Angel opened his eyes. He reached into the front pocket of his sweatshirt and pulled out a pistol. His finger was already inside the trigger guard. The other two froze and their eyes became glued to the black contraption. Angel calmly rested it on his lap. "I'm not going to let Rose ruin me. I wouldn't let her do it while she was alive, and I won't let her do it now."

"Angel…" Tony began.

"If you go to the police they're going to come after Amanda, and they're going to come after me." Angel stared at the wall over Tony's head, a faraway look in his eyes. "I'm as guilty as you are, and I don't want to go down like that. So if you promise me that you won't tell them... I'll put this away and leave."

Amanda looked to Tony. He sat with his hands clasped, and his eyes still on Angel's. She couldn't read anything from him except for heartache. The gun, which she had trouble keeping her eyes off of, didn't seem to bother him. It had the exact opposite effect on her. She wanted to advise him to listen to Angel. Though it was doubtful that he would let them go just because of a promise, one that could easily be broken, some chance was better than none. Amanda hoped Tony would understand that and comply.

"I can't do that," Tony replied. "I can't lie, Angel."

"Tony..." Amanda stammered.

"I'm sorry," He said.

"So am I," Angel stood up and walked over to stand in front of the door with his back to them. "You would die for Rose?"

"It's not just about her. My conscience won't let me do anything else. I have to go forward."

"You would die for her?"

"Yes."

"TONY!" Amanda screamed.

"Shut up." Angel turned and pointed the gun at her. "You want his parents to come down here and get involved?"

Amanda bit her lip to keep from screaming. The emotions welling up inside her craved a release, and holding them in caused her to tremble.

"I've given my life to the Lord now, Angel," Tony said. "And I know it's what He would want me to do. I'm serving Him... not a gun, or my own life. That's freedom. And power. You can't take that away."

"You sound crazy." Angel smiled, bitterly.

"You're the one with the gun, Angel. And I'm hoping you're not crazy enough to pull the trigger."

"I'll do what I have to do to protect my family. I am *not* spending my life rotting away in some hell hole because of Rose. I have a little girl at home depending on me, and a wife. They need me."

"How long do you really figure you'll last in the gang?"

"We'll see. I'll take my chances with them."

"Are you really going to shoot me? I know we haven't seen each other in a long time, but I'd like to think we were closer than that. You were a brother to me."

"We were all tight." Angel nodded. "My parents kicked me out for knocking up Arianna. You and your folks let me move in here over the summer until I got on my feet. Took care of me... fed me... Rose and Amanda watched the baby when I went out and worked. You guys were there for me."

"We still are."

"It's too late for me."

"I don't think so. No matter how low you've fallen, God can help you. I can help you."

"When you see Death face to face..." Angel aimed the gun at Tony's chest. "I've seen him twice in one night. He's coming for me. Just like the cops will."

"What are you talking about?" Tony shook his head.

"I have to keep moving. If I don't, one of them will catch up to me. I can't let that happen. I'm not ready."

"Do whatever you think you have to do, Angel," Tony said with a sigh. "But I want you to know that I love you like a brother."

"You're the best friend I've ever had... best friend I'll ever have."

BAM! Angel pulled the trigger and Tony and Amanda cried out. BAM! Tony fell from the stool and landed on his side, arms crossed over his chest. Blood seemed to pour from the wounds in his torso onto the carpet. It was also speckled on the couch, the stool, and the shocked face of Amanda. She gawked at Tony's motionless form, eyes stretched in disbelief.

"This wasn't how I wanted it to go," Angel said, lowering the gun to his side. He used the back of his other hand to wipe the tears from under his eyes.

"Why did you shoot him?" Amanda asked as she sobbed into her hands. "You didn't have to hurt him."

"God, going to the cops... that stuff doesn't work. I thought about it back after it happened. Justice and religion aren't real. There's only one way to escape the pain, and I found it. Tony's free now."

Amanda looked up to see the muzzle aimed at her. "Angel, no..."

"You'll be free, too."

BAM! The hot cylindrical piece of lead tore through her left shoulder. Amanda released a scream of desperation, shock, and pain as the impact knocked her onto the floor. She threw her hand over the wound and regretted it instantly when she felt warm blood pressing against her palm. Survival instinct alone kept her hand in place.

"I'll be the only one living with the pain," Angel said. "Because I've found something to deal with it."

"Angel..." Amanda wept. "Please don't... I don't want to die..."

"It's the only way for you. Sorry, Amanda."

Angel adjusted his aim and his finger started to tighten on the trigger. Amanda cringed and prepared herself for the second bullet, hoping that it would be quick and painless.

Angel's body jerked forward and his trigger finger relaxed. Blood sprinkled up onto his chin and he and Amanda looked at each other, both puzzled. Angel lowered his eyes and Amanda followed them to his torso. Blood had encircled and covered the tip of a double edged blade that protruded several inches from his chest. The weapon it belonged to had punched right through his body. Their eyes met again.

A quiet, hoarse voice spoke from somewhere nearby, "Whosoever sheds man's blood, by man shall his blood be shed." Angel's eyes briefly widened in disbelief as he stared into Amanda's. The blade retracted and disappeared into his flesh. He dropped the gun and slumped face first to the floor on top of it.

The Avenger of Blood stood in the doorway to Tony's basement, holding a doubled edge sword in his right hand. He'd heard the gunshots while he stood outside, contemplating what entryway to take. To his surprise, there was a survivor. Amanda sat on the floor, leaning against the couch and holding a bloody hand to her left shoulder. She stared up at him, her expression both weary and uncertain.

He kneeled in front of Angel's body and used the lower part of his shirt to wipe the blood from his sword. Then he stood, ignoring the sudden stab of pain in his ribs, and moved toward the other two. Tony lied on his back with his hands over his diaphragm. Blood covered the front of his torn shirt. His eyes were fixed on the ceiling.

"Do you have any other injuries?" The Avenger asked Amanda.

She shook her head.

The Avenger placed his sword on the couch and hurried over to the bed. He picked up one of the pillows, slipped off its white linen case, and headed toward the girl. She stared at him, a faraway look in her blue eyes. He kneeled in front of her and pried her hand off of her chest. He held the pillowcase against the wound and let go of her hand. She immediately grabbed the soft fabric and applied pressure. Her facial expression remained unchanged. It was probably for the best that she was in shock, otherwise he knew his appearance would worsen her condition.

"Tony!" A woman's voice called from somewhere upstairs. A pair of footsteps rushed in the direction of the staircase. "Tony, are you alright?"

The Avenger rose, took up his sword, and walked toward the exit. He stepped over Angel's body, grabbed the doorknob and pushed it open. Half a second later the door at the top of the steps opened.

"Tony? Amanda?" Tony's father yelled down.

Amanda watched the door across from her close behind the Avenger. The instant he disappeared, her mind was free to return to her present situation. Her entire shoulder hurt, but she could feel the bullet burning in her flesh like the tip of a lit cigar. It was unlike any pain she'd ever felt before and it immediately brought fresh tears to her eyes. Her entire body seemed to go numb.

Physical pain didn't mask the heaviness of her heart. Three of her best friends were dead. Two of their bodies, both of them bloodied, were sprawled on the ground before her. Tony's blank, empty eyes continued to stare up at the ceiling. Only the top of Angel's head was visible from where she sat. A small puddle of blood had formed under his mouth. Her third friend had died a more brutal death than the other two. She'd been buried seven months ago.

White began forming on the edges of Amanda's vision. Her right hand grew heavy and began to slip away from her shoulder. She fought the light overtaking her, the tiredness. She pressed her palm against the wound with all the strength she could muster. Then her hand fell into her lap and she closed her eyes.

17

A loud knock on her desk awoke Leslie from her slumber. She quickly lifted her head from the haven of her folded arms on the desk. The dim light from the small lamp in the corner of her desk blinded her. She blinked a few times to allow her eyes to adjust to it. Once they had, she wiped the corners of her mouth and looked up. The Avenger of Blood stood beside her, leaning on the desk with his hands.

"Hi," She said, groggily, and tried to shake her head free of the cobwebs. Briefly, she wondered if something was wrong with her. Anyone who woke up to the sight of *him* standing over them without getting scared had to have problems. "Kana called... she told me to wait up for you. I tried to."

"I'm going to see where Rose is buried, while it's still dark," He replied. His voice was quiet as usual, but without the intimidating rasp that usually accompanied it. "I thought you might want to come with me."

The last words snapped her out of her daze and she tilted her head to one side, peering up into his face. His eyes were concealed by the shadows of his mask. "Does that mean that you..."

He nodded. The simple gesture stirred a bundle of feelings in Leslie's heart. She was relieved, saddened, and weary all at the same time. Relieved that her conscience would no longer bother her, and that she didn't have to worry about the boys hurting anyone else. Tired from the long nights she'd had for seven months. Saddened by Rose's death, which she finally had the opportunity to mourn without guilt. She was overwhelmed by the prospects and hid her face in one hand. A moment later she began crying into it. The Avenger placed a comforting hand on her shoulder.

Three Days Later

The assistant pastor of the Faith Independent Bible Church sat at the end of a row of four blue chairs in the Our Lady of Lourdes Hospital. In the seat next to him was a younger woman with dark, frizzy hair and big framed eyeglasses. He sat relatively still, staring across the hallway at the closed door marked 303. His arms were crossed over his chest and his expression unreadable. The girl literally sat on the edge of her chair with her hands in her lap, gazing around at the uneventful setting.

They were on the third floor of the building, which was a far cry from the usually hectic ER. A handful of nurses and visitors had gone by in the last fifteen minutes. Two thirty something women couldn't help staring at the odd couple as they went. Lizzy had stuck her tongue out at them covertly, then glanced at the pastor to see if he'd noticed. Joe had seen her out of the corner of his, yet said nothing. Currently they were alone, besides an oriental woman in green scrubs who worked on a chart outside of another room a few doors down. She looked up at Lizzy and smiled. Lizzy returned it.

"I don't think I've had a better conversation in my life," Lizzy muttered.

"Sorry." Joe ripped his attention off of the door and turned to his young companion. "I'm a little distracted right now."

"Yah, you are." Lizzy nodded. "I'm glad you brought me along, though. I'd probably be getting yelled at right now by my parents, talking aimlessly with one of my friends, or both."

"This is taking a little longer than I expected."

"I'm hungry." She rubbed her stomach to emphasize. "Didn't eat much today."

"That means you'll have room for tacos in there when we leave."

"Whenever that'll be. What's Mrs. Miyoshi up to?"

"It's Mizaki now," Joe replied. "She's working late tonight. Her boss wanted to squeeze a few extra hours out of her before our vacation."

"So, where are you guys going? And for how long?"

"Probably to Shabath. One of her friends has a cabin up there she goes to during the summer. She offered it to us a couple of months ago but we were too busy."

"Shabath." Lizzy narrowed her eyes. "I hear a lot of weird stuff about that place. You been there before?"

"No. What have you heard?"

"That all of the people there have their own little community. I'm putting it nicely because some of my friends used the other C word to describe them. They don't send their kids to public schools, that's where Tony Russo—the 'prophet' who killed his wife and children—came from, they don't let certain people move in the area. And come on, they live in a forest at the top of a hill. Isn't that weird enough?"

"It could be," Joe said, shrugging. "Miyoshi tells me that most of the city was like that at one time. It was originally a Messianic settling. Now, the people who don't like what Minkin Capital has become stay there to themselves. But some of them send their kids to public schools. It's probably a pain for the bus driver who has to go up there. Personally, I'm not going to send my own kids to those schools when the day comes."

"Why not?"

"I'm teaching on that next week, so no spoilers."

"That stinks. So you guys aren't staying that long?"

"Just the three day weekend."

"Good. I'd be disappointed if you were gone next week, too. I'm going to have to find something else to do with my Friday night."

"Well, some of the younger folks are having a study at James' house."

"I can't learn anything from them."

Joe paused. "You have a point."

"And I know they're not going to want to hear anything from the cursed Agnostic."

"You went from complete denial to feigned ignorance?" Joe grinned. "It's a start."

Lizzy laughed. "You're a good teacher and with my friends, the Bible being anything other than some mythological nonsense never came up. I mean, the most I knew was about Noah and the Ark, and Charlton Heston telling Pharaoh to let his people go."

Joe laughed this time.

"That was the most understanding I had before. And I heard about all the supposed contradictions. But you've disproved at least half of them, which is cool. I still don't agree with some things."

"Which is why you're ignorant for now."

"Ha."

The door across the hall opened and a middle aged female nurse stepped out. She smiled at the pastor and his friend and said, "She's awake, and eager to see you. You've met her before, sir?"

"Yeah, briefly," Joe assented as he and Lizzy stood.

"Go on ahead." The nurse stepped aside and held the door open.

Joe thanked her as he and Lizzy walked past her and into Room 303. It was a medium sized room with pale blue walls and matching tiles. The space was split up into two sections. In the first, which they entered, a young woman lied on a bed, inclined so she was almost in a sitting position. On her right was a table with an empty tray, and a carton of orange juice atop it. To the left, in the other half of the room, was an empty bed with a large window a couple of feet past it. Two television monitors were set up near the ceiling across from both beds. The screens were blank.

The woman, Amanda, had been staring out the window when they stepped in. She appeared okay. Her left arm was supported in a sling and the shoulder covered by the hospital gown. The light fabric didn't conceal the form and color of the bandages underneath it. Her eyes were half closed, due to tiredness or grief. She turned to her visitors and managed a weak smile, "Hello Pastor."

"Hello, Amanda," He walked to her side with Lizzy close behind. "How are you feeling?"

"I've had better days," She admitted. "They've got me on pain meds, of course. As bad as it hurt that night I don't think I could live without them. I don't feel a whole lot now, though. The surgery went well. They removed the bullet. I asked if they'd let me take it home as a souvenir."

"What did they say?"

"First time someone's asked them that." Amanda's smile widened. "They're probably going to run tests on it and keep it for evidence, though." She nodded to Lizzy. "Who are you?"

"Lizzy," The bespectacled woman waved. "I go to his Bible Studies."

"Hm." Amanda blinked a few times, and looked to the pastor. "I'm going to start coming as soon as I get out of here. That's one thing I promised God in my head when I was lying there that night." She frowned and appeared to stare at something right above Joe's head. "I told him I'd go every Friday night from then on, and I'd stop messing around. I'd do anything as long as He kept me alive."

"It would be nice to have you there," Joe said.

"I didn't want to make it seem like I was just coming because I had nothing else. You know, I thought God deserved more than that. And I have lost everything. All of my close friends..."

"When it comes down to it..." Joe chose his words carefully. "I don't think any of us really has anything to begin with. It might seem like we do—we might have money, friends, power... but all of those things can be taken away. And sometimes they are. Sometimes God allows it to get our attention."

"Isn't there an easier way?"

"I ask myself that every once in a while." Joe swallowed down his own grief. As he'd told Leslie two nights ago, he'd learned a difficult lesson in the matter himself. And witnessed how God used it for His purposes. "But, maybe there's not. It's easy to get distracted to the point where He doesn't come to mind. And if he does, people put Him off and chose to stay in their sin. I know what you've been through is painful, but try to look at it this way. Do you think that you'd be anywhere near where you are now... considering devoting your life to Him, if not for everything that's happened?"

Tears ran down Amanda's cheeks. "I doubt it. I'd try to lie to myself and say I would've found my way eventually. But I don't think I would've. To me... I could just wait until I was on my deathbed and then say a little prayer or have a priest give me the Last Rites. It's been a tough example..."

"But nowhere near as bad as hell."

"Yeah, I just wish..." Her lips quivered. "I just wish Rose was still here."

"So do I." Joe frowned. "But she's in a better place."

"With better company," Amanda added. "And I think Tony is, too."

"What?"

"He... I went to visit him after I met with Mrs. Arturo on Monday. He called me while I was there and asked if he could see me. He said he was saved. Apparently, some detective gave him the verbal beat down of his life. Scared the hell out of him, literally. We were talking about it when Angel showed up..."

"So..." Joe was awestruck. He often wondered why God had allowed him to meet Rose that night in the first place. There were several other churches she could have gone to. One or two of them were decent.

He selfishly asked why he had to experience the grief he did because of their meeting. Now, it became apparent. Tony and Angel would have died immediately otherwise, and they'd have both ended up in hell. Instead, it sounded like Tony had repented. "Huh. A hard lesson."

"How are you holding up about it? About Rose? I know you didn't know her that long, but you definitely had an impact on her life."

"I've made peace," Joe replied, sadly. "I'm grateful to you for that. For telling me the truth."

"No problem," Amanda said. "I'm glad I ran into you. I literally have very few others right now... I thought I did, but... besides my family you're the first to visit me here. Both of you. It gets a little lonely."

"Since Pastor is going away for the weekend, I don't have any plans Friday at least," Lizzy told her. "Maybe we could hang out. Even if it has to be here."

"That would be awesome." Amanda's smiled returned.

Leslie stood five feet from the headstone over the resting place of Rose's body. Joe was right behind her, holding six roses by their stems in his right hand, and the Avenger of Blood mask in his left. They were near the center of the Gava Cemetery, the oldest burial ground in Minikin Capital. It resided at the top of a large hill on the way to Shabath. As a result, it was surrounded by forestry and other hills of various size.

The top of the sun peeked out from behind a hill in the distance. Its morning beams cast a dull orange glow on the cemetery and the land surrounding it. Due to the fall weather, its heat couldn't be felt yet. A strong, steady wind that had blown most of the night continued to move through the area. Leslie's hair and the bottom of her coat were swept about by the breeze as was the Avenger's cape. The material it was made of was silent, so all that could be heard was the wind and the birds singing their morning chorus in the distance.

Joe reached forward and held the roses in front of Leslie's chest. She accepted them in both hands, wrapping her fingers around the cold stems. The roses were beautiful, plush, and as red as she'd ever seen. She strengthened herself, then stepped closer to the headstone. The inscription read:

IN LOVING MEMORY OF

ROSE LYNN ARTURO

BLESSED DAUGHTER AND FRIEND

Sighing, Leslie kneeled down and placed the roses on the small platform under the headstone. She stood and slowly backed away, her eyes glued to the name. The name of the young woman who had suffered the last five hours of her life, and had since suffered slander due to Leslie and her clients. Both of them were dead now, and Rose rightfully avenged. That brought some measure of peace to Leslie, yet her heart still ached for Rose.

She backed into Joe's shoulder and leaned against him, exhausted. Her hair kept him out of her peripheral vision and his face remained hidden. Though she would ordinarily jump at the opportunity to see the face of the man she worked with, today it was far from her thoughts. She relaxed and bowed her head.

Joe raised his eyes to the reddish orange sky and searched the firmament. He imagined Rose up there somewhere, in a world hidden to his natural senses. If she was where he suspected, all of her suffering had ceased. All of her tears had been wiped away. Her smiling face appeared before his eyes, bringing a burning to his bosom. He closed his eyes and lowered his head.

Joe and Leslie stood quiet and motionless together before the grave of their friend. His cape continued to flap in the breeze as the sun rose higher in distance, casting its warming light on the serene landscape around them.

ABOUT THE AUTHOR

Ryan Callaway is a young writer who resides with his wife Lillian in South Jersey. Growing up watching horror-themed films and TV shows and hearing stories about local legend, The Jersey Devil, inspired his choice of genre. His first book, "Six Faces" was published in 2004. His second was a suspense novella, "Yearly Harvest: A True Story of Christmas". He is also the author of "Avenger of Blood", and has several other novels and short stories in the works. Starting in 2008, Ryan Callaway also ventured into the film production world, and has thus far directed several projects, with many more to come including upcoming feature film "The Watchers".

His books and films are available through

http://ryancallaway.webs.com

Also, keep an eye out for the rest of the "Avenger of Blood" series, including <u>The Bloody City</u> and <u>Vengeance is Mine</u>. <u>The Bloody City</u> will delve deeper into the Avenger's origin, his first meeting with Detective Kana Mizaki, and the history behind Minikin Capital. <u>Vengeance is Mine</u> is a direct sequel to <u>A Fallen Rose</u>, and features a confrontation involving the Mafia, the Yakuza, the police department, and the Avenger.

www.ingramcontent.com/pod-product-compliance
Lightning Source LLC
Chambersburg PA
CBHW050925120626
46552CB00001B/48